Ghost Light

A Grunt's Second Grimoire

Jay Peterson

This is a work of fiction. Some of the locations are quite real indeed. That said, names, characters, businesses, events, and incidents are the products of the author's imagination. Any resemblance to actual persons, living or dead, or actual events is purely coincidental.

Don't whistle backstage.

Don't wish someone good luck before a show.

And whatever you do, don't say The Scottish Man's name when you're in the building.

Dedication

For Sharon Morrow

Acknowledgements

Nobody makes one of these things alone.

I want to acknowledge my various alpha and beta readers, who did everything from laugh at a snippet to checking out everything I had and wanting more. Especially those who had the thankless job of telling me honestly where I wasn't measuring up.

Between my time as a theater kid and my career as a working actor, I've had the good fortune to work with and learn from an abundance of colorful characters over the years; from combat to intimacy and everything in between. I'm not naming names to protect the innocent and the guilty both, but they know who they are. Folks, I thank you from the bottom of my heart. And I hope I didn't roast any of you too particularly hot.

I want to thank Sydney at True Edge Art for going through a learning experience with me on Renfield Blues.

I especially want to thank the WGA and SAG-AFTRA for fighting like hell during the strike of 2023.

And all of the thanks go most especially to my family, for putting up with the nonsense in the name of storytelling.

Contents

Prologue

Guideline Twenty:
Believe in spooks. After all, they believe in you.

I told you at the beginning this would all make much more sense if you admitted you believed in magic. Those of you who did so found a much smoother ride than those of you who didn't. But, believer or otherwise, you're back for more. So I must have done something right. Welcome back. Now I'm gonna go asking you to believe in crazier things than magic, like ghosts and the theater.

Ghosts shouldn't be too much of a stretch. I mean, we all exist, though some of us are going to argue otherwise. And unless we somehow manage to outpace life, which has had a 100% casualty rating for all of human history, one day we're all going to die. The idea that something that makes us who we are goes off and does something else; when our bodies stop making chemical reactions for longevity and start making them for recycling, is both comforting and at least plausible.

That, and seriously, you've already seen me get up close and personal with vampires. And while I didn't go too in-depth with it, to the surprise of many, I at least mentioned the zombie wars from back in the 1870's. Kinda hard to have active undead if the concept of active dead wasn't on the table, you know? Ghosts are practically natural instead of supernatural like that.

The supernatural bit is when that part of us that makes us who we are goes someplace nearby but nowhere modern science has been able to quantify or navigate. Invisible, inaudible, almost undetectable. Unless it wants to be. Ghosts have a wide collection of ways to make themselves be noticed if the mood suits them. Knocking small objects off tables and pictures off walls is one thing. Anyone who owns a cat knows that can happen anytime. But ghosts don't stop there. Radios and TV's change channels and volume. Light switches? Ghosts can play with them all day. Then you read some of the older stories and realize ghosts could do that with candles and lanterns too. If a light switch can get creepy, imagine what a candle lighting itself feels like.

Imagine sitting somewhere all alone, thinking about quitting smoking. You've got the last cigarette in the pack, but your lighter is buried somewhere deep in your pocket. You think about this and you think about that, your potentially last cigarette just dangling there between your fingers. Then, without warning, your cigarette lights itself. Are you going to wait for the disembodied voice to say, "if you're going to quit, can I have this one?" Or will you be halfway down the block and accelerating already?

The thought of a superpowered voyeur would be disturbing enough. But most of our ghost stories deal with the spirits of folk who died with unfinished business. Oh, some of it's mundane enough: being honest with loved ones, telling opponents where to stick it, the awkwardness when they're the same person, that sort of thing.

But ghosts scare people. Not the least because, let's face it, our last resort in dealing with someone we don't want to deal with is to kill them. That's not really an option with ghosts. Ghosts have all the time in the world. No matter how long you live, they have time to wait. And by then, they'll have more experience being dead than you are. So now what are you going to do?

Nobody wants to be unfinished business. Or finished business, for that matter.

Theater, on the other hand, is easier to find but harder to believe in. There are just enough people onstage that they can perform and keep the lights on at the same time. The sets are built to last for show runs instead of lifetimes. The costumes are only worn for people to watch instead of for the wearers to live in. The makeup owes more to the masks of their ancestors than to the precision tools of expressing a daily life. The lights only illuminate what the storytellers want you to see, in the intensity and temperature they want you to see them. We all know that the most powerful heroes, the most passionate lovers, and the most dastardly villains are all just thrilled to be telling you what they're going to do about the doomsday plan. At the very least, it beats telling you what the specials on today's menu happen to be. You know all of this.

That is, until you sit down and the show begins. Done well, your brain takes a hike as effectively as any mind control I know of. Theater tells stories that skip our brains entirely and plays with our hearts like a kid with action figures. It builds other worlds from dollar store materials and raw human passions. Those passions burn bright. They burn hot. And too often, people get burned.

Mages have been arguing whether or not the theater is a form of magic for millennia. Bardic mages like my friend Seb say it's old magic in a similar way that written language is: it lets us know about things that happened centuries before we were born in places far away. It lets us know the innermost thoughts of people we've never met. It can convince us that things which never happened were the real truth. It rejects our reality and replaces it with something prettier and more energetic, like a tacky second marriage of convenience.

Theaters get a lot of ghosts. They mix like maple syrup and bacon: sweeter than you'd think, but with disturbing and naughty undertones.

Ghosts are souls with unfinished business and expired bodies. Theaters shatter dreams on industrial scales. Lot of dreams died before the dreamers walked in that door. A lot more were crushed within minutes of arriving. But some lasted for years. Handcrafted. Reinforced. And right when they were about to pass through the vale and come true, they shattered. And some just got worn down a piece at a time until they didn't even look like dreams anymore, just gossamer fantasies that died swiftly in the darkness.

Actors are always talking about how the show must go on. Most say that because that's how they wind up eventually getting paid. But some actors, the ones who've been treading the boards for so long they don't know any other life? They say it like a prayer to a vengeful God. They keep their furtive rituals and practice their few holidays as devout as any priest. They believe with all the fervor that true believers once thought the sun revolved around the earth. And they say, in the face of fire, flood, and disaster, that the show will go on.

Ply those actors with enough to drink, which most will gladly allow you to do, and they might even let their guard down. As if somewhere in the depths of their romantic little souls they still believe, even in absence of overwhelming evidence, that the show will. go. on.

And if you look very closely, and if you know what to look for, you can see, deep in the back of their eyes, the undiluted fear.

They're too scared to tell you about what happens when a show can't be stopped.

Chapter One

Guideline Thirty-Two:
If you can't train the way you play,
try to have fun with both.

Mages don't do therapy.

In our defense, there's only about six licensed psychologists in the U.S. that are read in on the Otherworld. Patronizing their couches means allowing another mage unprecedented insight into your own life, and they don't even need cognimancy to do it. At best, this makes things socially awkward, if not politically hazardous. Anyone else we'd have to lie to, which is kinda beside the point. That's without even addressing the financial plan. Magic is not a substitute for decent health insurance.

Fortunately, I find chainsaws immensely therapeutic.

Byron kicked in the door of the atrium and took out the first zombie with a wakizashi as I stepped into the fatal funnel, catching the second zombie with a draw cut across the face. The body jiggled with the chain's vibration until I'd cut off most of the head. The diagonal-cut skull bounced once, spilling remaining brains and ichor on the hotel carpet.

Byron smirked as only a hunter elf can. "You're enjoying this way too much."

I gave him an evil grin in return. "Hey, we don't have to clean this up. And it's not as heavy as I'd imagined."

An alto voice cut through the room. "Heads up!"

An unfolded entrenching tool, its handle tightly wrapped with hot pink paracord, flew between Byron and myself. The flight path left it embedding itself in the skull of a zombie that had lurched into the room. The corpse collapsed like the pile of rotting meat it was.

Connie tiptoed on heavy combat boots between us, letting something squish. I high-fived my covenmate as she passed, crouching to retrieve her e-tool. A Kbar knife was hanging loose in her free hand, ready to go. She gave the e-tool a little shake, letting brain fragments splatter on the floor. "Travis is right about cleaning up. It's still disturbing, but it's kinda fun."

Thumper slipped past her, hatchet in hand and sack slung over their shoulder. Crouching even shorter than usual, Thumper peeked around the corner into the next room. Without turning to the rest of us, Thumper gave a thumbs up, then slipped their free hand into the sack, drawing forth a fragmentation grenade.

Byron shook his head in disappointment. "You're just enabling him."

Thumper shrugged, still focused on the open doorway. Using the hatchet, they pointed to the grenade and said, in their thick Mississippi delta accent, "Tool." Then they pointed the hatchet towards the doorway. "Job."

For Thumper, that was inspiration worthy of Agincourt.

I took my space behind Thumper as the others stacked up on me. Thumper pulled the pin, threw the grenade into the open doorway, then scurried back to the end of the stack. The explosion was short and felt under our feet as much as in the air. A small cloud of dust and a few splatters of ichor emerged from the doorway. I revved the chainsaw and stepped through, leaving splatter patterns that would've gotten me a B-minus in a modern art class.

I wasn't lying about the weight. The chainsaw was kinda awkward, but fortunately, I've got the forearms of a blacksmith to go with my slowly growing paunch. Carving up zombies was good interval cardio, wasn't it?

Byron shook his head, disarming and then beheading a struggling zombie. "The best intimidation weapon in the world, used on things that can't be intimidated."

I rolled my eyes. "If I wanted to intimidate, I'd pretend to be a thunder spirit or something. I want to relax and enjoy myself. Killing slow and stupid undead counts."

Byron tried appealing to Connie. "You're a necromancer. Isn't this kind of offensive?"

She shrugged. "I didn't raise them."

Thumper whistled as the next wave began to arrive.

For the next several minutes, I enjoyed the cardio butchery with my friends. It might not be the kind of magic that inspires ancient legends, but it was incredibly satisfying.

As we geared up for another round, Jazz softly tiptoed into the living room. She was holding a smartphone at arm's length, as if at any minute a cobra was going to emerge from the screen and begin threatening her. Given our current lifestyles, the odds of that happening were better than zero. Fortunately my insurance agent hadn't figured that out yet.

"Master?" she said, "I've got another one."

I paused the game and got off the couch, leaving my chainsaw-wielding avatar in the lurch. My game controller fell off the arm of the couch and unceremoniously landed among the cushions. "You heard the lady, folks. Thumper, take the lead."

Thumper scurried past Jazz, eager to get their plan up and running. Connie, having only a vague idea of what was about to ensue, gave a stretch before dismounting the easy chair. Byron, easily the most enthusiastic of us, had already put his controller down and was on his feet. I could almost see the points of his teeth flashing in his smile. Leaving swaths of pixelated chaos in our wake was fun, but Byron was a hunter born and raised. And our newfound quest, even though it used different tools, was still a hunt.

The four of us followed Thumper down the hallway to their bedroom.

Thumper, Connie, and myself were all mages. Last summer, we'd all survived some ugly times around vampires. All three of us had tasted vampire blood, survived, and kicked the addiction. We'd had some help along the way, but the three of us understood each other's experiences in ways nobody else really did. So we wound up forming a coven. Renfields Anonymous isn't the most awe-inspiring name for a crew, but it works for us.

Byron started out as a combo bodyguard and parole officer, and wound up becoming my friend. Surviving high school meant that I made some badly one-sided bargains. At one point, I turned the Wild Hunt itself away from prime territory. In exchange, I agreed to hunt with them for a season. Byron was left behind both to make sure I didn't try to weasel out on the deal and make sure I had the skills to survive and keep up with them. We wound up joining the Marine Corps and fought in Iraq together. Someday, my marker will be called in, and Byron won't have a reason to stick around anymore. But until then, I couldn't ask for a better hetero lifemate.

Then there's Jazz.

As far as my coven, or anyone else in the local Otherworld knows, Jazz is an Iraqi witch Byron and I met during the war. Only Byron and I know Jazz is one of the few Djinn still on earth and still bound to a Solomanic talisman. Said talisman being the ring I wear on my left pinky. In Iraq, I killed her last master, took her ring, and then took her home. In that order. She's been working for me ever since. Djinn are insanely powerful by modern magical standards. Most also have a serious hate-on for Mages.

Mercifully, Jazz didn't seem to suffer from the mage hatred that dominated her species. Or hatred of anyone else, for that matter. She's sweet as a candy store to everyone she meets. She'd also been a scribe and archivist for various libraries for several centuries. Give her enough bookshelf space and tasks todo and she was content as could be. So I'd brought her up on the last century of current events and had her assisting me in magical theory. Having an assistant who could read a dozen languages helped a lot.

She'd helped so much that at one point I was under suspicion of demonic bargaining. Her cover and mine held up under investigation, but it was a close call. Revealing her true nature was a good way to make both of us international targets.

As it stood, we just looked mildly bizarre. My ethics won't let me become romantically involved with someone magically compelled to serve me, no matter the temptation. And make no mistake, she's extremely tempting. Deep sapphire blue eyes, a dangerous set of curves, a scorching case of bibliophilia, and a streak of service submission a mile wide. On top of that, I'm fairly certain she still doesn't own a shirt that isn't cropped. Temptation.

Unfortunately, wishing her freedom is physically possible, but it would be a temporary solution at best. The spell that bound her into my ring is easy enough to find. But once I freed her, there would be nothing keeping someone else from binding her into another ring or a bottle or something and serving them. All other options were just as complicated and dangerous, if not more so.

While I couldn't safely set her free, I could help her adapt to the modern world. I set her up in a spare room at my house. I introduced her to friends and acquaintances. Powerful glamours left her skin tan instead of blue. She'd gotten in the habit of wearing western clothes instead of bedlahs, at least publicly. I couldn't stop her from calling me "Master," but I could have her wear a black leather collar in public and let onlookers draw their own conclusions.

One way or another, she was going to be a free woman someday. And I wanted her to be confident in whatever choices she made when that happened. So we went to work building her new identity, using magic to make the way a bit easier when we needed to. She had her own ID, bank account, and resume. We were slowly building her online presence and getting her used to the internet world.

You heard that right. I took a sweet, pretty, zaftig, subby and wide-eyed girl who hadn't been dialed in to pop culture since the glory days of the British Empire and I let her dive into social media.

I. Am. An. Idiot.

Fortunately, I managed to keep her from calling down a public curse on any of the poor little morons thus far. If a string of creepy men started being hit by lightning, I'd have an SiS marshal on my doorstep wanting a word. Or worse, some fruitloop from the Nimuen wanting me to join up. What's the fun of being a wizard if you can't even get yourself off mailing lists?

By the time I made it to Thumper's room, they were already hard at work. Thumper was settled into their overstuffed office chair. Two towers, seven monitors, and a speaker array faced them like a church organ with all the options. Several more towers occupied a shelf under the desk. Cables were everywhere. The rest of us piled onto Thumper's modest bed to watch the show.

Thumper's been a good friend since middle school. Then our senior year teacher tried to murder our entire graduating class. Long story. Short version: The Blue River massacre wasn't a school shooting. That night, an explosion sent Thumper flying headfirst into a tree. When they woke up from the coma a couple of months later, they had a form of aphasia. They could understand people fine. And somehow, they didn't have much hearing damage. But they couldn't respond much. Something between Thumper's brain and mouth was screwy, and nobody mundane or magical could figure out how. Short answers they could usually pull off. But anything longer than a short sentence turned into a frustrating mess of word salad. Even sign language just devolved into charades, and nobody could tell them why.

But they could type just fine.

Thumper hadn't had a great deal of support when they recovered. The injuries combined with being nonbinary in a less than understanding family didn't help any. But they wound up becoming a fairly decent self-taught programmer. They'd even managed to mix the peanut butter of magic with the chocolate of programming to be a pretty stellar technomancer in their own right. And since communication had been their impetus for getting into programming in the first place, they were very good with phones.

Jazz's phone was plugged into a docking station with several indicator lights whose purpose I couldn't determine glowing like small Christmas decorations.

I wasn't into computers for their own sake. They were a means to various ends for me. But like any craftsman, I knew the importance of having good tools when I found them. So when Thumper moved in, I helped out on the hardware side. One USB stick plugged into a tower. Another one plugged into Jazz's phone. A few clicks later, the upper right hand screen showed a full text conversation between Jazz and the unfortunate soul who was now a target in Thumper's sights.

HIM: ur beautiful

　　　　　　　　　　　　　　　　　ME: Thank you.

HIM: Where ru?

　　　　　　　　　　　　　　　ME: Atlanta. It's very nice.

HIM: u wanna hook up?

　　　　　　　　　　　　　　　　ME: No thank you.

HIM: u sure?

　　　　　　　　　　　　　　　　　ME: Very sure.

HIM: u dunno what ur missing.

ME: I'm not interested.

ME: Please leave me alone.

HIM: All this is yours if u want it.

Below his final line was an up close and personal pic of a prominent erection. To the guy's credit, it was as well lit and shot as an amateur could hope for. Shame the guy had learned photo composition instead of modern etiquette.

Thumper's computer had a digital countdown going on the center-right monitor next to a copy of the phone's screen display. In the top center console, a large font type let Thumper text us details in all caps. The countdown fell to zero, only to be replaced with a banner declaring AC-TIVATING TATTLETALE.

Thumper texted, "AND HERE WE GO."

I couldn't begin to explain how Thumper's technomancy worked. What I did know is that the program was intuitive enough to make the next logical steps. Even if the next logical steps included a device or database it wasn't connected to at the time. That said, we could all pretty much guess as we watched Thumper work.

I sighed. "Crap. It's a burner phone."

Byron shook his head. "So he does have two brain cells to rub together." "WATCH."

Half of Thumper's monitors showed us the chase, jumping from computer to computer.

Connie pointed out a lit connection. "He bought it at a gas station in... Norcross, looks like?"

Byron munched popcorn as a camera feed popped up. "And here's the register camera."

Thumper picked up a headset and handed it wordlessly to Jazz, who donned it over her ponytail.

More data appeared. I smiled. "Say hello to Brandon."

Byron grinned. "28 years old. Lives at home."

Connie watched impassively. "Mother's name is Kathryn."

Byron read aloud. "Last known jobs: exterminator, pizza delivery, parking enforcement."

Another camera popped up. I grinned. "We got the cam in his TV."

The center middle screen opened up, showing Brandon. He had dirty blond hair and was dressed in dirtier raggedy shorts and a tshirt he might have slept in, possibly for multiple nights. The room around him was beyond a mess and well into filthy. When old laundry and old dishes meet, the results are never pretty. I was glad there was no way for us to experience the smell. Brandon was playing with a game controller, occasionally pausing to scratch himself.

I saw more data pop up. "We've got mom's phone."

"JAZZ, YOU'RE UP."

A window opened on the screen with Brandon's phone, now showing his mother's cell. After three rings, we could hear her pick up. "*Hello?*"

Jazz visibly blushed, and her tone dropped the way it did when she was convinced she had done something wrong. "Yes, hello ma'am. I'm terribly sorry to bother you. Oh my goodness. This is so embarrassing. It's about... Brandon."

"*What? Does he owe you money too?*"

"Oh, no no no. He's just..."

"*Just what?*"

"He's sent me some disturbing messages, ma'am."

"*... send them to me.*"

"I'm.. I'm so embarrassed, ma'am. I'm so sorry."

"*Don't worry about that honey, go ahead and send them.*"

"SCREENSHOTS INBOUND."

We were all on the edge of our seats. Kathryn hung up, sending all of our eyes to focus on Brandon's TV cam. I'm not sure what microphone Thumper was using, but we could hear Kathryn screaming easily.

"Brandon!!!"

The flip-flop came screaming into the frame like Connie's e-tool, nailing Brandon straight between the eyes as he turned to face the door. Kathryn charged into the room like an angry valkyrie, cursing a blue streak with her other flip-flop in one hand and her phone, shining with forwarded evidence of Brandon's misdeeds, in the other.

We all laughed ourselves silly as Brandon got his ass kicked for several minutes. Thumper got high-fives all around from the assembled. Jazz was blushing furiously but found the celebration infectious. Kathryn finally decided to show mercy, stomping out of camera range and grumbling to herself.

Thumper held up a hand, then typed quickly, "STAND BY. THIS MIGHT GET UGLY."

Brandon picked up his phone, fury in his eyes, and began to text. The screen duplicating Jazz's phone lit up with a new message.

HIM: Bitch wtf you think you doin?

Jazz reached for her phone. Thumper stopped her with a raised hand, then started typing again. A response popped up on that screen.

ME: I told you to please leave me alone.

Through the TV cam we could hear Brandon snort as he kept texting. "Fucking bitch think she is?"

HIM: Fuck you!!! ugly bitch I'll cut your fucking face. Fucking flabby whore.

Jazz began to swear in Arabic, making several insinuations about which barnyard animals Kathryn must have pleasured in order to conceive Brandon. Thumper typed away.

"UH OH! DADDY'S HOME!"

On one of Thumper's screens, duplicated on Brandon's home TV, now depicted a grinning green animated skull. Cartoon fires burned in its eye sockets. It's voice was a guttural baritone that matched Thumper's all-caps typing perfectly.

"*THE LADY SAID TO LEAVE HER ALONE, BRANDON.*"

Brandon stared at the screen, dumbfounded. "What the fuck?"

The skull continued under Thumper's puppeteering. "*THERE ARE WORSE PUNISHMENTS THAN MOTHERS AND FLIP FLOPS, BRANDON. USING A BURNER GAINED YOU NOTHING BUT MINUITES. FINDING YOU WAS SIMPLE. FINDING YOUR MOTHER WAS SIMPLE. IMAGINE WHAT ELSE WILL BE SIMPLE.*"

The fury in Brandon's eyes melted into fear as he frantically looked around, wondering how he was being treated like this.

"*LEARN HOW TO BEHAVE AMONG LADIES, BRANDON. YOU ARE NOT UGLY, ONLY CRUDE AND FOOLISH. CORRECT YOURSELF. THIS WORLD HAS NO PLACE FOR EUNUCHS.*"

Thumper typed a quick command, and Brandon's phone made a series of sharp pops. Smoke began to curl from under the casing, and Brandon dropped the suddenly hot phone.

"*DO NOT COME TO MY ATTENTION AGAIN.*"

Brandon's TV blipped, then returned to the game screen he had been playing.

Thumper cut the connection, restoring the home screen on Jazz's phone.

"THANK YOU FOLKS, I'LL BE HERE ALLWEEK. BE SURE TO TRY THE VEAL AND TIP YOUR SERVER."

Byron started golf clapping. "Well done."

Connie smiled, but it didn't reach her eyes. "One down, hundreds of thousands to go."

Jazz was still flushed, and looked at her nervously. "Truly?"

Connie nodded. "Unfortunately. Most of em ain't even worth this much effort."

Thumper sighed, then started typing. "IT WORKED THIS TIME. EVENTUALLY, I CAN REFINE IT TO SOMETHING YOU'D JUST KEEP LOADED ON YOUR PHONE. THEN I CAN SHARE."

I tried to give an encouraging smile. "Altruistic of you there, old friend."

"THE GIFT THAT CAN KEEP ON GIVING. UNTIL DUDES LEARN MANNERS."

Mages didn't usually share their custom spells. Constructing new ways to use magic was a time-consuming and often dangerous undertaking. Which is why most learning after high school goes from Master to apprentice. Or within a faction.

Which Thumper didn't belong to.

I tilted my head in confusion. "Wait a minute. Share with who?"

My pants began vibrating before Thumper could answer. I checked the number on my phone when I drew it out. I was being called by someone I hadn't seen since high school. I hit the answer circle. "Rocky?"

Thumper tilted their head in confusion. They hadn't heard from Rocky in years either.

An alto voice emerged from my phone. *"Hey Travis. It's Rocky. Sorry to bug you out of the blue, but I got a problem. A Blue River kinda problem."*

That raised my eyebrow. "Sure. What's up?"

"*My theater is haunted. And I'm pretty sure the theater ghost killed my assistant.*"

Chapter Two

Guideline Twenty-Seven:
Cultural taboos are there for a reason.
Find out what that reason is before you go breaking them.

Atlanta's Fairlie-Poplar district isn't a neighborhood of its own so much as a way of feeding people with business at the state capitol. That made it a great place for a discreet lunch. Connie and Thumper were coming with me. This definitely sounded like a full coven mission. We'd taken a Marta train to the Five Points station, mostly as a way of not having to find a place to park. A short walk west brought us to a Mediterranean hole-in-the-wall with amazing cooked meat smells coming from the kitchen.

"Travis!"

Rocky was a short, curvy girl with doe eyes that belonged on a cartoon princess and royal purple hair held back by a black headband. She stepped out of the crowd, wrapping her arms around me without a moment's hesitation, though she had to reach a couple of extra inches to do it. Depending on how you looked at it, puberty had either been abundantly generous or particularly cruel to Rocky.

We lingered for the handful of extra seconds you give to an old friend you hadn't seen in too long. Then she let go and I was able to exhale again.

Rocky's lifestyle had given her the kind of back muscles normally found on longshoremen that took plenty of overtime.

"Rocky, not sure if you remember Thumper here."

Thumper gave her a grin. Rocky's eyes lit up in recognition. "I do. Hey!"

I gave them a moment to de-hug and pointed out the last member of our party. "And this is Connie. Not sure if you know each other."

Rocky tilted her head and squinted. "I don't think so, but you look kind of familiar."

Connie kept her quiet smile. "You're probably thinking of my sister. Heather McKay."

Rocky's cheerful look dimmed like a cloudy day. Heather, who had been my girlfriend and Thumper's best friend, had been killed at Blue River. "Oh, I'm sorry."

Connie shook her head and gave a rare smile. "It's all right. I love your hair."

Lunch was cafeteria style. We grabbed our food and found a quiet alcove. It wasn't quite like a Wa'cross or Warwell's, but the owner clearly knew a lot of their business consisted of lawyers and bankers. Moderate privacy is almost as attractive as a good menu in a place like that.

About halfway through my lamb calzone, I washed it down with a soda and figured it was on me to get down to business. "On the phone you said this was a problem with ghosts? Did I hear right?"

She nodded solemnly. "Yup. I got a problem with ghosts. A big, angry, nasty one. And I think you can help me with that."

I hated playing dumb. But at times like these, you had to do the dance. "Not sure what you want me todo, Rocky. I mean, ghosts?"

Her look told me she wasn't buying it one bit. "I saw you kiss one."

I dropped my fork. A lot of nasty memories hit me in the back of the emotions. I tried to blink them away before they reached my eyes and doubled down on the dumb. "Really?"

She nodded again. "The night of Blue River."

Blue River. So much of my life came down to Blue River. It had been too dark, too fast, and too bloody for most people to realize what was happening. Rocky must have seen me spend time on memory lane, because she kept going.

"I'm sorry I'm dredging all this up, Travis. But give me some credit here. I know a lot of ugly shit happened that night. I also know the official story is bullshit. We don't talk about it, even among ourselves. But we know that much. I know whatever happened that night is something I can't explain. And I also know that you, and Thumper, and some of the others are the reason I'm still alive."

I dropped the act and nodded. She kept going.

"And in the middle of all that mess, I will swear on a copy of the completed works of Shakespeare that I saw you kiss a girl who'd already been dead for a year that night. So either I saw you cheat on Heather McKay within an hour of her death, or I saw you kiss a ghost. And I don't think the man I saw tearing up attack dogs with a shotgun all night is a cheater. So own up. Did I see what I thought I saw that night?"

There was no point to further charades. "You did."

She cracked a smile. "Then if you can't help me, you know who can. And I need help."

I nodded. "We can. Connie especially. She's the medium."

Rocky's shoulders de-knotted a bit in relief. "Really?"

I nodded. "Absolutely. I'm a 3XL at least."

Connie rolled her eyes. Thumper blew a raspberry at me.

I kept a poker face with my eyes on Rocky. "Fill us in."

Thumper opened a notebook and started scribbling as Rocky began. "I'm stage managing a show at the Pencil Factory. A rock opera version of Romeo and Juliet. Big stuff. The director slash producer is Max Roman."

Connie frowned a bit. "Isn't he the guy from that show?"

"He's the guy from a lot of shows. Since the late 80's. Never made superstar fame. But he was an investment genius and never had expensive habits, so he's worth a fortune. He didn't just lease the Pencil Factory for a show. He bought it lock, stock, and barrel. And he had it renovated himself."

I was impressed. "Pricey real estate even if you don't have a theater attached."

Connie nodded. "And the ghost?"

Rocky shrugged. "Pretty much all theaters got em. And they're usually pretty harmless. Shadows of people who aren't standing in the light. Lights will turn on or off, you'll hear footsteps or voices, see people out of the corner of your eye... Things you can shrug off. They don't hurt anybody. You chalk it up to being in the theater, like not whistling backstage or not talking about the Scottish Man or always leaving the ghost light on, that kinda thing."

Connie was more focused now. "Never heard of a theater ghost killing anyone."

Rocky nodded. "Me neither, until three weeks ago. We started rehearsals a week before that, everything seemed like it was going well. We'd taken a break and I was just about to call the company back in when Grover, the lyricist, just loses it. Screams his head off and runs full speed out the front doors. Some clown in a pickup smeared him across Mitchell street all the way to the stoplight. Dead the moment he stepped off the sidewalk."

I grimaced. "That incident report had to suck."

Rocky slammed her empty cup on the table. "Ya think? I'm barely out of my twenties and I got 'Lyricist in vehicular homicide' on my resume."

I nodded. "What did the cops say?"

Rocky threw up her hands. "Everyone who saw him, including me, saw him run right out into the road. The truck driver got charged with vehicular manslaughter, but I think he's gonna get off easy."

Connie asked. "And nobody saw what spooked him?"

Rocky shook her head. "Nope. He'd dropped his stuff in the lobby and took off."

I nodded. "And that wasn't the only accident."

Rocky seemed to get smaller by the moment, her natural cheer gone. "No. My assistant, Greg. Two days ago, he fell from the grid without a word."

I listened. "No scream, nothing?"

Rocky shook her head some more. "Just some movement out of the corner of my eye and then his body smashed into the house."

I nodded, starting to do math in my head. "What kind of distance? Height, I mean?"

Rocky bit her lip and thought. "From the catwalk to the middle of the house? Forty-odd feet."

I took that in. "What did the cops say about that one?"

Rocky snorted. "He died on impact. His safety line had snapped. Cops took one look at it and saw it worn away near the break."

I nodded, still thinking heights and distances. "Does that make sense to you?"

She shook her head emphatically. "Not since I watched him buy a new harness just a few months ago. Greg had his problems, but he looked out for himself."

I looked over to Connie, who asked. "Either of them have any enemies?"

Rocky shook her head again. "Nobody on this cast or crew that I knew of. Which is how it usually goes."

I raised an eyebrow. "Really?"

Rocky nodded. "Doing a show means living in each others' pockets for a few months, then scattering to the winds. A couple of theaters have regulars, but even then people come and go unless they're also a staff member. So most people try and at least get along long enough to do the show, but after that, you're competition again. Not a whole lot of deep friendships, but no enemies willing to kill, either."

Connie nodded. "Anything that would've made someone go that route?"

Rocky sighed in embarrassment. "Greg was handsy. Grabbed my ass at a wrap party once. I told him I'd twist his sack off with a multitool if he ever did it again. Goddess rest his greasy soul. He was a good rigger and a good follow spot, but he'd creep all over the ladies if I didn't keep him in line."

I nodded. "And Grover?"

Rocky shook her head. "Only off the clock. Consummate professional at the office, but get a couple of Mai Tais in him and he thought that gave him a license to play with other people's boobs. Which was all the more weird, given that he was gay, but that's showbiz for you."

I shook my head. "The tortured lives of artists."

Connie waved me off. "OK. Anyone see this ghost around?"

Rocky grimaced. "Physically see it? Not that I know of. But this ghost, it's... stronger than usual. Angrier. I hear doors slam when I'm the only one in the building. I've heard singing at night while I'm locking up. Temperature drops in weird places. It's creepifying."

I nodded. "And the cops are letting the show go on?"

She shrugged. "Why not? Two accidents that could each be suicide."

She had a point there. Connie asked. "Anybody quit?"

Rocky shook her head. "Nobody would dare quit a show like this, ghost or not."

That was weird. "Why? Everyone reads it in High School. Romeo and Juliets are a dime a dozen."

Rocky looked at me like I'd tried to eat my fork. "Nonunion ones? In Georgia? paying twenty percent over Broadway rates?"

That description meant nothing to me. "That's a lot?"

Rocky nodded solemnly. "That's unheard of."

I frowned. "You're shitting me."

Rocky shook her head again. "I shit you not. New musical. No out-of-towns, but an eight week rehearsal and workshop period and open-ended performance season at the Pencil Factory. All nonunion, all way above union minimum pay."

Rocky gave me some numbers. I did some math in my head and twitched. "How the hell is that possible? Even with... how many seats?"

Rocky was on the ball. "Fifteen-fifty. Bigger than the Alliance, about a third the size of the Fox."

"Even then, you'd have to sell out night after night for... " The math of it silenced me.

Rocky's hands went up. "I think Max is bankrolling the entire thing himself. His big project is this show in this theater."

I frowned. "Weird. What, is he screwing the ingenue or something?"

Rocky shrugged. "Dawn? Probably. Girl's built like a bomber's nose art. Not that she can't do the job, she's got the pipes to match the tits. But outside of work it's anyone's guess. Maybe she is a mattress and Max is just being a sugar daddy, but I don't think so."

Connie nodded. "Let's go with the idea that these ghosts are into handsy dudes. Who'd be the next target?"

Rocky thought. "Right now? Either Tim or Danny."

Connie asked. "What do they do?"

"Tim's playing Tybalt. He's pretty and he's got buckets of charm. But he's a love em and leave em type. Between you, me, and the wall, he's a lousy lay, too."

I nodded. "Makes sense. Danny a letch too?"

Rocky nodded. "Yep. Danny Larus. Smooth as a silk bathrobe. But he's a lot like Grover. Charming as hell, but gets way too familiar way too quick. He's playing our Mercutio."

I nodded. "Two hot-blooded gents, no waiting."

Rocky grimaced. "Yeah, and replacing either of them would suck."

Connie spoke up. "Can you get us inside?"

"Easy. I need to hire a replacement for Greg, and ASM's, assistant stage managers, can go anywhere."

I nodded. "Can you hire two?"

Rocky grinned. "For what they're paying me? Easily."

Connie and I traded glances, then Connie turned back towards Rocky. "OK. I can't make any promises, Rocky. But if it is a ghost, we got a pretty good chance of taking care of it before anyone else gets hurt."

I could almost see some of the weight leave her shoulders. "Thanks, Connie. When can you guys start?"

Connie spoke up. "Tomorrow, if possible."

Rocky's eyes were bright with relief. "Sure. Remember the three big rules?

I frowned. "Wasn't one of them never whistle in a theater?"

She nodded. "That's rule one."

Connie frowned. "Isn't there one about not saying good luck?"

Rocky held up two fingers. "That's number two. You don't have to say 'break a leg.' You can say whatever kind of encouragement you want. Except 'good luck.'"

I looked skeptical. "Well, don't leave us in suspense, Rocky. What's the third rule?"

She glanced both ways, then looked me dead in the eyes. "Never, and I mean ever, say The Scottish Man's name inside the theater."

I cocked my head. "The guy from Braveheart?"

Thumper rolled their eyes.

Rocky grimaced. "No, dumbass. The one from Shakespeare."

I thought, then it hit me. "Macbeth?"

Rocky winced and held up a hand. "We're not in a theater right now, so it's OK. But ...don't. Just don't."

If there's one thing magic and theater both teach you, it's to take taboos seriously. No matter how nonsensical they look at first value. "No whistling, no good luck, no Scottish Man. Got it."

"You got it. Anything else you need?"

Thumper gave her a business card. Connie nodded at it. "Info. As much about the show as you can tell us. The script, the libretto, if there's recordings of rehearsals. Oh, yeah, and everyone's headshots and resumes."

"For a ghost?"

Connie looked uncomfortable, then took a long breath. "Ghosts usually aren't homicidal. And when they are and they're this powerful? It's usually because someone is making them that way. We might not be looking for just a ghost. We might be looking for a necromancer."

Rocky blinked. "That sounds bad."

I bit my lip, then nodded. "Blue River was a necromancer. And we're lucky they killed as few people as they did."

Rocky's eyes got wide and her voice got small. "You mean something like that is running around in my theater?"

Connie and I traded looks. I broke the silence. "We don't know yet. We know that's the first answer that makes sense to us. But like we've said, ghosts like this usually don't kill."

Connie held Rocky's hand. "I'll do what I can with your ghost. If it's more than that, we'll figure it out as we go."

* * *

We got back to my house and found our relaxing spots, having spent the ride home thinking in our own heads.

Connie kicked it off, her feet up on the coffee table. "Well, this is definitely a double-G."

She was referring to the law of magi: We Guide, We Guard, We Never Rule.

I accepted a soda on ice from Jazz and nodded a thank you in her direction. "Rocky sounds convinced it's ghosts. It could still be a Scooby, though."

A Scooby was an Otherworld problem that turned out to have a mundane cause.

Connie nodded. "There's probably ghosts involved, just not sure how. And I might be jumping to conclusions, but ghosts that are no-shit killing people is just suspicious."

That raised my eyebrow. "How do you know? It's a theater. There's a lot of ways for people to get killed in there."

Her immaculate purple lipstick pursed into a smirk. "What do you know about ghosts outside of what they taught in study hall?"

A flashback hit me like a dodgeball. "Just the ones that crashed Blue River. We didn't have much time then."

"Gotcha. This theater older than, oh, a decade or two?"

"Yeah."

She nodded. "Then there's ghosts. Always are."

I frowned. "How does that work? I've done roadie work off and on since high school, I've never seen hauntings."

Connie moved her hand in a circle. "But you've felt the energy in there, right? You noticed how magic flows through the buildings easier?"

I nodded. I was an alchemist and an engineer. I knew enough building design. "Yeah. I figured it was a bonus of the same old designs being used for centuries. That magic flow gets affected the same way acoustics does."

"Maybe. But that's not why they're ghost magnets specifically."

I raised an eyebrow. "Enlighten me."

She started talking with her hands as lecture mode engaged. "Theaters are lightning rods for hopes, for wishes, for dreams. Every actor, every dancer, every musician who walks in the door comes full of passions. And showbiz being what it is, a lot of them get left behind. For every one dream that comes true, dozens never make it. And it happens again every single show, every single season, every single year."

"Yeah?"

She folded her arms in a way she usually did before handing me my ass in a chess game. "To make a simplistic definition, ghosts *are* passions that were left behind."

The implications of that set in. "Oh."

Her look softened. "I don't think it's a question of whether we have ghosts. The question is, are they the ones who've started killing people? And if that's the case, who got them started?"

Chapter Three

Guideline Nineteen:

Respect the local customs.

At least until you find out why they're the local customs.

It was about eleven the next morning when Connie and I rolled into the parking lot. It was my turn to drive, so I was behind the wheel of my Yukon. The sun was up, still chased by the persistent clouds. It could rain, scorch, or both before we went home today. The fun of springtime in Georgia. We parked in the open-air lot Rocky mentioned and unbuckled.

Connie handed me an eyeliner pencil with carvings in it I didn't recognize.

I frowned, accepting it. "What's this for?"

"You need to know ghosts are therebefore you can work on them."

"With eyeliner?"

Connie shrugged. "It's a quick fix, but it works."

"How do I put it on?"

"Like any other eyeliner."

I shrugged and lifted it up to the edge of my eye when Connie touched my wrist to stop me.

I frowned. "What now?"

She blinked carefully at me. "You've never worn eyeliner before, have you?"

I shrugged again. "Never needed to before. How did you know?"

She flipped down the driver's side visor and opened up the mirror. "If you can see what you're doing, it's harder to accidentally stab yourself in the eye."

I blinked. That made sense. I looked at my eyes through the mirror and raised the pencil.

"Gimme."

Connie had her hand opened. I raised an eyebrow. "Now what?"

"It'll go faster if I do it for you. Now gimme and turn towards me."

I handed over the pencil and looked into my covenmate's eyes.

"Close your eyes."

I shut them obediently, then felt a weird sensation of a small point rubbing across my eyelid. I opened my mouth to say something when Connie spoke up again. "Stop squirming. I'm working in tight quarters here."

A few more rubs, then, "OK. Open your eyes and look up."

She was holding the pencil closer to my face than I was comfortable with. I looked up at the fabric ceiling of the Yukon. She moved in and I could feel more rubbing, this time on the bottom of my eyelid. Then she moved to what feltlike right next to my eyeball. I held still until she stopped, then sat back and nodded. "That'll do for now."

I looked into the visor mirror. It was thick enough to be noticeable. "I look like a cartoon pirate."

She smirked. "Rather dashing, I think."

"So I'm supposed to see ghosts now?"

She nodded. "You can. When you think some may be around, call up a bit of magic to activate it. You'll be able to see any nearby. And see through any illusions they throw up."

"How do I know it's working?"

"You'll recognize the underworld when you see it. Everything turns kind of gray-green. Everything's kinda dull. Rotting here, falling apart there. Like all the wear and tear we hide under paint and maintenance all comes to the surface."

"Useful. How long does it last?"

She shrugged. "Fifteen, maybe twenty minutes?"

"Just enough to be handy. Thanks."

"Got one more for you."

She dug into her purse and came up with three packets of burgundy fabric, each small enough to fit in a shotglass. They were tied off at the ends with rubber bands.

"There's no time to teach you proper necromancy. These are just shit hitting the fan charms."

I frowned. Connie continued. "Not a whole lot that's physical harms a ghost. But a ghost can still hurt you. You get in deep shit, pop one of these open and spread it around. It'll banish whatever's screwing around with you. It doesn't last forever. An hour, maybe a day, tops, and it will come back. But if it's doing their best to kill you, this will save your ass long enough to get something more effective."

I nodded and tucked them into a pocket. "Thanks again."

We stepped out into the warm breeze as Atlanta traffic went about its rounds. Across from the parking terminal was a pair of middle school aged kids standing next to a white cooler. As I was punching in the code Rocky gave us, the taller one held up a bottle of water, glistening in the sun.

"Hey, Big Man! You and the lady want some water?"

I tucked away my receipt and looked him up and down. He looked human, but it always paid to check. "How much?"

The kid didn't take his eyes off me, but grinned in anticipation. "Five bucks each."

I nodded. "Gimme two."

I pulled a pair of fives from my front pocket. The kid put the bottle he had back in the cooler, pulling two fresh ones from the ice inside.

I accepted both. "Thanks, kid." I passed one to Connie, who watched the whole exchange with a poker face.

The kid made the cash disappear, then grinned again. "Anytime you're thirsty, Big Man. Nice guyliner."

Connie and I went on our merry way. Once we were out of earshot, she murmured at me.

"Ten bucks for water?"

I shrugged. "They could be selling worse. Plus, the truck's less likely to be fucked with this way."

I hated parking this deep downtown. I could take a boot off a truck just by looking at it funny, but I tried to keep that kind of thing to a minimum.

A haggard new voice called out. "Hey, Big Man!"

I cocked my head. "Why does everyone call me that?"

Connie shrugged, her elbow barely rising above my belt. "It's a mystery."

Staggering towards us was a bum that had been napping against the wall. He had all the marks of someone who'd been out for a long time. The lines in his face were deep enough to have been carved. Maybe four teeth were left in a mouth surrounded by scraggly beard. His head was permanently swaying forward as if mounted on a broken spring, but his eyes were focused enough to notice us. His arm was out and his hand was open. "Can ya help me out, Big Man?"

He'd probably seen me with the kids and pegged me for an easy mark. I didn't care. I could afford it. I shrugged and dropped a ten in the old boy's hand.

"Just a little bit, man. But it's enough to get some lunch in you."

Somewhere in the swaying was a smile as the worn fingers closed on the bill. "Heyyy, thanks, Big Man! Nice guyliner. Looks good on you."

I wished him luck and we moved on.

* * *

The theater itself was in a part of downtown that kept getting failed attempts at revitalization. Nobody wanted to use Marta, Atlanta's shell of a subway system. But trying to park downtown was like playing Russian Roulette with your tires. Here and there we'd find a barber shop, shoe store, or family owned restaurant. But most of it was a sparsely populated no-man's-land between the capitol building and the stadium.

The Pencil Factory Theater, on the other hand, was easy to recognize. Structurally, it was the same size as the other buildings on the block; four story brick blocks with boarded up street retail places on the ground floor. But in the middle of the block, an old-school marquee jutted out of the first floor roof. Unlit in the middle of the day, but the recessed lights in the burgundy facade looked newly installed and ready to go. A "coming soon!" sign was already in place for "Romeo &Juliet: The Rock Opera!"

There was nobody in the ticket kiosk, but the door was unlocked when we tried it. We pushed the glass-front door open and slipped into the glorious air conditioning. The lobby looked like an old-time movie theater. All burgundy velvet and soft, warm lighting. The concession stand was clean but empty. It smelled like an old bookstore, modern cleaning chemicals with the hint of ancient paper beneath. I was surprised at the lack of popcorn among the scents. The windows had a haze to them, like they were still getting used to being cleaned.

Connie and I both gave the place a once-over. I shook my head. "This looks like the kind of movie place you only see in old movies. Y'know, where the ushers are dressed like old-timey bellhops."

A gravelly voice asked. "Can I help you?"

Both Connie and I twitched. Neither of us were used to someone being able to get that close without noticing them. Standing behind us was a man with an advanced case of monitor slouch. A horseshoe of white hair lay around the back of his head, and thick glasses rested on his nose. He wore a set of used but cared for dickies, with a rag hanging out of his back pocket. A mop was clenched in his hands like a knight's sword. A bucket was at his feet. Central Casting couldn't have sent a better janitor.

I recovered first. "Uh, yeah. We're here for Rocky?"

The janitor's frame bounced slightly as a coughing sound emerged from his chest. It took me a second to realize it was a laugh. After a pause to look Connie up and down, the janitor vaguely waved further inside. "She's around somewhere. Watch your asses, though. The ghosts have been jumpy lately."

A familiar voice spoke up. "I got 'em, Roscoe."

Rocky emerged from the depths behind the concession stand. A ring of keys hanging on a bright purple lanyard bounced off her chest like a Lilliputian daredevil.

Roscoe shrugged noncommittally. We had briefly interrupted his day to no consequence.

Rocky, on the other hand, was all energy. "Guys, this is Roscoe, our janitor. Roscoe, these are my new ASM's, Travis and Connie."

Roscoe gave a single wheezing chuckle. "Heh. Hope they turn out better than the last one."

Connie looked him in the eye. "How have the ghosts been jumpy, Roscoe?"

His jaw set deeper as he looked her up and down. 'Heh. Most of 'em scare people away. This one's gone straight for the throat. You heard yet?"

She slowly nodded, not looking away. "About Grover? About Greg? I have. You seen this ghost, Roscoe? Heard it?"

Roscoe sneered. "Heh. Yeah. Heard a girl crying here and there. Course that could just be an actress. They go off like sprinklers in a smoking section." He snickered at his own joke, then squinted to look at me. After a second, he nodded. "Nice guyliner."

Without waiting for a response, he returned to the display window. A spray bottle and squeegee were drawn from the holsters around his bucket, and a slow assault on the window dust began.

Rocky motioned us to follow her and led us through the double doors into a room twice the height of the lobby. A pair of grand staircases led up to the second floor, and hallways stretched in either direction.

"Don't let Roscoe spook ya. There's still a lot of cleanup from the renovations, so he's here pretty much full time."

Connie was already checking the corners. "Where'd you dig him up?"

"I didn't. He came with the building. I'm pretty sure Harry, the business manager, hired him. We've got some time until people start coming in, so lemme give you a quick tour."

Connie looked around the foyer. "Place is bigger than I thought."

Rocky nodded. "Oh yeah. This was the old factory, then some storefronts with offices and warehouses in the back, then a theater and some stores, then it was a theater off and on, got used for a movie set or two, and now it's a theater again."

Rocky pointed back the way we came. "We're actually standing right where Grover lost it."

We lingered. I'll admit I didn't really know what to look for. Spy cameras and hidden compartments were more my jam. I saw Connie checking out the area, though it looked like she hadn't found anything more interesting than I had. After giving the place a good once-over, she looked back to Rocky and shrugged. "Nothing so far."

Rocky nodded and turned left, heading down the hallways. "I'm waiting on permanent signage, but you'll get used to the rooms we're actually using."

We passed a door with a hand lettered sign saying "Harry's office." Similar signs adorned offices for Max and Rocky.

Going down two flights of stairs at the end of the hall, we hung another left. First door on the right was a sign labeled "Grover's office." Then an open door on the right leading to what looked like a gym with no machines in it. One wall was covered in mirrors. The other held a line of folding chairs. An upright piano was positioned at the far end.

"That's the rehearsal hall on the right. And over here is Mabel's domain."

Next to an open door was another paper sign reading "Wardrobe." The sign had a growing collection of colorful graffiti, including glitter and gold star stickers. The open door led to a room with rows of mannequins draped in costumes at varying stages of construction. Bins lined shelves up to the ceiling along one wall. Racks upon racks of hung-up clothes lined another. I noticed the same model of embroidery machine that I used, ready for action on a long bench that housed a few other machines.

Rocky yelled through the doorway, pointedly not entering the room. "How ya doing, Mabel?"

A seasoned voice replied. "On schedule, honey."

Opening the door completely revealed a pear-shaped figure working at a shiny purple costume hanging on a dressmaker's form. Her hair was done up and short, most of it riding the edge from silver into white. The exception was a streak of bright blue two inches wide, sweeping back from over her right eye to the back of her neck. She wore thick glasses with a pair of jeweler's loupes clamped on the left side. They hung on a chain of irregular plastic shapes in matte colors. She jabbed a pin back into the tomato-shaped pincushion strapped to the back of her wrist.

"It's everything for the ball scene. Max has me tarting it up like prom night in Vegas. I got enough sequins in here to outfit a biopic of Liberace. You need anything, darling?"

Rocky shook her head. "Just showing the new ASM's around. Travis and Connie."

Mabel's magnified eyes gave us both a once-over with a side of shining smile. "Well, they look sturdy enough. Welcome aboard. Try not to get yourselves killed."

I raised an eyebrow at that one. "I'll do my best."

She gave a short laugh that would've made a great cackle from a witch, if we went with stereotypes. "I like this one. He rolls with the punches. That's a good attitude to have, young'n. Keep being that positive. It might save your ass when the ghost goes after you."

Connie tilted her head. "You think the ghost will go after him?"

Mabel looked closer at me, then flipped down one of the loupes on her glasses. "Hrm. Older than I'd think. But still a nice thick slice of American beefcake. Nice guyliner, too. I think he'd piss her off more than the others around here."

Connie's gaze didn't falter. "So the ghost is a she?"

Mabel turned her look to Connie and flipped up her loupe. "If it's a ghost, how much does it matter? I've never heard the ghost speak, but I've heard a woman crying when I thought I was alone. And no, it wasn't me. I checked. Besides, it's had weeks of opportunity and only killed men so far. I figure even money it's a woman."

Connie nodded in noncommittal agreement. "Would you respond if she did speak?"

Mabel gave a grin that was somehow even quirkier. "At my age, it's a pleasant surprise talking to someone who's not dead. But I probably would, just to be polite."

Chapter Four

Guideline Thirty-One:
Caution won't save you every time.
It's still a good habit.

The rest of the tour was relatively uneventful. The scene shop was occupied by a pair of surly carpenters focused on their jobs. Metal frames were in various stages of construction, with the usual wall of tools. Finally, a place I understood.

The prop shop, on the other hand, looked like a time traveling thrift store had exploded, then been stuffed into a random room. The occupant, a red bearded little man with hornrimmed glasses and a tricorn pirate hat, was supervising a 3D printer as it buzzed away.

We made another left at the end of the hall and headed past several closed off and unlabeled doors. Something about the place was making me itch between the shoulder blades, and I didn't know why. I was a master alchemist. I could feel things about how buildings worked that modern materials science hadn't figured out yet, let alone modern architecture. But something about this theater was put together in ways I couldn't describe. They were almost like the wards that covered the walls of my own house, or the spell work that went through the walls of the study hall in High School. But they weren't material or structural. They weren't electrical or magnetic.

They weren't plumbing or gas. Something I couldn't identify was here. In the walls, the floors, the ceilings...everywhere.

Connie spoke up. "How many levels does the building have?"

Rocky shrugged. "At least six. We're in the original sub basement, which is below the stage. That door there leads to the orchestra pit where we're keeping the band. There's also trapdoors in the stage we can access from here."

Rocky opened a door and flipped on a light switch, A handful of incandescent bulbs spaced far apart illuminated the dusty room. There were piles of old cardboard boxes filling the space to our right. Strips of glow tape marked a pair of doors to the left. Dust and cobwebs covered everything.

I clicked on my flashlight and started shining it in various corners. Connie looked the place up and down, noting the stanchions that held up the stage every couple of feet. She turned to Rocky. "Are we using any of those trapdoors?"

Rocky shook her head. "Not for this show. It's not on my priority list. Or on Roscoe's. I don't even know what most of this stored stuff is. Those doors go to the orchestra pit, but it has it's own entrances from the hallway, so we're not using them."

I sniffed. There was suddenly an odd scent in the air. "Anyone smell that?"

Rocky tilted her head. "Decades of dust?"

I shook my head. "No, it's more like... old man cologne. Some kind of aftershave or something."

Connie frowned. "Yeah, I smell it too."

Rocky shrugged. "These boxes could be full of it for all I know."

I scratched my temple. Connie shook her head. I shone a flashlight into a few more corners before shrugging. As I turned to go back, I swore I could see a shadow out of the corner of my eye slowly growing. I aimed my flashlight at it underhand and clicked the tail cap on. The shadow, and whatever was manipulating it, vanished, leaving a pile of cardboard boxes and cobwebs behind.

Rocky led us back out and locked the door behind us. We turned left and headed for another stairwell.

Rocky pointed at the ceiling. "Next up is the basement, where the stage, loading dock, green room, and dressing rooms are. Next level up, even with the street, is the box office, house, lobby, and admin areas. Next level up is the house and the upper salon. Next level after that is the balcony, next after that is the booth, catwalks, and fly system. Plus some storage units I haven't poked around in yet. And I'm pretty sure there's at least one floor above that before the roof."

I mapped the place out in my head. "That's a lot of room. Like the theater is just the core of the building and everything else is wrapped around it in layers like a cake."

"I know. I think Max is planning on renting out some of the spaces after the show run ends. Or maybe the entire venue."

Connie glanced behind us. "A lot of nooks and crannies to hide in."

We came up the staircase, followed the hallway and ended where we began.

Rocky checked her watch. "We'll have to hit the other levels later. Looks like the cast is about to start rolling in. So we'll end with the house for now."

Rocky opened one of the big double doors and led us into the auditorium, which I'd already started mentally calling the house. Row after row of velvet upholstered seats led down to one of the bigger stages I'd ever seen. Two massive aisles led down the middle of the seats, with two more aisles splitting them on the sides. Halfway towards the stage, the balcony ended and the ceiling rose at least twenty feet. The three of us walked down the entire length of the aisle until we came to a wooden barrier between us and the stage. I glanced over the barrier and saw a lower area strewn with a band setup: keyboards and drum kit in the back, spots for guitars and horns closer to me.

I looked up from the orchestra pit and saw the set. It was just a skeleton, but a multi-story steel structure in the middle of an open theater is impressive all by itself. A second-level catwalk met in a staircase heading down to center stage. I could see a pair of stairways offstage to let the cast make their exits safely. At some points, I saw cables linked to the structure, rising up into the maze of lights, pipes, and miscellaneous supports overhead. It looked sturdy enough. Which meant I would need to check it out myself later.

I glanced over at Connie and gave a questioning gesture. She responded with a negative one. No immediate ghost threat here. Before I could say anything else, the doors opened and a crowd began heading down the aisle.

The cast introduced themselves in a flurry of extroversion. It was like getting welcomed aboard by an influencer convention. I recognized faces and roles only because I'd studied the night before. Kenny, who was playing Romeo. Danny, who was playing Mercutio. Tim, who was playing Tybalt. Ron, who was playing Paris. All of them bright-eyed and dripping with charm. A few of the others were older, heavier, or both. I mentally matched them up with Friar Laurence, the parents, the Prince, and the Nurse. A half-dozen pretty and fit folks of both sexes filled out the ensemble. Then the door kicked in and the stars approached.

Coming through the doors, they looked like a prom king and queen who reigned well into their twenties. She was in a sundress that looked grateful to be worn by the likes of her. He was in a polo shirt and a waistcoat that looked just tailored enough to not be ostentatious. They looked like what they were: casual clothes that took a lot of effort to design and wear. Only the gray in Max's hair showed their age difference, and he was enough of a silver fox that I had to work hard to notice.

Rocky saw them coming. "Hey Max, Dawn, these are my new ASM's."

Their smiles lit up the room on cue. He stepped forward with his hand out.

"Max Roman. Welcome aboard."

His handshake was the clenching grip of someone determined to show he could take it with the big guys. I'd never seen this kind of raw charisma. Old instincts I hadn't used since high school told me this guy would seduce my girlfriend just to watch my heart break, and a part of me liked him anyway. I made a note to have myself checked for mind control later. It took me a half second to remember to respond. "Travis Wayland. Glad to be here."

He moved on with practiced ease and I was suddenly spellbound by a pair of bright blue doe eyes. She was just shy of petite, with a willowy build. I could see just the hint of knowing amusement in those baby blues. Her blonde hair was straight and pulled back in a ponytail, expertly tightened enough to frame her face. Probably in her late twenties now, she'd look like a naive teenager well into her forties. "Hi! I'm Dawn!"

I found a stronger handshake than I expected. Women usually didn't play that stupid game.

"Travis. I'm working for Rocky. Guessing you're the leading lady."

"You got that right."

She flashed another smile that ad agencies would kill to have hawking for their clients and moved on. The composer had entered the pit and began plinking away at the keyboards. An electric guitar and amplifier were set up next to him.

The stage was full of bodies. Some were stretching, others tumbling. A few were adjusting braces or pads. Others were double-checking 3-ring binders, presumably their scripts. Onesies and twosies turned their phones off, tucking them away.

Max turned to Rocky, looking for all the world like a starship captain consulting a bridge officer. "Where we at?"

Rocky checked her diver's watch. "Twenty seconds."

Max nodded a thank you to her, then paused to stretch, making a few focused breaths. Then I could almost see his game face come on, like he was donning a helmet. "All right folks! Hope everyone's been safe and focused. Welcome our new ASM's, Travis and Connie. Jerry, warm us up, then everyone at places for the top of the ballroom sequence."

A slim guy with long sandy hair had pushed back from the piano and slung the guitar over his shoulder. Without a word, he began the opening riff of an old song. I vaguely remembered it, but the entire cast seemed to. It was old-school call and response, the kind you heard in a church sometime, but with a rock sound to it. Jerry would drawl out a verse, and the entire cast would sing the response.

I'm not one to lose myself in a performance, but something put a tingle down my spine. The same kind of tingle I felt when someone was casting a spell. I strained my senses, but couldn't notice any obvious magic. Something I didn't understand was going on. The cast began to move and dance spontaneously, not missing a word or a breath. It was like being in the same karaoke bar a cast full of professionals had just happened to crash for dinner that night. They were warming up their own voices and showing off for each other at the same time.

At the side of the ensemble, one of the ladies caught my eye. She was curvier than anyone else on stage, with bright blue eyes and auburn hair. Her confidence radiated through her voice and movement both. She reminded me of Jazz, and was just as good at catching my eye. It took me several seconds before I remembered where I was and came down. I felt like I'd just been enchanted. Again. And that was a possibility that worried me.

I'd spent about a year as a renfield, being very susceptible to vampiric mind control. I'd also altered my own memories with a spell that backlashed hard on me. Long story short, I'm a little paranoid whenever something affects my thoughts or emotions that I didn't see coming.

The cast and band wound down before setting up for the next scene, satisfied with their warmups. I blinked, trying to wrap my mind around what had happened. I had legit lost track of time. Had I been hit with a spell? Was a ghost screwing with me? I resisted the urge to activate my eyeliner and settled for checking out all of the corners in the house I could see. Sitting on Rocky's right, Connie caught my eyes. I let my eyes circle the room, then ask a question. She gave me a slight shrug in return. If I'd been hit with magic, she hadn't noticed it.

I tried to focus on where a ghost would watch from, if they had a choice. Rocky had a folding table setup in the house as her domain, with a small mixing board, a gooseneck lamp, and a 3-ring binder thicker than my fist. Different colored post-it notes were stuck to various pages in the binder. Currently, she had it open to the page of the script that began the ballroom scene. On the other side, she had a legal pad open to a fresh page.

To Rocky's left, at the end of the row, Max sat at another table with his own script. It was odd to see him alone. He looked like the kind of guy who naturally had an entourage. But he'd only showed up with Dawn, who was onstage rolling her shoulders and neck like a prizefighter. He looked focused more than anything.

Rocky reached past Connie to tap me on the shoulder. "Can you grab my kit from my office? Toolbox with my name on it."

I nodded, took her massive keyring, and headed back up the aisle to the foyer.

Coming into the foyer, I could see daylight coming through the lobby windows for the first time in an hour. One side of the lobby windows was distinctly letting in more light than the other. Clearly, Roscoe's war on dust was being fought in stages. I turned right, heading for the row of offices. The sound of the rehearsal vanished as the door closed behind me.

Rocky's office was where I remembered it from the tour, at the end of the hall before the stairwell. The lock was easy to open, but the hinges of the doors creaked like an old-fashioned haunted house. I made a mental note to oil those hinges ASAP. Inside, it was dominated by an old fashioned steel desk. The kind executives would bend a secretary over back in the fifties. It had come from the factory in classic battleship gray. Someone, with an engraving tool and various paints, had painted "The Arts" across the front. It leaned slightly to the left. Everything else was a thrift store rescue, from the comfortable-looking sofa to the filing cabinet. Only the pristine phone on her desk and a Wi-Fi router in the corner seemed new.

Rocky's kit was unmistakable as advertised. It was a big tackle box festooned with a decade's worth of band stickers. I made sure the latches were closed, then grabbed it. I'm not sure why I imagined it would be heavier. I'd never rummaged around in a stage manager's kit before. How many tools could you need to make actors behave? One cattle prod and a fresh set of batteries and I could do it easy.

As I was closing the door behind me, I could hear a baritone voice sing. But it wasn't accompanied. And it seemed to be coming from upstairs instead of onstage.

What have I done?
What have I ruined?
It was only for fun.
The thing to be doing.

Puzzled, I crept closer to the stairwell. As I got to the doorway, I could hear more clearly. Someone was singing on the upper level.

If I could court you without courting disaster
I could brave the storm, scandals, the rumors, disgrace.
If I could ask now and just hope for what's after
I could step in the light and reveal my face.

Not wanting to interrupt if it was someone who'd gone off to rehearse privately or something, I stepped inside and climbed the stairs warily. Halfway through, the singing faded away, replaced with the sound of wracked, ugly crying.

At the next floor's landing, a young black woman was curled up in front of the door, weeping. She was in an old-fashioned skirt and jacket in the old gray-tan color they called butternut. A mane of long black hair covered her face like a veil. One hand was pressed against the door, as if she'd been locked out and slid down it before landing where she was.

I stopped at the top step and put down the kit, just loud enough to be noticed. My eyeliner wasn't on, but she could still be a ghost. She was almost definitely an actress. And from the look of things, she was armed and set to go off at any moment. If I was quiet and didn't make any sudden moves, I might be able to escape the brunt of the explosion. I licked my lips carefully, then waited for a pause in the sobbing to quietly ask.

"Are you OK?"

She turned rapidly, screamed like something inhuman, and charged at me.

I was blinded. Then horribly cold. And then I felt nothing.

Chapter Five

Guideline Forty:

Finding the truth and finding everything are two different things.

"Travis? Travis!"

I was sitting up against the landing in the middle of the stairwell. The crying girl was gone. In her place was Connie, crouching above me with a flashlight in hand. What looked like half the company was gaggled in the stairwell below and behind her. She was slowly moving a pair of fingers across my eyes.

"Travis, you with us?"

I managed to speak. "Yeah?"

Connie's fingers stopped moving. "How's your head?"

I tried to shrug, which was painful enough to make me grimace. "Still attached."

Someone snickered. Connie just nodded.

"Great. Gonna shine a light on you for a sec."

I only winced a bit as her pocket flashlight clicked on. I squinted as she shined the light in my left eye, then my right. After a moment she turned the flashlight off, then flipped it upside down.

"Follow the flashlight with your eyes, not your head."

I obeyed, focusing on the light moving in a slow arc.

Connie nodded to herself, then to Rocky. "He's got a decent goose egg, but no concussion. He's thicker than he looks."

I focused on them both. "What happened?"

Max spoke up first. "Mabel heard you falling down the stairs and found you here. How'd you land like that?"

I blinked. The crying girl was standing right behind Max. But instead of crying, she looked furious. I licked my lips and turned back to him before answering him. "I heard someone singing in the halls and thought it was on the upper level. I came up and saw someone crying by the door. I thought it was Bekah at first."

Bekah, one of the two young black women in the ensemble, frowned at her name. "But I was onstage."

I shrugged, playing up the hapless lummox. "Same size, same hair. Different clothes, though. Old fashioned. Crouching down and from the back. I didn't get a good look at her."

If I hadn't been looking right at him, I would've missed the fear in Max's eyes. I looked to the girl behind him, who was slightly translucent but unmistakably the one I had seen before. She scowled at me, then lifted a single finger to her lips.

Max's mask of cool was firmly back in place as he clapped once. "Well, good to know you're all right. Rocky, can we take a ten and return to the mainstage afterwards?"

Rocky nodded. "You got it, Max. Take ten, everyone."

There was a chorus of, "Thank you, ten" as the company dispersed. The girl glared at Max one more time, then disappeared through a wall.

Connie caught my eyes, then flashed hers to the spot where the girl had vanished.

I nodded. Connie had seen her too.

* * *

An hour later, we took a break. I headed for the stage door and the smoke pit.

The loading dock had been decorated with a handful of folding chairs swiped from inside and a park bench acquired gods only knew how. The light over the door had a metal cage surrounding the bare bulb. Next to the light was a security camera I'd already discovered was fake: just a red LED on an empty box with a lens glued on. Between two of the chairs was a coffee can half full of sand, with a handful of cigarette butts here and there.

I immediately relaxed into one of the folders, which cradled me like a grandpa's easy chair. You could take the grunt out of the smoke pit, but you couldn't take the smoke pit out of the grunt.

The door opened and one of the actors stepped through. She was the curvy one I'd seen in the opening number. Out of the stage light, her hair was darker than the auburn I'd seen earlier, but the baby blues were just as brilliant. Without missing a beat, she dropped to one edge of the bench, crossed her legs, and leaned back against the brick of the building. Letting out the deep breath of the decompressing, she reached into her top and pulled out a pack. Drawing a cigarette with a polished fingernail, she nodded in my direction.

"Got a light?"

I tossed her a lighter. She caught it, lit up, tucked the pack back in the depths of her bra and tossed the lighter back without a wasted movement.

I caught it and tucked it back in a pocket. "Hey."

I could sense rather than see her chest rise and fall like an approval rating with her first drag. Afterwards, she looked me up and down. I wasn't used to being checked out, but wasn't complaining. Satisfied with the view, she flicked the first ash in the general direction of the can. "You're Rocky's new ASM, right?"

"Yeah, I'm Travis. The other one's Connie. You?"

"Hannah. I'm playing the Nurse."

I almost did a spit take. "The fuck? How?"

She gave a smirk, a quick shrug, and a flick of an ash. "I auditioned and I got it. Like everyone else." She paused, tilted her head and looked to the sky for a second before continuing. "At least I think it was like everyone else. Some shows can get weird like that."

I closed my water bottle. "I meant how did it make sense? You're barely thirty."

She shrugged, which would have had my eyeline drop involuntarily if I hadn't been living with Jazz for the last couple of years. A smile cracked at the same time. "Glad you noticed. But in the industry? The pickings are slim when you're not."

That confused me. "And here I thought the theater was all inclusive and diverse and such."

She rolled her eyes. "Oh, they like to talk it. But when it comes to who gets hired? Straight, twenty-something, skinny, and pretty WASPS rule the day. One or two deviations from that and they can pat themselves on the back and call it progress. They're better than Hollywood, but not by much."

I shook my head. "Shit, at least the Marines had a vague excuse for giving me shit about my weight."

She gave me another once-over look. "Extra pushups?"

"Held back for promotion."

She smirked. "Heh. At least you had the job for as long as you wanted it, honey. I was lucky to get a gig that implies I was a working wet nurse at fifteen with these things. Not flattering, but the money on this gig's a lot better than usual."

"That's what I keep hearing about this gig. Anyone said why?"

She shook her head. "Nobody looks a gift horse that profitable in the mouth."

I made a mental note of that one and said the first thing that came to mind. "Good thing I'm not an actor."

She gave a one-shoulder shrug. "I dunno, you got the timing to do comedy. There's probably a studio suit that looks like you somewhere. If you had the confidence, he'd pair you with some fresh out of high school bikini model to bankroll his own vicarious wish fulfillment."

It had been shaped like a compliment, but I had no idea what that had actually been. "Um, thanks, I think?"

Another shrug, another ash flicked away. "Better than what the girls get, honey. Once you hit 130 pounds or 30 years, you disappear."

I grimaced. "That bad?"

If she'd had glasses, she'd have looked over the top of them at me. "Name more than three. That worked in the last few years."

I thought for a moment, and kept hitting a wall. After a moment, I gave up. "Well, shit."

"Used to be one a decade. Now it's about three. And the rest of us heifers got to wait until one of them gets hit by a bus."

"Do I wanna ask what happens to the thin ones who turn thirty?"

Another shrug. "They take a break for a few years, maybe have a kid or two and come back when they're 40, playing 50-year-old first wives."

I wondered if this was how disgusted normal people felt when I told gory sea stories. I shook my head slowly, apologizing to the universe for my ignorance. "Shit. Even the Marines didn't expect you to smile when you got fucked over like that."

She flashed her teeth in a winning smile, the sarcasm failing to impact her makeup. "That's showbiz for you, honey."

I took another drink and shook my head. Seeing a chance, I jumped on it. "Sucks about Greg, huh?"

She flicked another ash into the can. "Your predecessor? Yeah. Creepy. Did you know him?"

"Not really. You?"

She nodded. "Did a couple shows with him." She paused for a moment, gave one of those chuckles that could start laughter or tears, then looked over at me with shining eyes. "Between you, me, and the wall, he was like a lot of sound guys. Plenty of stamina and didn't mind a screamer."

I cracked an awkward smile. "He make any enemies or something?"

She flicked another ash away and pointed the cig in my direction. "If you're an undercover cop or something, you're not subtle, honey." She smiled, then shrugged. "You don't last long in this business without pissing someone off. Usually for stupid stuff. Greg was no different. He could get handsy before he got permission sometimes. I never needed to tell him to back off more than once, but who knows?"

I mentally filed that note away for later. "He just fell right out of the grid?"

"Yeah." She closed her eyes and shook her head. "Spooky stuff. Not even a scream."

"Think it was a ghost?"

She shrugged. "Good an explanation as anything. You believe in ghosts, Travis?"

I took a second to center myself. Talking about the supernatural with standers always makes you rewire your brain a little. At least if you'd prefer not to be thought of as wearing a tinfoil hat. "I think every superstition is there for a reason, even if it's not the reason given. I try and keep an open mind."

She gave a nod of tepid approval. "Good attitude. Because I've never worked a theater that didn't have a ghost. Then again, I've never seen a theater ghost kill before. If you've ever thought about whistling backstage, I wouldn't start experimenting now. Nice guyliner, by the way."

Rocky's voice came in over the intercom. "Back in five."

I thumbed the call button as Hannah and I both responded. "Thank you, five."

Hannah ground out her butt on the sole of her shoe, then tossed it into the can. "Nice talking to you, honey."

She hauled open the door and vanished into the darkness of the theater, leaving me outside in the light.

* * *

The cast went home, and the stage management reconvened in Rocky's office. She flopped in the leather office chair and put her feet up on her desk. Connie and I took the couch.

"So," she asked, "any ghosts in this room?"

Connie looked around, then got up and fished a permanent marker out of her bra. She pushed a spare toolbox over to the door, then stood on it. Now that she could reach, she drew a series of markings above the doorframe, took a breath, and murmured a word that I couldn't make out.

Satisfied, she turned back to Rocky. "Not for the next hour."

Rocky shrugged. "Good enough. What can you tell me?"

Connie and I traded nods and I started off. "Well, you've got at least one ghost in the building."

Connie stepped down from the toolbox, shook her head, and held up two fingers.

I frowned. "No shit?"

Connie nodded. "But the one that smacked you is the most active."

I snorted. "Ya think?"

Rocky pointed to me. "The girl he saw earlier?"

Connie nodded again. "Whoever she is, she's pissed."

I tried contributing. "Never seen her before. But she's definitely got something to do with Max."

Connie flopped back down on the couch. "But there's at least one more that I can sense. I don't want to say it's benevolent, but it's definitely not as hostile as her."

I snorted. "My biggest worry is a hostile crying girl. It's like living in barracks all over again."

Connie raised an eyebrow. "You know she was honestly trying to kill you, right?"

I blinked. "Wait, really?"

She gave a wry grin. "You managed to fall down, back, and roll. You've only got a headache from smacking your head on the wall after slowing down that much. You'll be black and blue by morning if you don't heal up, but you're OK. Probably fell right on instinct when she hit you. If you'd fallen straight back, you'd have flown for a second. Then all two hundred and excuse me pounds of you would've landed head or neck first. If she'd knocked you over the side, same thing with twice the height."

I managed a dry chuckle. "Glad my carcass let us narrow down what we're dealing with. Think she did similar to Grover and Greg?"

Connie nodded. "Absolutely. Now we know five things about her." Connie counted off on her fingers. "She's female. She's powerful and angry enough to kill. She can apparate. She prefers to scare her victims into killing themselves; and she can manipulate small objects, which accounts for Greg's safety line."

I held up one finger. "And Max knows who she really is."

Rocky frowned. "Really?"

"Saw it on his face when I described her. That and the Crying Girl was scowling at him."

Rocky nodded. "Well, that's more than we had. Any problems with my cast or crew?"

I shrugged. "Too early to tell, really."

Connie concurred. "They seem nice enough"

Rocky snorted, opening a can of soda. "Of course they are. You're crew and none of them are A-listers. They can't afford to be assholes to the crew. Except for maybe Dawn. And she's too invested in being nice to be an obvious bitch."

Connie tilted her head. "That bad?"

Rocky took a swig of her soda and winked. "Fuck with us and they dance naked in the dark."

I smirked. "Reassuring."

Rocky waved it off. "Don't let it get to your head. It's enlightened self-interest, not friendliness."

Connie shrugged. "They seem tight enough."

Rocky nodded. "They have to be. They're stuck here."

I made a face. "How? The contracts that bad?"

Rocky shook her head. "Not the contracts. The industry's that bad. I'll guarantee you every one of them's been rejected fifty or a hundred times for the one appearance they're making here and now."

I nodded. "So it's money."

Rocky shook her head again. "Max probably arranged it with that in mind. But no, it's money and it's hunger. They want this so bad the thought of turning it down isn't even occurring to most of them."

Connie tilted her head in confusion. "They want what now?"

Rocky waved in the direction of the stage. "This. Being on stage. Performing. Doing what they do. Being who they are. The rest of their lives, they're stuck in whatever survival gigs let them eat and whatever they think will get them cast. Here they know who everyone is. They don't have to jockey for position in a social hierarchy because it's right there in the cast list. They all know their place and don't have to worry about it."

I frowned. "It's that addictive?"

Rocky finished her drink and nodded. "Yeah, usually. For the next few months they'll have a community. People who have to give a shit about them because they're part of the show. The night it closes?" She snapped her fingers. "It's gone. They vanish with their stuff that night. In the morning, the dressing room is empty and there's no sign they were ever here. And the only way they'll ever talk to each other again is if they wind up doing another show together somewhere else."

It sounded cold. I only had one way to describe it. "Fuck."

Rocky shrugged. "Why do you think theater still exists? It wasn't designed to be pop-up community and do-it-yourself therapy. But it works just enough at being both that thousands of souls use it that way."

Connie steepled her fingertips. "And that's why they're staying with this show even though it's already killed two people?"

Rocky shook her hand noncommittally. "Column A, Column B? The money drew them here. But the chance to do what they do was just as much a draw."

I snickered. "That sounds somewhere between cultish and just plain nuts."

Rocky grinned, dropping her can in the recycling bin. "See? You really are starting to understand the theater."

I shook my head. "At least I'm ghost bait for a good cause."

Connie spoke up. "Better than some scenarios. You can fight back better than anyone else here but me. As long as she's focused on you and we're keeping you alive, we're keeping everyone else safe until we figure out the next step."

Rocky looked concerned. "What next step? Do you banish her or do an exorcism or something?"

Connie sighed. "That's part of the problem."

I held her hand. She gripped it. I turned to Rocky. "After Blue River, active necromancy was banned in North America. Listening to ghosts is OK. Small favors, maybe. But compelling them? Controlling them? Big no-nos. Not to mention the thousand and one scary things you can do with corpses. The authorities know what Connie can do. And once word gets out about this ghost they'll be all over her. Which limits what we can do to stop the Crying Girl."

Rocky grimaced. "That's... not good."

I shrugged. "Blow up that bridge when we get to it, I guess."

Connie looked over at Rocky. "Anything else you got for us before we finish the tour?"

Rocky blinked, then snapped her fingers. "I almost forgot."

She reached into a drawer and tossed something on a chain towards Connie. Connie caught it easily, holding the small medallion at arm's length.

I frowned. "What's the St. Christopher's medal for?"

Connie looked at it critically. "Good guess, but it's not St. Christopher."

Rocky gave Connie a finger gun and pulled the trigger. "It's St. Genesius. Patron saint of actors. Grover dropped it just before he ran out the door. I found it with his papers."

Connie was nearly scowling at it. I blinked. "Connie?"

She grimaced. "Someone's enchanted this. I'm not sure with what."

She pulled out a white silk handkerchief and folded it up neatly around the medal.

Rocky looked concerned. "Can you guys use that?"

I shrugged. "Solid maybe. Thanks for letting us know about it. Confirms something we've already suspected."

Rocky looked confused. "Confirms what?"

Connie tucked the hanky away. "We're not the first mages to come here."

Chapter Six

Guideline Thirty-Five:

If you can, find out why the local Chesterton's fences were put up.
It'll make life easier if you have to knock them down later.

The sun was still out when we headed back into the lobby. Roscoe had cleaned the other half of the windows during the day, so we had a homogeneous view out into the street. With the cast gone and Roscoe nowhere to be seen, it was still vaguely creepifying. We knew we were being watched now, it was just a case of what was watching us at the moment.

We went up one of the two staircases that flanked the entrance to the house. Empty frames with light sockets on the insides had once held posters for upcoming movies. Now they had dust and cobwebs that Roscoe hadn't gotten around to evicting yet. At the top of the staircase, where the lobby was below, there was another concession stand and set of public restrooms. That level had it's own entrances to the house, with identical sets of double doors.

Rocky waved a hand. "This is the balcony level. Figured I'd show you this on the way to the booth."

Hallways went down to the right and left, identical to what was on the lobby floor. "Are there wraparound hallways like this on every level?"

Rocky nodded. "Yeah. The house and stage are where the old factory floor used to be. The wraparounds had offices, storage spaces, even rented apartments. Zoning wasn't as much of a thing back then."

We went through the double doors and into a vomitorium that emptied into the balcony. There were about half as many seats up here as there were on the main level. It was raked the same way, with the back of the balcony higher than the front, so there were more seats where you could see the entire show. Four emergency exits were lit at the two back corners and the far ends of the balcony. If I was following right, there was another wraparound hallway on this level, above and behind us. Rocky led us up the aisles to the back.

I ran my hand along the old velvet upholstery. "Not bad for cheap seats."

Rocky nodded. "Yeah. Whoever rebuilt the place into a theater knew what they were doing."

"That was what, 1920's?"

Rocky shrugged. "I think so, maybe, but I'm not sure."

Connie was looking into dark corners. "We'll ask Thumper and Jazz about it when we get home."

There was one level below the first level of seats. I stepped onto it to find the barrier up to my waist. I nodded in approval. I was a big guy. Falling over the railing to the house below would've taken a serious accident or deliberately trying. On a hunch, I closed my eyes and touched the rail. I extended my senses into the building, looking at the strength of the balcony itself. I focused on the rail and the wall just beneath it, checking for any weaknesses in the materials or any stress points. I found old age and some thin paint, but on the whole it seemed well made and remained that way. Magic would never be the basis of an inspector's signature, but I was satisfied. If a ghost was going to threaten someone on the balcony edge, it was going to have to work at it.

Connie and Rocky were already well past me heading back and up towards the booth. I let go of the rail and headed up the stairs.

Halfway up, there was a barrier between one level of seats and another, like a mini-balcony in the middle of the level. I stepped past the barrier and a chill ran through my body. I blinked, but the chill didn't dissipate. In fact, it sank into my bones. It felt like something horrible was standing just behind me to one side, and if I turned my head just enough, I'd see them. I considered activating my eyeliner, but I wanted to be sure.

I licked my lips and spoke up. "Did you feel that?"

Rocky turned. "Feel what?"

I tried not to move. "The temperature just dropped a good ten degrees or more. It's in this row. And I don't see an air conditioning vent or anything."

Connie nodded. "I felt it too."

Rocky thought for a second, then asked. "Is it between row R and row S?"

I looked down and saw the little bronze plates engraved on the armrests. They were so dark with tarnish that only their shapes kept them from blending into the antique wood. I could just see the capital letters engraved on each one. "Yep. Row R, row S. Right around this barrier thing. How'd you know?"

Rocky grimaced. "This theater used to be whites-only. Then it segregated at the end of the forties, trying to make more money. Only made more money after a couple of nasty fights, here and outside. That barrier is the old color line."

I stepped down a few levels and the chill dissipated like I'd never felt it. Stepping back up and the chill went back up my spine, with a renewed intensity. It felt like the chill knew that I'd noticed, and enjoyed the attention. I checked my left and right, knowing I wouldn't see anything that hadn't been there before. I looked a question at Connie and she shook her head. I nodded back, then kept on going, following Rocky to the booth.

* * *

The booth was about half the size of a shipping container, but it only needed to be. Five seats for three stations, none of which would be our problem. But because Rocky was a good boss, she put us through it anyway and pointed out the lighting and sound consoles. Among other things, there were security monitors showing camera feeds from the box office, lobby, center stage, loading dock, and the green room.

Now I was in my element. A lot of juice was flowing through the building, and it was all controlled from here. I'd gotten to be on the bridge of the *USS Wasp* once on a tour at sea. Show the junior enlisted grunts how the Navy did things, that kind of deal. Just being in the room and knowing all of that power was in arm's reach was a rush. Not that I'd admitted it to the squids at the time. Being in the booth felt a little like that.

It was also kind of like being in an old bookstore. Or maybe the bathroom of a dive bar. The booth had been the projection room back when it was a movie theater. The walls were covered in old posters, newspaper clippings, stickers, flyers, and pin-up postcards. All manner of graffiti covered every nonworking surface. It was a collage that had grown over the decades like a bonsai tree. Some art history major would have a field day with the place.

Rocky tapped the monitor showing us center stage. "Camera's just under the balcony. We've also got monitors showing this just offstage, at the box office, and in the green room. Makes it easier for the actors to get their cues."

Connie asked. "Any other cameras setup? Or monitors?"

She shook her head. "None that I know about."

I remembered something I'd seen before, then looked at the monitor showing the loading dock. It took me a couple seconds, but I finally got it and smirked. "Clever."

Rocky frowned. "What?"

I tapped the screen. "See the camera over the smoke pit here? It's a fake. Just a battery powering a red LED. The wire leads nowhere. But this camera is watching the entire area."

Connie frowned. "A decoy?"

I nodded. "An obvious camera to block or destroy while the one you don't see watches you do it. One of the previous owners was nicely paranoid."

Rocky nodded. "Makes you wonder how many fake cameras are in the building."

I waved my hand back and forth. "Makes me wonder if there are more real cameras with feeds leading elsewhere."

Connie frowned. "Who's going to be in this booth during the show?"

Rocky shrugged. "One running lights, one running sound, and me. If I still have you two, you'll be just offstage on either side."

I got an idea and threw it out in the open. "Thumper could run one board or another. Probably lights. They could probably figure out this rat's nest in the cameras while they're at it."

Rocky tilted her head. "Thumper knows how to run a board?"

Connie shrugged. "Even if they don't now, they'll learn fast. They can't respond on a mic, but they can listen on one."

Rocky thought about it for a sec, then nodded. "I'll hire them either way. They'll probably be working with one of my usual crew up here. At least for as long as you're on the job. I'm going on a limb and assuming you two will be done once our problem is fixed."

Connie smiled. "We'd give you notice, but yeah, pretty much."

We all pondered that before Connie noticed something and pointed downstage. "What's that floor lamp doing downstage center?"

Rocky glanced at it. "Oh. That's the ghost light. We'll turn it on just before we leave."

I blinked. "That a fire code or something?"

Rocky shook her head. "No. It's just a tradition and a good idea."

I smiled. "You've got a lot of those."

Rocky shrugged. "It's theater. It's easier to convince actors to appease the ghosts than it is to pay attention to safety rules. So we say it's to keep the ghosts comfortable. In reality, that's a big space with a lot of ways to have nasty falls. Keeping just enough light to maneuver around safely helps."

I nodded. That one made sense. "What's the one about whistling for? I got nothing there."

Rocky smirked. "Old school safety reg that stuck around. Before we automated everything, there was a shitload of manual counterweights in the fly system. The guys working the rigging were out of work sailors. No radios back then, so the stage manager would give them cues by whistling. As long as the stage manager and only the stage manager did it, the work went smooth."

My mental light bulb ignited. "But some asshole actor comes by and starts whistling whatever's on his mind, you court disaster. Smart reason to have a taboo."

Rocky opened her hands in a tiny flourish. "I know, right?"

Connie tilted her head. "How about breaking a leg? Where does that come from?"

Rocky stepped over to the light board and moved a few of the sliders, bringing up some of the stage lights, then pointed out into the empty theater. "See those lines of curtains? The big burgundy one in front and the black ones on the sides going upstage at intervals?"

Connie squinted. "Yeah?"

"The big burgundy one's called a Grand Curtain. The black ones at intervals are called legs. Back in vaudeville, it wasn't just one big cast. It would be a bunch of individual acts. A comedian, then a singer, then a magician or whatever. And because, surprise surprise, performers can get a bit flaky, theaters would book more acts than they could show on any given night. But you only got paid if you went onstage. So if you break the line between backstage and onstage, marked by the leg, you get paid. So the preferred replacement for good luck became break a leg."

Connie cracked a smile. "That's a pretty good wish."

I did the same. "Especially with a cursed show like this."

Rocky tilted her head. "The Scottish play is the cursed one, Travis."

I snorted. "Sure, if you wanna be lazy about it. This one has so much potential. Knife fights, horny teenagers, useless voices of reason, poor communication, bad drugs...there's a reason I hated this damn play in high school. Stupid people get other people killed. The friar, who's supposed to be the literate one here, doesn't get the right message sent. But even then Romeo can't die stupid and simple by offing himself the moment he thinks Juliet's dead. No, he's got to make it about him and do it right on her body, because that'll show her parents they were wrong. Because of that, he has to go kill that dumbass himbo Paris for the crime of being emo. And of course, because he's lingered that long, then Romeo's dumb ass offs himself at the speed of plot just in time for her to wake up as the hypotenuse of an even bloodier love triangle. Of course she offs herself rather than explain that one to her mom. Although, given what a rotating bitch her mom is, I'll give her a pass on that one. The survivors think it's romantic. And Max goes and thinks adding electric guitars will somehow help. Like dying stupid to a nice tune is somehow dying less stupid."

There was an awkward silence. Then I remembered how I sounded. How I had firsthand experience about how dying young and in love being romantic was bullshit. This place was starting to get to me.

Connie broke the silence. "Much as he's being a stick in the mud, Travis is right. There's room for all sorts of chaos here, and I don't even have to make a zombie."

Rocky was starting to look nervous. "Please don't make Mercutio a zombie."

Connie pouted. "Spoilsport."

"Connie!"

Chapter Seven

Guideline Thirty-Nine:

If someone you hate wants you to do a job you're going to do anyway, keep negotiating.

Their inconvenience alone is your bonus.

Rocky gave us the next day off. We didn't bother protesting. We'd both had a long day and I'd gotten my bell rung in the process. Despite Jazz plying me with various remedies, I woke up more stiff than usual. If she hadn't, Connie's prediction about my being black and blue would've come to pass. We all agreed to chill for the day, then compare notes with Thumper and Jazz after dinner. Which made it all the more annoying when another video game battle with Byron was interrupted by a knock at my solid oak front door.

Two men and a woman stood waiting on my porch when I opened up.

The first man was a tall, heavyset fellow in worn jeans and broken-in hiking boots. A battered black ball cap shaded his eyes. He had the broad shoulders, thick arms, and paunch of a football lineman who'd retired and gone to seed. He looked like a long haul truck driver more than anything else. I recognized him as regional SiS Marshal Jimbo Sims.

There are only about ten thousand mages living in North America. Most of us live a low enough profile that federal governments don't take too much interest in us. A very limited number of US Marshals are mages in their own right, who handle what little law enforcement the community needs.

Standing next to him was someone I was used to seeing in formal robes standing on a dais. Of course, for preference I liked knowing he was in a different zip code even better. Councilor James Neary was about a foot shorter than the Marshal, with a turkey neck and a graying buzzcut. His face was weathered enough to look like carved leather. His eyes were locked in an almost perpetual squint. His tweed suit would've made him look like an old-timey academic if I hadn't known any better. He even had the chain of a pocket watch dangling from his waistcoat. There were only 13 Councilors that formed the closest thing that mages had to a government in North America. The chances that one I'd already pissed off had spontaneously come over for tea was unlikely.

On the end was a woman the same height as Neary, and the only one of the three I didn't remember meeting before. She wore a dark pantsuit and had a mane of chestnut curls held back by an industrial strength scrunchie and an assortment of pencils. Big brown eyes were magnified behind glasses that screamed quirky academic, and her lipstick was a shade of purple dark enough to be designed to fly under someone's dress code.

Ages were hard to determine with mages. Sims and Neary looked to be around my father's generation, while the woman looked maybe six or seven years younger than myself. They could all have a century and change on me for all I knew.

I let them watch as I took my time reholstering my sidearm, which I'd been hiding behind my back, then nodded to them in inverse order of apparent rank. "Ma'am, Marshal, Councilor. Dare I ask?"

I deliberately did not start with a welcome, just to let everyone know where we stood.

Neary nodded in turn. "Mr. Wayland. I'm actually here to speak with Ms. Chandler."

Which begged the question of why they weren't at her house, but I let it slide. Connie and I being covenmates was common knowledge. My curiosity was piqued. "Who'd she irritate this time?"

Neary gave a politician's smile and indicated inside my home. "If we may?"

Sims, snickering behind his ostensible boss's back, gave me a short nod.

I opened the door, calling inside. "Jazz! We have guests!"

The Iron Council's power over North American mages was fairly loose. As long as I wasn't up to some seriously evil shit, I could tell Neary to pound sand and leave him on the porch. Unfortunately, there was plenty of evidence lying around that I could be up to all manner of nefarious things. And Neary was just the kind of jerkoff who would take the excuse to raid my house. Being polite, at least for now, was cheap insurance against me having to be bloodstained and powder burned later.

Mages go to school like everyone else. Then we turn twelve, find out what we are, and almost always have to transfer schools. Regular schools. There's not enough of us for an all-mage school. Most of our time after that is still spent learning what everybody else learns. We also have a study hall from seventh grade through senior year, where we learn magic. It's supposed to teach us to control our abilities, help our communities, and generally live our lives without serious havoc. In exchange for their time and expertise, instructors are given a lot of leeway and almost complete hands-off treatment by the Council.

Well, my senior year teacher tried to sacrifice my graduating class in a necromantic ritual. All of my graduating class, not just the mages. We managed to stop her, but got butchered in the process. Half the mages I graduated with were killed, including my best friend and my girlfriend.

Thumper was left irreparably scarred. By the time Sims' predecessor and other authorities got there it was all over but the paperwork.

Which is how the Blue River Massacre really happened. There wasn't enough evidence to charge anyone in the mundane world. The mundane authorities had a handful of dead and wounded graduates, over a hundred terrified and screaming graduates, and exactly no suspects. The Council went through the motions of trying and convicting our teacher of mass murder and such. She'd been rotting in a cell in a dungeon deep underground in Missouri ever since.

Unfortunately, the Council seemed to be more concerned with the egg on their face than what had happened to us. None of us had good political reputations after that, and two of my fellow survivors committed suicide that summer. The biggest change was a ban on active necromancy by mages living in Iron Council territory. A small community and an even smaller subculture suffered because a bunch of stuffed shirts in robes really dropped the ball when vetting some job candidates.

Have I mentioned Connie is one of the better necromancers on the continent?

Anyways, Neary and his entourage were here. Better to face them as a coven and on our terms. Most people in the Otherworld are big on hospitality and the responsibilities of hosts and guests. I could be reasonably certain that Sims didn't have a hit squad waiting down the block, and Neary could be reasonably certain I wouldn't hock a massive loogie in his tea.

While I'd closed the door and led our guests up the stairs, the others had sprang into action. Byron, not being a mage, was ignoring the political elephant in the room and occupying himself playing another video game on the couch. Thumper and Connie had taken their places on the far side of the dining room table. Like me, they trusted Neary no further than they could throw him, and regarded him as solemnly as if he'd farted in the elevator. Shrapnel, my smoky gray rescue cat, opened an eye from the back of the couch where she'd been curled up. After giving our guests the stinkeye, Shrapnel decided the newcomers weren't there to give her tribute and went back to sleep. Jazz was pouring water glasses all around and reheating some leftover biscuits from breakfast.

Why was Jazz acting like a servant? Because she was my servant. She'd been a servant ever since some jackass had bound her into her ring centuries ago. Now she was mine, and determined to do a good job of it, especially in front of company. I, for one, was standing back and letting her do it. I was refusing to take sexual advantage, yes. But I wasn't going to leave her feeling completely useless.

I'd tried stopping her, once, before I realized what I was doing. Once. I'd been around service submissives enough to know better, but did it anyway. She wound up being both hurt and insulted. It took a while to reassure her that I didn't think she was doing such a bad job that I might as well do it myself. After that mind-boggling mess, I did the smart thing and stayed out of her way. If there was serving to do, it was her job to do it.

Neary and his entourage took their seats opposite the one left for me. I found my own chair between those of my covenmates just as Jazz brought out a plate of biscuits, accompanied by a butter dish and a saltshaker. Our guests went quietly through the small ritual of buttering, salting, and eating a biscuit apiece. Jazz remained standing a pace behind me on my right side.

When we had all finished, I closed my eyes for a moment, opening my hand on the table before nodding and taking them all in. "Welcome to my home. Councilor Neary, first time we've had the pleasure. Marshal Sims, a comfort as always." I stopped to look at the woman. "You're new."

She seemed surprised to actually be addressed, startling for a moment before giving a little wave. "Oh! Chucky Brubaker. I'm a Council archivist. You've got to be Travis Wayland. I've seen some of your device work. Awesome stuff. You're really a pioneer in practical alchemy."

I hadn't expected a fan. I nodded politely out of a lack of anything else to do. "Glad to have you join us." Then I turned to Connie. "The Councilor claims he's here to speak with you."

Connie somehow managed not to sneer. "Who did I irritate this time?"

Chucky went almost cross-eyed, visibly trying not to snort.

Neary folded his hands like a preacher. "The Council has received word of some serious indiscretions you've committed."

Connie stopped bothering to hide it and sneered freely. "What indiscretions? I've followed the ban."

Neary slowly shook his head. "The death of Tasha Marazzi…"

I raised a finger in objection. "…was not due to necromancy. Both Prince Byron and myself witnessed it. She merely disarmed Tasha with a spell that appeared necromantic."

Byron, ignoring his royal title, snorted. "Yeah, disarmed her at the wrists. She killed her with an e-tool, and it looked awesome. I wish I had video."

Thumper snickered until Neary tried again. "Nonetheless, Ms. Marazzi…"

Connie folded her arms. "… was responsible for my abduction, intended to be responsible for my murder, was indirectly responsible for my intended rape, gave every indication she was willing to do so again, and tried to control my mind before I cut her head off."

"Nonetheless…"

Thumper flipped him off with both hands. Chucky worked hard not to snicker, then pushed her glasses back into place with a fingertip.

I decided to chime in. "With all due respect, Councilor, you can probably imagine where your nonetheless can be inserted."

Neary was almost openly scowling. "There are rather powerful interests demanding Ms. Chandler be punished. You're not the only one who has to live among vampires, young lady."

I shook my head. "Everything we did to the Marazzis was sanctioned by Lord Chittenden himself. I've been his consultant ever since and he's said nothing about this."

Neary had managed to calm down. "Lord Chittenden is far from the highest authority among his kind that one can find."

Connie hadn't moved. "You can definitely get fucked if you think you're feeding me to some vampire I've never heard of."

Byron looked up from his game. "Hear him out."

Connie and I replied in stereo. "What?"

Byron waved his controller in the table's direction. "He wants something from you. If he really wanted to arrest Connie, he'd have come with a couple of pipehitters ready to throw hands. Instead he brought a Marshal we like and a clerk with nice buns. He's just stupid enough to offer the stick first instead of the carrot. Or he's too much of an egomaniac to ask politely. Possibly both. Ask him what he really wants."

Neary glared. Chucky blushed bright red. The Marshal snorted.

I just raised an inquisitive eyebrow at him.

Neary took a breath and relaxed a bit. "Prince Byron is correct. I am actually here for your assistance, Ms. Chandler."

Connie's expression didn't change. "You're not getting it. But go ahead and elaborate."

Neary continued smoothly. "We've received word that a powerful conjurer is coming to Atlanta on a mission of vengeance. His name is Dr. Gull."

Connie wasn't impressed. "Isn't that what SiS is for?"

Marshal Sims had the decency to look embarrassed. "Necromancy is a rare skill even among the SiS. The few I have are being kept busy in other states."

I nodded. "And Babs is a good cop, but she doesn't know the dead from her ass."

Deputy Marshal Babs Ward was a former classmate of mine, and a protégé of Sims. I had been wondering why she hadn't been invited to the party.

Neary grabbed the conversation back. "If you can kill or capture Dr. Gull before the dead start slaughtering humans indiscriminately, the Council is willing to overlook some of your questionable actions."

Sims joined in. "Or at least drive him back to Conjure territory. Getting him out of a major Council area before he wreaks havoc is the driving goal."

Connie laughed harshly. "All right. You want the Doctor gone? Lift the ban. Full pardons for any convictions. Update every Monitor and Marshal in Conus by sundown."

Neary grit his teeth. "This is not a negotiation."

Thumper snorted.

Byron laughed. "Like hell it ain't."

Connie just stared. "You keep acting like I somehow take orders from you, Neary."

I could see a vein in Neary's forehead throb. "I cannot overturn a Council decision unilaterally."

Connie didn't flinch. "You seem perfectly capable of threatening me unilaterally."

Neary almost growled. "Your insolence..."

I joined in. "...is what you earned with your incompetence, old man."

Sims' voice cut like a knife. "Enough."

In the silence, he turned to Connie. "He's right about the Council. He can't overturn it himself. And time is of the essence, so he can't maneuver the rest of the Council into doing it even if he was willing."

I found my tongue. "Then fuck him. He's trying to throw us under the bus. Again. We're more than happy to beat him with it until he figures out how to not do that anymore."

Connie held up a hand. When she got the silence she was asking for, she looked Neary dead in the eye as she held up two fingers. "Two things. One, you want death or capture before indiscriminate death of standers. You might have to settle for banishment. Even given free reign, kicking his ass back into Conjure territory may be the best option I can give you."

Sims gave Neary a pointed look. Neary looked even more angry, but nodded. "And the second?"

Connie steepled her fingers, not taking her eyes from him. "You will grant me an exemption from the ban on active necromancy. Full, unconditional, retroactive, and in perpetuity. That's the bare minimum I'll need to get the job done. Oh, and it covers me, my coven, and any students, apprentices, or mercenaries I take on. I dunno how much firepower I'll need to take down Dr. Gull, but for all I know I'll need an old-fashioned posse."

Neary reared back as if he'd smelled something nasty. "Out of the question."

I cut in. "Bullshit, Neary. If Connie wasn't one of us, you'd be offering her a badge and a deputization. The thought makes your skin crawl, so you're here trying to bully her into it instead."

Neary squinted even harder. "Much as the Council is in need of your services, Mistress Chandler, I am not about to fulfill your every want."

Connie wasn't having it. "I'm not asking for what I want, Councilor. I want that stupid, useless ban rescinded. I want your bully boys to stop terrorizing schoolchildren because they have power you fear. I am settling for a blanket exemption for myself and immediate associates, guaranteed by you. And I'll handle your conjurer problem in the process."

Neary snorted. "That's blackmail."

Connie folded her arms again. "Hi, pot. I'm a kettle. Besides, you got another necromancer waiting in the wings?"

Thumper held their arm out in a "she's got a point" gesture.

Sims turned to Neary. "Give her what she wants, boss."

Neary sneered. "Impossible. It's far too dangerous."

Sims rolled his eyes. "Save it for Council sessions. Everyone in this room knows the ban is horseshit, but there's no politically feasible way for you to back down on it. This coven's already here and they have the skillsets to take down Dr. Gull."

Neary huffed. "I am not doing this."

Sims turned to Connie. "You want a badge?"

Connie snorted. "Hell no."

Sims turned back to Neary. "Give her the damn exemption."

Neary sighed, then somehow squinted even harder. "Very well." His lips twisted into a godawful smirk of his own. "However, there is an additional rider."

Connie's look didn't change. "Go on."

"There are those in the vampire community who dispute your claim surrounding Ms. Marazzi's death. And they have witnesses to back up their disputation."

Connie looked puzzled. I tilted my head in confusion. Byron snapped his fingers. "Damn."

I looked over at him. "What?"

Byron tapped his temple with his fingertips, "Tasha's henchmen. The ones who took off in the truck. They must have survived. Long enough to be interrogated, at least."

Neary nodded. "Lady Mariah of Los Angeles was very distraught. And of course, I wouldn't dare sanction a rogue necromancer killing the citizens of an ally."

I sneered. "Lady who? Tasha lived in Atlanta and was trying to overthrow Chittenden! We did him a favor."

Neary sniffed in disgust. "Nonetheless, I cannot risk an Otherworld war. Particularly not one instigated by the same Nimuen who have been so loud about how they were able to break the renfield bond."

I shook my head, appalled. "You'd throw an Iron Council mage under the bus on a vampire's say so?"

Neary somehow stuck his nose higher in the air. "If it prevented a war? Yes."

Connie grimaced in disgust. "You son of a bitch."

Neary sniffed. "Spare me. Ms. Chandler. Take your exemption. Dispatch, deliver, or drive away Dr. Gull. Or I will let the vampires declare open season on you and call it self defense."

Connie smiled impudently. "Done."

I nodded. "What do you got on this Dr. Gull?"

Chucky pulled a notebook out of her pocket. "Oh. Very little, I'm afraid. As you know, the southeast coasts of the continent and nearly all of Florida are Conjure territory."

Neary huffed. "Disputed territory."

I raised an eyebrow at him. "If it was disputed, you wouldn't be here."

Chucky continued. "In any case, Dr. Gull is based somewhere in Florida, but he's been seen anywhere from Miami to Jacksonville."

I nodded. "Any description? MO?"

Chucky flipped over a few more pages." The last description we have comes from the 1950's. He was a middle-aged black man with a medium build and average height. No scars, tattoos, or other distinguishing marks. And even that might have been a glamour. We know he's a powerful necromancer, and he's a mover and shaker in the conjure world."

I thought for a moment. "Would you be able to recognize one of his works?"

Sims shrugged. "Maybe?"

Connie took a folded silk handkerchief from her pocket and slid it over.

Sims took what looked like a jeweler's loupe from his pocket and held it to his eye as he unwrapped the hanky. When the St. Genesius medal was revealed, he backed away a bit.

Connie noticed. "Is it Dr. Gull's work?"

Sims shrugged. "Can't tell for sure. It's definitely cursed. And it's definitely a Conjure work."

Neary frowned suspiciously. "Where did you find this?"

"We're helping a friend with a double-G problem." I said. "A theater ghost killed two people in as many weeks."

Chucky frowned. "Theater ghosts don't kill people."

I shrugged. "That's what we said. But the first victim dropped this right before he was killed. Theater ghosts might not kill. But a necromancer controlling them damn well can. We might be hunting him down already."

Sims rewrapped the medal in the hanky, sliding it back.

Connie nodded as she tucked the hanky away. "So what's this mission of vengeance?"

Chucky flipped a few more pages. "The man who killed his daughter has come to Atlanta."

She slipped a few more pages, blushed, and apologetically shrugged. "That's all we've been able to find. We have no idea who she was or what the circumstances of her death truly were."

Chapter Eight

Guideline Forty-Four:

Research isn't the be-all or end-all, but you're not getting very far without it.

Neary & Company left quickly after the deal was made. Byron left soon after that, after kicking my ass two out of three falls in the fighting game I'd just bought the other day. Jazz made an amazing shepherd's pie for dinner that night. At the table, Connie and I brought Thumper and Jazz up to speed on the previous day's adventures. Jazz visibly resisted the urge to go at me with another round of healing potions.

Dinner finished, we all adjourned to Thumper's room. While Thumper brought up visuals on the top screens, Jazz stood to the side to take the lead on the briefing. She spoke with the ease of a natural lecturer.

"First up, the Pencil Factory itself. It's on a part of Atlanta that was built up after the Civil War, hoping to support a subway system. The rail lines destroyed by General Sherman in the war were rebuilt quickly, and this part of the city was where some of the first lines were laid. Most of the area was factories and warehouses, taking advantage of being close to the railway station. It remained that way until 1915, when it was the site of an unsolved murder."

Several pictures accompanied her speech, showing the building as it appeared now and as it had been in the 19th century. After several pictures of the building itself, a black and white portrait appeared, showing a brunette girl in an old-fashioned dress. A locket hung on a thin chain around her neck. Large bows did her hair up on either side of her head. She neither smiled nor frowned.

Another picture came up on the next screen. This one showed a gentleman in a suit and tie, with a straw boater on his head. He was young and clean shaven, with delicate features and eyes that could have been soulful. His lips were drawn in a taught line that looked almost painfully polite.

I frowned. "I've heard about this one. No shit, that's where it got the Pencil Factory name?"

That surprised Connie. "You heard the story in school?"

I nodded. "Oh yeah. If you know anything about local history, you know about this case. He was convicted of her murder, but the case against him was beyond sloppy. The judge commuted his death sentence to life in prison, hoping he'd be exonerated on appeal. Then an angry mob broke him out of prison. He was lynched a few hundred yards from the Big Chicken."

Northwest of Atlanta is a KFC built to look like a giant chicken. Locals use it to give directions. There's also a little historical marker describing the lynching.

Connie grimaced. "I remember the story too. But they're not who we're dealing with. At least I don't think so. Neither of them look or feel like who I was feeling when we were on the site."

Jazz picked up where she left off. "They weren't the only tragedies. The Pencil Factory closed in the wake of the trial. It was first reopened as a theater in 1922. It was raided more than once during prohibition for holding speakeasies in the lower levels."

Some newspaper clippings of raids went through the slideshow. One of them had a sketch of the interior. I did some orientation in my head and made a connection. "In Mabel's costume shop, no less."

Connie smirked. "Now I kinda want a gin and tonic."

Jazz nodded with a shy smile. "There was some considerable rivalry when the Fox opened less than two miles north. Both were closed and reopened during the Depression, then the Pencil Factory reopened again during World War 2. It would close and reopen several times for the rest of the 20th century."

The pictures got more sharp. Some of them appeared in color. The marquee went up, then in old-fashioned incandescent lights. I nodded. "Lemme guess? Max Roman played there."

Jazz flashed a dazzling smile. "He did. In 1990, he was set to open a new staging of Romeo and Juliet."

A poster advertising "Romeo and Juliet: The Rock Opera!" came up on the screen.

Connie smirked. "Familiar."

Four head shots appeared on the screens. One was Max Roman in his prime, oozing charisma. One was of a rugged-looking white man with a lantern jaw, one was of a big-haired blonde with bedroom eyes, and one was the spitting image of the girl I saw in the stairwell.

Jazz continued. "Three of his friends were set to appear alongside him. George Burbage, Maria Clive, and Ginny Kemp. Kemp and Roman were linked romantically on several occasions around that time."

Connie nodded. "Now we have one name to go to a face. Ginny Kemp's the one that threw Travis down the stairs."

I looked at the pictures, then traded looks with Connie. "Lemme guess: there was bad blood and something happened to some or all of the others?"

Jazz nodded with a shy smile. "While Roman was set to direct, the four of them were to be double cast. Roman and Burbage were to play Romeo on alternate nights. Clive and Kemp would do the same, both playing Juliet. This was considered unusual, but a sign of how deep the friendships between them were. Kemp, although she was often mentioned alongside Roman, was seen as arising star in her own right. Burbage and Clive were seen more as character actors."

Connie frowned. "Any idea what happened?"

Jazz clicked her remote a few more times. Newspaper clippings popped up on the screens. "Roman abruptly canceled the production and enlisted in the US Army, a few weeks before the show would have opened. There's not much that mentions the others after that time. I found one tabloid article claiming that the others suffered financially as a result. But the others don't appear in any news sources we could find after Roman's enlistment."

I frowned. "That's a surprise. Even has-beens crop up every now and then."

Jazz gave a diplomatic nod. "I did find a death certificate for Kemp dated less than a week after Roman enlisted. Cause of death was listed as a suicide."

I nodded. "Left in the lurch when she was just about to be a star? Or dumped by a lover who left her?"

Thumper typed in their text screen: BOTH?

I nodded at Thumper. "Exactly. Anyway, she's got plenty of motive to go after Max. Any word on what happened to the others?"

Thumper shook their head. Jazz did likewise. "Nothing that I've seen so far. From what I can tell, they're both still alive. But I haven't seen any mention of them."

Connie stared at the headshot of Ginny a little harder.

I blinked. "Something on your mind, Connie?"

She shook her head. "I'm wondering. What's holding her back? What's stopping her?"

All of us had some experience in cognimancy, magic affecting the mind. But Connie was in grad school to become a psychologist. Out of all of us, she had the best handle on how people worked.

I cocked my head. "What's stopping her?"

She nodded. "From killing Max Roman."

I frowned. "You said theater ghosts usually don't kill. Maybe she can't kill him?"

Connie shook her head. "She killed the other two, and tried to kill you, but Max is still alive. Why? She dies, and the Pencil Factory is where her dreams died, so she stays tied to it. That part makes sense. It goes unused all this time, so she stays dormant. Now, Max is back, in the same damn theater, no less, and she can finally get revenge on him. But she kills a lyricist and a stagehand instead, then tries to kill another stagehand. That's what I don't get."

I frowned. "Is Dr. Gull influencing her somehow? I mean, if he's making her powerful enough to kill, maybe he's also affecting her choice of targets?"

She shrugged. "Maybe? No idea."

I nodded. "Which begs the question. Who is Dr. Gull?"

Connie threw up her hands. "Again, no idea. Could be anyone in the cast, really."

I frowned. "Yeah, Rocky says she's known everyone in the crew for years. That eliminates them. One of the older actors, maybe? Gull had a grown daughter who died years ago."

Connie shook her head. "Someone as powerful as Dr. Gull could easily change their appearance. Wear a Gorlois pendant or something."

I nodded. "True. We don't even know if the Dr. is male, female, or enby. If Rocky hadn't vouched for her, I'd think it was Mabel. Woman's got a vibe to her that's putting me off."

Connie grimaced. "I'd be more inclined to think about Roscoe. Rocky said he came with the place. And he's always off on his own program. He's got the means at least."

I pointed at her. "You got a point there. But everyone in the cast has big stretches of not being onstage. Except for the musicians."

Connie sighed. "So we're at square one."

I shook my head. "No. We definitely know it's not a Scooby. This is definitely a double-G problem. That said, it's your turn."

Connie tilted her head. "My turn?"

I shrugged. "We're facing at least one each of ghost and necromancer. You're the one with the best knowledge of what they're capable of and how to beat them."

Connie let out a breath. "That's two big ones, but OK. Broad strokes. Ghosts are mostly dangerous in that they can't be killed. They can only do small things. But small things in the right places can do a lot of damage. A door here, a stairwell there, you get the picture. Manipulate objects, cast illusions, some can possess living people and manipulate their bodies. But it all takes a lot of effort, so they're more effective when you don't know they're coming. They can be warded. They can be banished, temporarily. If you're gutsy you can bind them to places or objects. But getting rid of them entirely usually means finishing whatever unfinished business they have."

I frowned. "Difficult, if their unfinished business is murder."

Connie nodded. "There might be a greater banishment that might do something, but I've never done one. Most heavy rituals like that are used for demons. The thought of using them on human souls isn't something a lot of people are comfortable with."

Thumper visibly shivered. Jazz grimaced.

I nodded. "Understood. And necromancers?"

Connie sighed and threw up a hand. "Well, if you listen to the Council, there's passive and then there's active. The differences are kind of arbitrary, which is one of the many reasons why the ban is such bullshit. Passive is listening to the dead. Watching them. Talking to them. Pretty low-key stuff. Active is... not low key. Binding. Banishing. Compelling. It also covers a lot of what's in the real world. Corpses. Zombies. That kind of thing."

I bit my lip. "I got to ask. Tasha..?"

She nodded. "Active. The Council got me there. I can make things rot. It's easier to do with small things. But given that Tasha was technically a corpse... I didn't kill her with it. But only on a technicality. Not that I gave a rat's ass at the time."

Thumper took Connie's hand. She returned the grip tightly.

I spoke softer than I planned. "Not that we blame you. And Dr. Gull can do all that?"

Connie nodded. "Better than me. I'm more... more talented than skilled. I learned in bits and pieces, lots of trial and error. And it's not like I had cadavers to practice on in school. But the Conjurers specialized in necromancy and never had a ban. Dr. Gull's older than me, probably more powerful, and definitely more skilled."

I smiled a bit. "Good thing there's more of us with a broad skill set, eh?"

Connie blushed a little, then cracked a smile. "Yeah." She let out a deep breath before continuing. "That's about it on those. Guess now we sleep on it, hope we find something in the morning."

I let my smile grow. "Thanks, Connie. Jazz, Thump, this is all good info. Thanks a lot."

Thumper gave me two thumbs up from their chair.

Jazz glomped me before I could blink, let go the second she felt me wince, but met my sheepish grin with one of her own, bubbly as ever. "I'm glad it helped, Master."

* * *

Connie and I stepped outside to the sound of the crickets and frogs, the streetlamps punctuating the starlight. I tried not to let the stiffness in my muscles show. I was really going to need whatever healing tricks Jazz had waiting for me.

We reached Connie's jeep, then she turned to stop me. "I'm worried about you."

I blinked. That was confusing. Then again, looking out for a covenmate was a good thing and deserved to be encouraged. "Okay..."

She took a deep breath and folded her arms uncomfortably, looking at the dirt. "Look, I do my best not to analyze my friends. It's just not a good idea. But I'm worried about you. And Jazz."

I frowned. "Less okay, but I'm listening..."

She looked up at me and spit it out. "Do you love her?"

I blinked. That, I hadn't expected. "How do you mean?"

She nearly glared at me. "Are you in love with Jasmine?"

I took a beat before asking. "Why are you asking me this?"

She took another breath, and I could tell she was trying to relax. In fact, she was trying not to scream. "You've been together for months now. She wears a collar and calls you Master. In public. All the time. From what I can tell, she's been doing that since she came to this country."

I raised an eyebrow. "I've never known you to kink shame."

She met my eyes and didn't let me turn away. "You barely touch her."

My anxiety fired off several neurons. "What?"

Her look softened, but didn't let up. "Every time you two show affection, she's the one instigating it. I barely see you kiss her. There's love in her eyes. I think there's love in yours too. But you're keeping her at arm's length. It doesn't make sense. You're touchier than you admit, and you're comfortable when anyone else gets close. Me, Byron, Thumper, yeah... but not with Jazz."

Now I was nervous. "Yeah?"

She opened her hands. "I know you've been in lifestyles where titles mean something. But you don't act like someone with that title. In fact, you restrain yourself more than you restrain her. I don't know what's going on, but from where I'm standing, it doesn't look healthy."

I nodded, not wanting to go further but helpless to stop it.

She looked sheepish. "Travis, I like Jazz. She's brilliant and a sweetheart. And you're my covenmate, so I'm supposed to give a shit about you. I don't know what your arrangement exactly is. But I know she's very far from her home and everything she's ever known. And I know she's in love with you. And you... you look like you're trying to keep yourself from falling in love with her."

I bit my lip and nodded again. She kept going.

"I don't know if you're still getting through something Eva did or what. But if you're in love with Jazz, you need to start showing it. You're not all she's got, but you're damn close."

I licked my lips uncomfortably. "Have you asked her about this?"

Her gaze went right through my eyes again. "Doesn't that collar mean I should be asking you first?"

I broke into an embarrassed smile. "Touché."

Connie reached up and touched my face. The annoyance in her eyes melted away to show the concern beneath. "Travis? Whatever you're doing now is hurting both your hearts. If you're in love with her, you need to start showing it. If you're not, for whatever reason, then you need to get that collar off her neck and let her be an unrestrained adult."

I bit my lip and nodded. "Got it."

"Good." She jumped close and hugged me. Surprised, I let my own arms curl around her, then gave in, letting out a breath I didn't know I'd been holding. I held on for longer than I expected. In fact, I lost track of time. It could've been a few moments or several minutes later. But, eventually,

Connie's grip on me loosened. I let her go, then silently watched her jump into her jeep and off into the night.

Chapter Nine

Guideline Forty-Two:
When you have a chance, check in on your people.
And yourself.

"Damn Neary!"

I heard a long streak of muted swearing as I took another sip of coffee. Babs must have lowered the phone along with her voice. From what I could tell, she was calling into vulgar question the Councilor's respectability, gentility, and finally ancestry. Several sentences later, she addressed me where I could hear her.

"So, how's it going so far?"

I shrugged, even though Babs couldn't see it. "Double-G. Confirmed and ID'd a ghost. Not sure on the doctor, but more likely than not it's him too. Got my bell rung by said ghost. Working on the suspect list. Not bad for a first day at work."

"Typical."

"Any idea what's driving this on the Council's end? It just feels weird."

"It's jacked up is what it is!"

I shrugged again, petting Shrapnel as she headbutted my hand in a bid for attention. "Not arguing here, but I'm wondering why a theater ghost has Neary out of bed, let alone on my doorstep."

I could almost hear her shake her head. *"It ain't the ghost, it's Dr. Gull. They're a big name in the Florida Otherworld."*

I shrugged. "Yeah, but he's not plotting an invasion or anything. He's supposedly going after whoever killed his daughter. Whoever she was."

"The daughter of a powerful necromancer, who is now in Council territory."

"And posing almost no threat to standers. Unless you count the two she's already killed. But Neary was ready to feed Connie to some California vampire I've never heard of unless she dropped everything to take on Dr. Gull. It doesn't make any sense from where I'm standing."

There was a pause from the phone. *"Look, you didn't hear this from me, but Blue River was a bigger screwup than we thought. Neary used necromancy as a scapegoat for everything that happened. The anti-Necromancy mages are a big part of his power base in the Daedeli. A necromancer as powerful as Gull coming in isn't something he can let go unchallenged."*

I frowned. "So he sends his biggest career embarrassment at it? Neary gave Connie a blank check to use active necromancy on this case. And she's damn good at it. Big force multiplier there."

"I'd still keep it to a minimum. Even if you've technically got your asses covered. Sounds like Neary's using you as a cats-paw for something."

I scritched Shrapnel behind the ears. She collapsed on her side in enjoyment. "Of course he is. It just isn't a big deal. We were going to end up helping Rocky out under double-G anyway. The license to reanimate just makes it easier."

I could hear her sigh. *"Any other dumb questions?"*

I bit my lip, then decided to go for it. "No, but I was curious as to the Iron Council's take on Djinn."

I could hear her stop to think. *"I said no dumb questions, you jackass... Wait, are you serious?"*

I winced and tried to keep it out of my voice. "Yeah."

She didn't hesitate. *"Kill the master on sight, then confiscate the anchor."*

I looked down at Jazz's ring, still on my finger. "What's an anchor?"

"The lamp or ring or whatever it's bound to."

I grimaced. "Harsh."

Babs was now completely in cop voice. *"Keeping reality in the same spot it was in this morning is like that."*

I shook my head. "I can imagine."

"Why do you even want to know?"

The lie flowed easily from my lips. "Jazz asked about them. Apparently there's still onesies and twosies of Djinn floating around Iraq. Brass Council territory. I didn't plan to bring one home or anything. I had enough adventure last time I visited."

"Try not to. Your gun collection alone is dangerous enough. Even without all the ordnance you think I don't know about."

"I love you too, Babs. Take care of yourself."

"You too."

I hung up. Shrapnel, seeing my phone hand had stopped being occupied, started demanding attention from that appendage as well.

* * *

"Hey Oz, Travis. Got to run some things by the boss tonight."

The renfield on the phone didn't react. *"Anything in particular?"*

I mentally shrugged. It was no big secret. "The Pencil Factory Theater."

I could almost hear his mental note. *"Anything else?"*

I shrugged, rattling it off like I was ordering a pizza. "Visitor from Florida, probably hostile. Speaking of hostile, is there a Lady Mariah in town?"

"Yes."

He hung up. I shrugged and put my phone back in my pocket.

In my younger days, I'd have gone out of my way to fuck with Oswald. He had absolutely no sense of humor or visible ability to relax. However long he'd been Chittenden's renfield, he'd had a stick up his ass the entire time. These days I didn't bother. He might not have had an open or informed choice, but a choice he had made nonetheless. His choice gave him a place he was confident that he knew and understood. If stability was your priority, working for a powerful vampire did have that going for it, I guess.

Going to work in this case meant going out to a vampire salon. Vampires and mages generally don't mix. There aren't many examples of either of us, and we're both well outside of human norms. But every now and then, our interests aligned. Chittenden, the vampire lord of Atlanta, had done me a considerable favor back in the day. I repaid it with what I considered interest. When we were square, we agreed to continue our relationship on a consultancy basis. He paid me a comfortable cash retainer, and I gave him a heads-up on any metaphysical goings-on in and around his territory. It meant attending his parties on occasion, which were full of people I didn't like, but I didn't mind.

One thing we did make clear was the subject of renfields. Most vampires had at least one: a human who had tasted that vampire's blood and now was subject to a form of mind control. As my coven's name suggested, the three of us had all experienced that at one point or another, and had no intentions of doing so again. Ever. I'd made it clear to Chittenden, and he agreed, that future attempts to make a renfield out of a mage in his territory would end poorly.

It was Connie's turn to drive, so I rode shotgun in her purple jeep while Thumper had the backseat to themselves. We were all dressed to the nines. I normally hate formal clothes, but hobnobbing with the undead had given me a chance to dandy up a bit. I'd started with a three-piece suit in navy blue made of synthetic spider silk. It wasn't quite bulletproof, but it was tailored, was light and comfy, but about as protective as a firefighter's coverall. My jacket was more of a two-button wizard's robe, which gave me a bit more air as Georgia started to warm up for spring. Satin stripes of dark burgundy went down my outside trouser legs as an accent. By astonishing coincidence, they happened to be placed the exact same way as the bloodstripes on a Marine dress uniform.

Connie's outfit was black with purple accents, and her lipstick matched. Leather miniskirt and stockings ending just below the knees, topped off with her usual jump boots. Above the waist, I couldn't tell if she was wearing a top with dozens of cutouts or a web of sewn-together straps, but the effect was dazzling. I should've known that taking a goth to a vampire party meant extravagance. The surprise was what, for Connie, was a distinct lack of jewelry. She had plenty of rings on her fingers and assorted piercings, but her neck was bare. And the only decorations on her wrists were a pair of fingerless fishnet gloves that didn't quite reach the elbow.

I was moderately surprised. Connie was no prude, but she wasn't an exhibitionist either. She also rarely did anything without purpose. I could have just asked, but I needed the practice. Out of the three of us, Connie didn't use as much cognimancy. But she was the best of us at reading people. Working on her PhD in Psychology probably helped a lot.

After a second it hit me. We were walking into a vampire gathering. She was deliberately exposing all of her pulse points for any to see. Compounded with her reputation, it was a giant middle finger to their entire species. Look at me, leeches. Don't I look tasty? Try it and die screaming.

Thumper, by comparison, was almost mundane in their black tie and tails cut along century-old lines. Their hair was gelled down into a flapper style tight to their head. Lugosi himself would've been proud.

All three of us wore enamel lapel pins with our coven's sigil: A white capital R, a red-and-white slash, and a crimson capital A on a black field. As Renfields Anonymous, we believed in simplicity. We also believed in swift and brutal retaliation, as shown by our trophies. I wore a vampire fang wrapped in gold wire as an earring. Connie had another fang decorated in a similar fashion dangling from her navel piercing. Thumper, alas, had yet to take down a vampire themselves, but the night was young.

Of the three of us, Connie had the most fearsome reputation where vampires were concerned. I had killed three vampires by myself, and I'd needed a lot of firepower and gotten my ass kicked in the process. Connie had made one painfully rot with her bare hands before taking her head with an e-tool. She hadn't even hadn't broken a sweat. A night later, we'd gathered some friends and killed over a dozen vampires, including one enormous bloodsucker named Moose. I'd knocked Moose off the summit of Stone Mountain with a homemade rocket launcher and blown him into cheap salsa.

Word of us had gotten around. Both Connie and myself had technically been under the renfield influence at the time. A rumor had it we'd figured out ways to make it ineffective, and we weren't about to correct anyone who spread them.

I took a breath, then turned off the radio. "Headspace check."

Connie let out a breath of her own, then nodded. "I'm doing OK. First time doing one of these was pretty creepifying, but I think that's just the lingering post-kidnapping issues. The only thing I'm really on edge about is this Mariah person Neary was babbling about. I don't think we're walking into a trap. But I'm gonna be smart about it, not paranoid. They don't try to disarm or mindfuck us, it'll be just like a faculty event. Only less judgy."

I glanced in the rearview mirror at Thumper. They put two fingers of one hand to their temple, then held a thumbs-up in the other hand, their eyebrow quirked inquiringly. I nodded as Connie spoke up, "Audio only, Thump. I need my eyes staying on the road."

Thumper nodded, smiling reassuringly. Then they reached out, touching my shoulder with their right hand, Connie's with their left. In our heads we could hear Thumper's telepathic Mississippi drawl. "*I'm all right,*

I guess. If Victor shows up, that might change quick. But I don't think Chittenden's letting him out of a box anytime soon."

Victor Marazzi, Tasha's brother, had kept Thumper as a renfield for the best part of a year before we'd taken him down last summer. Given that he'd tried to usurp Chittenden as Atlanta's vampire lord, I didn't think he was going to be let off with a slap on the wrist. But it was all up to the whims of Chittenden. Which sucked for Thumper. Connie and I had the closure from having killed our tormentors personally, even if we'd needed a lot of work to recover ourselves since. Unlikely as it may seem, Thumper's former master was still undead and still out there somewhere.

I nodded. "Makes sense. Chittenden could drag him out and make an example of him anytime. Or he could lock the dumbass away for the next couple of decades. Even money."

Connie didn't take her eyes off the road. "Your turn."

I leaned back and looked up at the green spiderweb patch that decorated the roof of the jeep on my side. "I'm pretty decent. I don't owe Chittenden a thing for the first time since high school. If I tell him to pound sand, all I'll lose is some easy money and a neutral contact. With any luck, we can just hobnob with some vampires and call it a night. Hell, Chittenden might know something about the theater or Dr. Gull that we don't. It's not as if the Iron Council consults him."

Connie stopped at a red light. "Agreed. Let's get this over with."

Chapter Ten

Guideline Forty-Seven:

If you're being thrown in a lion's den and can't bring a weapon, bring snacks.

Then bring a weapon anyway.

Connie stepped out of the Jeep, her boots heavier than mine. They worked on her.

Tonight's shindig was being held at some country club house at a golf course I'd never had reason to approach before in my life. Not that I have much of a reason to approach any golf course. I hated golf. It felt like an excuse for a sport. Not to mention a waste of a good KD range. The clubhouse was done up in the same neo-antebellum style as Warwell's. Only it had none of the warmth and extra helpings of sneering at the peasants.

As the valet drove Connie's jeep away, I saw a familiar face at a podium by the door. Said face had the lines of a life ridden hard but the smile of one glad to be there. She tilted her head and inhaled slightly at our arrival, then smiled wider. "Hey, Travis."

I gave her a smile to match. "Hi, Linda. How's the pack?"

She shrugged casually, her windbreaker with SECURITY printed on the left breast rustling slightly. "Thriving, these days. Chittenden's one of the best clients we ever had."

I made a show of looking around and nodding. "He does run a tight operation. Glad to hear you're doing well. Ryan around?"

Linda smirked, pointing a thumb behind her. "In the back with the other team leads. Still cranky at you, though."

I held my arms open. "I can only apologize for shooting him in the face so many times."

Linda was the alpha female of a werewolf pack. We'd had some misunderstandings before I'd put in a good word for them with Chittenden. Now they headed up his security detail. They all seemed happier and better fed than when I'd met them, which was good to see. Chittenden may be an amoral parasite, but he was pretty decent for a boss.

Linda kept her easy smile. "Well, have a good night, Travis. Duty calls."

Linda nodded to the doorman and keyed her radio, looking away as she quietly reported us to whoever was on her net. The doorman opened the glass-fronted entrance for us.

Once into the atrium, Connie and Thumper each took one of my arms and we all began to strut. It let us take up space, look powerful, and played to the stereotypes of the older vampires in the room. They weren't quite outnumbered by the renfields attending on many of them, as well as the ordinary humans serving. I didn't bother using magic to double-check. In a place like this, body language said who was who. Vampires were here to see and be seen. While some of them could wallflower, none of them would dare look like a servant when there were renfields and humans to do that for them.

The three of us were breathing and walked in like we owned the place. That was enough to turn some heads even before whispers began coming from those who'd figured out who we were. There weren't a whole lot of supernatural people of any kind wandering around. We didn't hold conventions. Social events like this were a way to meet people without blatantly trying to kill each other. Normally. And if I was really lucky, nobody would notice how hard we were working to keep three sets of legs, all different lengths, keeping in stride with each other.

The air conditioning was going full blast, as most indoor places in Atlanta did after Valentine's Day. With over a third of the bodies in the room not giving off the heat to compensate, it was only going to be more noticeable as the night went on.

"Travis!"

I turned from the buffet to see a tall fellow in a leather jacket approach. He looked to be in his early twenties, with dirty blond hair slicked back in a way that was trying to be Sid Vicious but didn't quite work. With him was a rosy-cheeked young woman in one of the more ridiculously ostentatious gothic ensembles I'd ever seen. And given that I was in a coven with Connie, that said a lot.

Flense and Calista were some of the more obvious vampires I'd ever met. They flew under the radar by being exactly that: obvious. They were at every goth and alternative event they could find, and played the part of club kids to the hilt. In Chittenden's court, they were useful enough to be allowed to stay, but not so useful that the other vampires bothered using them as pawns. Which sounded lonely to me, so I always made a point to say hi when I saw them. We'd talked enough that I was convinced they just liked having someone to talk to that wasn't playing human chess. Which is how I knew their real names were Gary and Lisa.

I shook Flense's hand and air-kissed Calista's, giving them each a smile. "Flense, Calista. Good to see you both."

Flense had just enough swagger to look pleased but not eager to be. "You're looking well, being your own man these days."

"You're not so bad yourself. These are my covenmates, Connie Chandler and Thumper Buchanan."

Flense gave each a polite nod while Calista managed a curtsy. "Ladies."

Thumper gave a sweeping bow. Connie nodded politely. "You two're looking good."

Flense and Calista both tensed. I pretended not to notice. "Oh, you've already met?"

Connie smiled languidly. "Last Halloween."

Both of them smiled nervously as I nodded. "Oh. Cool."

They'd not only heard about Connie but encountered her personally. No wonder she scared them shitless. Flense didn't offer his hand and neither of the others took it. Word hadn't quite gotten around about the nuances of proper mage-on-vampire etiquette. They were probably playing the long game the way they had with me. When we'd met, I'd been a renfield. They'd treated me with distance but dignity, like leaving good tips to a waiter. Now that I was no longer a renfield but a fellow courtier, they were being friendly and egalitarian.

I tucked my thumbs into my pockets, Marine-style. "So, how's your night been? From the looks of things, someone farted the moment we stepped in the room. Can vampires fart? I never thought to ask before."

Thumper smirked. Connie's poker face didn't move. I could almost see Flense's brain stutter, but Calista recovered nicely, giving a shiny-fanged smile. "Our diet and digestion precludes such things, to the best of my knowledge. Given your choice in jewelry, I'd reckon you've more insight into our biology than most. As for the room, it's been rather boring tonight. The three of you are the most exciting thing to happen since the sun went down."

Connie's smile grew. "How scandalous. The vampire lord of Atlanta throwing a boring soiree? My fellow goths would be so disappointed."

Calista folded her hands over her heart in scandal. "Absolutely."

"Enjoying Chittenden's pets, Flense?"

I turned to get a good look at the speaker. If Flense and Calista were stereotypical vampires, this guy looked ready to steal a main character's girlfriend in an extreme sports movie. Blonde waves, deep blue eyes, and arrogance that could probably be smelled from the parking lot. He kind of reminded me of Victor, and for a horrible second I wondered if he was family somewhere up the bloodline.

As Flense tried to find the words, I smiled. "Just an old contractor, I'm afraid. Nothing so exotic."

The newcomer oozed smug as he smirked. "Excessive modesty from the man who supposedly killed every country vampire from Florida to New England."

I kept the easy smile going. "We had help. And you are?"

"Oh, where are my manners? Brian Quanor." I shook his hand. He hadn't bothered to warm it up to seem a little more human.

"Travis Wayland." I gave the little who's who indications. "Connie Chandler, Thumper Buchanan."

Quanor gave a little bow. "Ladies."

Thumper quirked their lip at the slight. Connie looked him up and down. "What brings you to Atlanta, Mr. Quanor?"

He opened his arms. "I'd heard the witches who brought Eva Marazzi down were due to make an appearance. I've never met one before. The notion intrigues me. You're quite the topics of conversation these nights."

She smirked. "You're out of luck if she was a friend. Girl had it coming."

He gave what I could only call a shit-eating grin. "I'd expect nothing less from an ex-renfield. Another mark of distinction."

I was really starting to not like this guy. I shrugged casually. "Oh, you know how it is. Uppity slaves are always a concern. Break one little shackle and they go thinking they're people."

If I hadn't been looking right at him, I'd have missed the twitch in his eye. That got him. Then the slimy smile was back in place. "Oh, not if they're kept in line."

Flense looked a touch uncomfortable, Calista even more so. I could feel a tingle in the back of my mind. Something I hadn't felt in over a year. I nodded at Quanor. My right hand, dangling at my side, slowly pointed two fingers towards the floor. "I bet the mind control y'all use on renfields is a whole lot more peaceful than physical methods. We ought to be taking notes."

Thumper held up a finger, then drew a pencil and notebook from their tuxedo pocket.

Quanor's smile grew. "You know, you're the only human I've ever met who realized that from the get go."

My face started to hurt trying to match his grin. "Well, when you've been on the receiving end of it, you can realize the possibilities."

I snapped my fingers. The pencil in Thumper's hand vanished.

Quanor blinked, looked strained for a moment, then fell over backwards, the eraser of Thumper's pencil just barely emerging from his pec.

As Quanor hit the floor, conversation came to a dead stop. I could see Flense and Calista slowly backing away from us, their hands in plain sight. Thumper pointed a finger gun at Quanor's stiff body, then blew imaginary smoke off the barrel. As I shook my head in disappointment, Thumper put the notebook away and opened a multitool. From behind me I heard the metallic sound of Connie drawing the folding entrenching tool she kept in her purse.

I refused to let myself show fear. We were in a room full of predators who'd just discovered they had challengers to being on the business end of the food chain. None of them were happy about it.

I opened my arms and addressed the crowd. "Does this dipshit belong to anyone?"

An angry and shocked murmur ran through the air. We had pointed out the elephant in the room. I could see one or two of Linda's packmates appear in corners of the room. They were watching, but they weren't about to interfere. This was a measuring contest, not an assassination or a war. They were going to make sure it didn't spread beyond that, then clean up the losers.

It was time to grab the narrative and run. I smacked myself in the forehead dramatically. "Oh shit! I must have forgot."

Connie, checking her makeup in the mirror-polished blade of her e-tool, raised an eyebrow. "You forgot?"

I snapped my fingers, biting back a laugh as some of the vampires in the crowd flinched. "Yeah. I could have sworn I told Lord Chittenden that mages can sense when someone's attempting mind control."

She nodded. "Oh yes. It's rather tingly."

"And on top of that, we do consider attempting such on a mage to be an act of war."

She smirked. "Makes sense, given that the Marazzis tried doing that to overthrow Chittenden's rule."

I waved a finger in agreement. "That's right! Good thing we slaughtered most of them in the end. I guess dipshit here just didn't get the memo."

Connie shook her head. "His loss. But hey, Thumper can get some cool new jewelry of their very own now."

Thumper held up the multitool with a shameless smile, clacking the handles like a pair of salad tongs.

"He's my dipshit."

The crowd parted. A curvaceous black woman strode towards us, high heels clicking on the marble floor. Her dress was a Rorschach pattern in black and white that hugged every curve. She stopped just out of lunging distance while meeting my eyes.

I raised an eyebrow. "Your son, I presume?"

She nodded. "He is. After being my renfield for a long time. He's still sowing his oats when it comes to being one of us."

I shook my head regretfully "I see. He tried to invade my mind, Ms...?"

"Fields. Mary Fields."

I tilted my head in a nod. "Travis Wayland. As mentioned, he tried to invade my mind."

She nodded. "I noticed."

Connie regarded her. "We killed most of those who've tried that."

She nodded. "Understandably."

Connie tilted her head down. "And Thumper over there's been looking forward to a trophy."

Mary held her gaze. "Please let him go. I will see to it he's... properly educated."

Now I was confused. Vampires were usually more than happy to let their children get themselves killed. After all, if they were smarter, they would have survived.

Something occurred to me. "Where's your usual stomping grounds, Ms. Fields?"

She blinked in surprise. "Biloxi."

That explained it. I wasn't sure how long she'd been a vampire, but if it was any longer than a decade or two, she'd have needed a pet white boy to make her unlife smoother. Which explained why she wasn't trying to get into a measuring contest with us.

I let the silence linger as I traded looks with my covenmates. We'd made our point, didn't feel like starting a fight, and could use a good favor. Consensus reached, I spoke for the benefit of the room.

"Thumper," I said, "I think dipshit here deserves a second chance."

Thumper gave an exaggerated sigh and put the multitool away.

Fields turned to Thumper and nodded. "Thank you, Thumper. I owe you a favor."

Thumper nodded magnanimously, then stepped away from the body of Quanor.

Mind control was a source of endless ethical debate among those who lived in the Otherworld. Many creatures capable of it, especially those older than fifty or so, tended to regard such powers as an adjustable wrench in the toolbox of dealing with humans. Iron Council Mages regarded such powers as being along the lines of a pistol: something to be used in dire emergency. Reckless or selfish uses of it was deeply frowned upon. Unfortunately, Mages being more or less human had left many vampires with a somewhat lax attitude towards using it. At least, until word got around about us. Quanor had just made the vampiric equivalent of trying to take selfies with a bison. Fields was grateful we hadn't very reasonably stomped him into a bloody mess. The crowd was taking in the spectacle with varying reactions.

But the only opinion that truly mattered here was Chittenden's. The room, and as far as anything that drank blood was concerned, the city, was his domain and his law reigned supreme. He was still in the corner where I'd last seen him, watching the display with a poker face firmly set.

As conversation began to pick back up, the crowd all somehow made certain not to look directly at us for more than the most brief glance. Flense and Calista had, out of good sense, disappeared into the masses. Fields had thrown Quanor over her shoulder like a sack of potatoes and carried him off without a word.

From the crowd, Oswald emerged. He was a handsome middle-aged black man, though from what I knew, he'd been all of those things for a very long time. He wore a simple charcoal three-piece suit, with a matching tie and no pocket square. It was an outfit carefully put together to not outshine any of the guests, while making it clear he was a notch above the servers.

He politely inclined his head in my direction as if we hadn't just caused a scene. "Lord Chittenden will see you all now."

The three of us traded looks, shrugged, and headed for Chittenden's reception corner.

Chapter Eleven

Guideline Thirty-Three:

If you can't make friends out of your enemies, you might still be able to make informants.

"Y'all sure know how to read a room."

Lord Samuel Chittenden looked like your typical hefty Southern man in a white suit. His accent played up the stereotype perfectly. But you don't rule every vampire in a region by collecting trading cards. Chittenden had ruled Georgia's vampires for decades, and he had both the brains and the ruthlessness to keep doing so for decades to come. I didn't laugh at his clothes or his accent for the same reason I don't laugh at apex predators at the zoo. Besides, I wouldn't admit it, but Thumper's drawl is worse than his. At his side was a glamorous woman who looked to be fighting the effects of age tooth and claw. She looked at us the way a cat looks at birds.

I opened my hands, chagrined. "Sorry about that, Sir. But we couldn't let it go unanswered."

He waved a hand, dismissing the idea. "Some young buck was bound to go testing what was possible. They always do. Y'all handled it rather well in the end. Now Ms. Fields owes you a favor, which is not to be sneered at."

We traded looks, acknowledging this.

He cut to the chase. "What y'all got for me?"

Connie spoke up. "We've been told there's a necromancer in town. Goes by the name of Dr. Gull."

That got us a raised eyebrow. "Dr. Gull is back?"

My train of thought derailed. "Back?"

Chittenden waved an arm dismissively. "He ran around here causing trouble back in the 50s and 60s. Nineteen-sixties, that is. I didn't quite have my finger on the pulse of magical politics back then, but I remember him."

I nodded. "We're told he's back in Atlanta. Something about revenge."

Chittenden snorted. "So he finally found out who killed his daughter?"

Connie shrugged a bit. "Presumably. You heard about that too?"

"Yeah, pretty young thing. Got loved and left. Broken heart. Don't remember the details."

Connie nodded. "Thank you for confirming the few details we have."

"Y'all got any leads?"

I nodded. "Maybe. The Pencil Factory Theater."

He tilted his head in mild surprise. "Is that opening up again?"

Connie chimed in. "It is. Max Roman bought and renovated it."

That brought a cruel sounding laugh from the next chair. The woman clapped her hands. "Old Maximus is finally putting on his old vanity show, is he?"

I nodded. "If his old vanity show is a rock opera of Romeo and Juliet, then yes, ma'am."

Chittenden grunted. "Where the hell are my manners? May I present Lady Mariah of Los Angeles? Lady, this is Renfields Anonymous, my magi consultants."

She offered a hand without getting up. "Charmed, I'm sure."

I took her hand lightly and nodded in it's direction. "Lady."

Connie actually curtsied. Thumper made a dapper bow. Mariah took her hand back.

"So you're going to go make sure Max works with a net?"

Connie nodded. "As best we can."

Mariah continued to smile with no warmth at all. "You may need magic for that, darling."

Connie smiled innocently. "That's what we've been called in for."

Mariah's eyebrow rose like an enemy flag. "Oh?"

I nodded. "Two people have died in that theater since rehearsals for a new show began. The stage manager thinks it may be ghosts."

Chittenden actually looked surprised. "Ghosts that can kill?"

Mariah chimed in. "Theater ghosts that kill, no less?"

Chittenden huffed. "Well, that will keep everyone wide awake."

Connie smiled. "I'm good with dead people."

Mariah's resting bitch face almost cleared the room. "Is that so?"

Connie didn't miss a beat. "Well, not when they're siccing the Iron Council on me."

Mariah laughed humorlessly again. "Word's already gotten to you? Lovely, dear."

Chittenden raised an eyebrow. "Y'all seem to have me at a disadvantage vis-a-vis the latest news."

I turned to him. "It seems the Lady objected as to the way Tasha Marazzi met her end."

Chittenden's looks got dark. "Is that so?"

Mariah waved him off. "Oh, don't get your knickers in a twist, My Lord. It's not my fault the little gothlet used forbidden magic to cut down the Marazzi girl."

Chittenden's look did not lighten one bit. "The Marazzi girl was trying to overthrow my rule. The young lady was quite helpful in ending her and delivering her equally traitorous brother to me."

Connie shrugged. "I'll tell you the same thing I told Neary. I just disarmed her with magic. I killed her with an e-tool."

Lady Mariah was puzzled. "What's an e-tool? Some kind of fancy torch?"

Connie reached into her purse, then shook her arm. Her e-tool unfolded and locked into place with a ratcheting sound. She'd wrapped the handle in fresh pink and black paracord. She saluted Mariah with it. "A bit more simple than that, Lady."

Another flick of the wrist, and the e-tool folded back up before Connie slid it into her bag. The rest of us relaxed all around.

Mariah sniffed, as if smelling something foul. "How vulgar."

Chittenden sat back, snickering in amusement. "Well that's just practical, now, ain't it? A zombie wrangler bringing her own shovel is just common sense. Now we know the fancy folding ones got their own name. Miss Chandler, are you facing repercussions as to this forbidden magic I hear about?"

Connie smiled. "Necromancy? Funny you should mention it, Lord. With Dr. Gull at large, I've been granted a blanket exemption from the ban. As have my coven, my students, and my collaborators."

Mariah's look darkened. Chittenden looked intrigued, then smiled. "Ah. Sending a necromancer to catch a necromancer, are they?"

Connie nodded. "Got it in one, sir."

"Well, I'll consider it a kindness for you to not to melt any of my constituents or guests, but the best of luck and good hunting to you."

It was a dismissal and we accepted it as such. With respectful nods to both of them, we made our way back among the crowd. Not that the crowd was interested in mingling with us. Even Flense and Calista had made themselves scarce. Without making it too obvious, we made our way outside onto the veranda.

The weather was nicer than usual for a Georgia spring, where storms can pop up at a moment's notice. The few other people were at shouting distance and beyond.

Thumper and Connie both looked all right, but I wanted to make sure. I curled my right hand into a cylinder, looked them both in the eyes, then looked down at my hand. Thumper kept their hands where they were, but curled in their thumb and pinky on their right hand, showing three fingers. Connie did the same, as did I. Yeah, we could've used telepathy. But a few small hand signals let us say simple but important things. Like, "on a scale of one to five, how bad do you need to get out of here?" All of us were relatively OK, all things considered.

I leaned back against a railing. "I'm thinking Wa'cross after this."

Thumper nodded emphatically. Connie started counting on her fingers. "We've educated an idiot, checked in with Chittenden, and scandalized a lot of people we didn't want to talk to anyway."

"You're also on the right track, for what it's worth."

Lady Mariah was standing in the doorway, a goblet of what probably wasn't wine in her hand.

I raised an eyebrow. "How so, Lady?"

She sauntered towards us. "A theater ghost killing someone? Not on their own, darling. Presumably a necromancer can arrange such. And if Dr. Gull is avenging a murdered daughter, then Max Roman is definitely his ultimate target."

I frowned, lying through my teeth. "They're connected? I haven't seen anything in Roman's background about a dead girl."

Mariah shrugged. "It didn't make the papers and it was largely before blogs. But it hit the rumor mills. Girl's name was Kemp or Kent or something like that. Lovely girl, for a negress. Dark hair, sweet disposition. Unfortunately she was too good for this cruel world onstage and off. Max did the typical wine, dine, and get stars in her eyes. Then when she was going to be a star, he dropped her like a used hanky."

Thumper and I traded skeptical looks. Having Mariah lecture us was like having an evil talk show host bring you the latest gossip.

Connie looked wary. "When was this?"

Mariah turned her hand in a circle, like she was trying to shoo away the details. "Oh, around the Gulf War or thereabouts. Max decided to make like Elvis and enlisted. How brave. So patriotic. It might have even worked. Backfired on him, though. He took a few years off, then made not so much a comeback as got back on the horse. Always made money, but he was never a star again."

I frowned. "Being rich didn't make him a star?"

Mariah laughed with no humor and less warmth. "Money's not enough to make a star, Boy."

I let the insult slide. "Whatever is?"

She grinned, mostly at the prospect of an interested audience. "Prestige is a good word. Clout. Influence. Popularity. Who knows you. What you can make happen. Money's no good in Hollywood if you can't make it do what you want. Roman has made steady money, but he's been sliding gently down the call sheet ever since he returned."

I mulled over that. "And the girl?"

Mariah shrugged. "The girl died penniless soon after he left. Suicide is what the rumors were saying. Whether it was over Roman or over her stillborn career is anyone's guess."

I frowned. "You're saying Miss Kemp or whatever was Dr. Gull's daughter?"

Mariah raised a manicured finger. "I'm saying it makes sense."

Connie frowned. "Why are you helping us?"

Mariah shrugged. "Clearly it's an important mission. I might as well be a good guest and help my host's consultants."

Connie didn't buy that for a minute. "But you tried to have me killed."

Mariah gave a dazzling smile. "Oh no no no. Don't sell me short, darling. I tried to get permission to kill you. That's a different thing entirely."

Connie shrugged in confusion. "Why? Tasha Marazzi your grandchild or something?"

Mariah laughed. "That Russian dingbat? Hah! I'd rather turn a patchouli-riddled granola rancher than that one."

Connie shook her head incredulously. "Then why?"

She gave the smile a cruel teacher gave to a particularly dim student. "General principle, darling. You've forgotten which link in the food chain you really are. If a cow kicks your idiot cousin in the head and kills them, you bury the cousin. Have a nice funeral, kind words, very sad. But if that cow gets it into her little bovine head that she can kick who she pleases? Then you put steak on the menu. And the world turns as it should."

The coven all traded looks. Connie took the lead. "Seriously?"

Mariah took a sip from her goblet. "Of course, darling. You're an uppity little heifer. And I'm going to eat you the moment it's feasible."

I checked the corners of the room in the blink of an eye, then chuckled at her. "Funny. Only thing I ever knew that sucked blood out of a cow was a mosquito."

Thumper snickered.

Mariah's look darkened. "I didn't say I was going to now."

"No? Damn." I snapped my fingers, which made Mariah flinch before I continued, deepening my southern accent. "Thumper and me are both raised country. Zapping mosquitoes is quality entertainment."

Thumper giggled, then bugged out their eyes, wiggled, and made buzzing noises. Connie cracked a smile.

Mariah shrugged again. "You're not killing me tonight either. I haven't lifted a finger against you. None of us are stupid enough to truly start a fight at Chittenden's party like that young moron earlier. I'm just admitting what you asked me."

Connie frowned. "Try to have me killed one minute, help us the next? That still doesn't make sense. Why waste time like that?"

Mariah laughed. "I have time, darlings. I've heard of all of you. You're clever, but too easily become desperate. How long did Chittenden hold your oath, Mr. Wayland? Ten years and more? You spent your twenties waiting to become a renfield. And because you got the drop on a couple of depression and vodka wannabes you think you're at the top of the game? You had a half-dozen of your fellows and a prince of the Wild Hunt with you taking down Victor, and it was still a near thing. Someday you won't be Chittenden's shiny new toys. Someday you'll have made enough enemies that you can barely watch each other's backs."

She'd made an uncomfortable point. I gave her my best unimpressed look. "At Stone Mountain, I was coming off of a year as a renfield. My friends and I still took out more vampires than there are in that room behind you. In another ten years, we'll be even better."

She finished her goblet, then tossed it onto the lawn. "Will you? I rule the City of Angels, darling. I've seen more relapses than you've had blowjobs. And I can tell you that in a lot of them, it's just a matter of time." She turned to Connie. "If you ask nice, I might even let you have a taste before I finish you off." She gave a predatory smile to us all. "Happy hunting, darlings."

We watched her strut away into the crowd. Then traded looks.

After long moments I said, "Waffles?"

They both nodded faster than I thought possible.

Chapter Twelve

Guideline Forty-Five:

Pick up every puzzle piece you find.

Even if they're not for your puzzle.

I considered chickening out and having Jazz do my eyeliner, but stubbornness set in, and I wound up doing it myself in the bathroom before Connie picked me up. I don't think I did too badly, but I still felt kinda weird. I climbed into the shotgun seat of her jeep as she turned down whatever dark metal band she was listening to.

After buckling up, I gave her a smartass grin. "How's my eyeliner?"

She took a glance and nodded before pulling out of the driveway. "Not the sharpest in the world, but not bad for a newbie."

I nodded. "That's what Byron said."

"That doesn't sound like Byron."

I moved my hand in a kinda-sorta gesture. "Well, first he said he'd do me."

She snickered. "Now that does sound like Byron."

I rolled my eyes. "If only I was out to seduce elves instead of hunt ghosts."

She shrugged. "The day's young. You never know."

"I'm more amazed you never dated him."

She gave a half shrug before turning at the green light. "Not really my type. Or rather, I'm not really his. To give him credit, he knows that, and dialed it back to a dull roar."

I nodded. "That's Byron for you. Do you even have a type?"

She smirked. "Yeah. The type the spectral peanut gallery shut up about when I date them."

I blinked as the implications of that hit me. Like all mages, Connie's magic had manifested itself when she was about twelve. If she'd been hearing ghosts give a running commentary on her life ever since? I twitched.

She winked, then cranked the music back up a bit as we rolled deeper into town.

*　*　*

The sun was out and the heat was only somewhat less humid. Fortunately, finding a parking spot was easy enough.

The kids with the water bottles were right where we'd left them.

One recognized me with a mercenary grin. "Hey, Big Man!"

I smirked, nodding a greeting. "Hey kid. I'll take two."

I passed the kid a ten as he handed over the bottles. I passed one over to Connie, then looked over the kid. "Hey, kid?"

"Yeah, Big Man?"

I opened my water and took a swig. "How long you been selling water on this spot?"

He shrugged. "Couple weeks. Before that, it was too cold half the time. Nobody want cold water when they need a jacket in Georgia."

I nodded. That made sense. "Seen anything weird?"

The other kid sneered, beyond unimpressed by the resident grownup. "What's weird, Big Man? I see weird every day."

"What about the guy who got killed by a truck over there?" I pointed down the street in front of the theater.

The first kid's eyes got wide. "Awww, shit! How you know about that, Big Man? It was awesome!"

The other kid nodded emphatically. "Like nailing a watermelon with a baseball bat!"

The first kid held his hands like he was holding a ball, then blew a raspberry as he shoved his palms together.

I nodded, trying not to laugh. "He just ran out into traffic?"

The first kid kept bobbing his head positively. "Oh yeah. Something scared the hell out of him. He never saw it coming."

I nodded. "You guys are gone when we get off work. When do you pack up?"

The first kid didn't hesitate before speaking up. "Before dark."

His eyes were wide again. Something was spooking him.

I took another swig. "Yeah? What happens at dark?"

The other kid muttered, trying to keep his voice down. "The Crying Girl."

I blinked. "Never heard of her."

The first kid was looking more scared by the moment. "You got a girl wit you, Big Man! You safe! We ain't got no girl with us!"

A quick glance around told me the bum that saw us the other day was nowhere to be seen now.

Connie tilted her head. "What's the Crying Girl do?"

The other kid checked both ways, then looked Connie dead in the eye. "She hunts for the man who did her dirty. He broke her heart. So she comes to take his. And if you did a girl wrong, she come to take yours too."

The first kid nodded, looking up at us with terrified eyes. "Yeah. She reaches right in your chest, stops your heart. Cops say it's just a heart attack. It ain't. You lay there stone dead on the pavement. The Crying Girl walk away, carrying your heart in her hand. Don't go nowhere after dark without your girl here, Big Man. It ain't safe!"

Connie took my arm possessively. "Don't worry. I won't let him go wandering off."

The kid didn't look too reassured as I nodded to him. "Thanks for the water, kid."

I looked around until we got to the theater, but didn't see any sign of the bum.

* * *

Walking by the door labeled "Harry's office," I heard some talk radio wafting past. The door was open, so I poked my head in.

Sitting at another vintage steel desk was a small balding man with delicate glasses. His tweed suit jacket was draped over the desk, and he sat in his waistcoat and tie, sleeves rolled up to the elbows. A second monitor and a wireless mouse were hooked up to a powerful-looking laptop, and some financial program played as he worked.

"Harry?"

He didn't look up. "That's what they call me."

I'd already poked my head in, might as well double down. I offered my hand. "I'm Travis, one of the new ASM's."

He finally looked up, stood up, and shook it. Firm enough to not be thought weak, easy enough to show he had no inclination to stupid grip strength games. "Harold Dun. I'm Mr. Roman's personal assistant, as well as the managing director of this lash-up."

I let go of his hand. "I don't know what that means."

He sat back down, etiquette satisfied. "It means I make sure Mr. Roman doesn't bounce checks in the middle of the run."

I nodded. "As a recipient of one of those, I appreciate it. That said, I was kinda curious as to how. Unless I'm missing something, it seems like he's paying a lot more without charging a lot more."

That got his attention. His eyes widened in a mix of pleasant surprise and mockery. "A theater person who understands economics? I've never seen one of you in the wild before. Are you sure you're not an undercover tax investigator?"

I spit on the floor. "Do I look like a fed to you?"

His eyes narrowed. "There are feds of all flavors, young man."

That got a smile out of me. "Not like me. So own up. How's Max planning on making any money off this show?"

He looked over the top of his glasses at me. "What do you care?"

I shrugged. "I like to know where my next meal ticket comes from. Looks like you're the one paying the bills around here."

Harry sighed. "Far too many bills for my taste. And most of them about caffeine. You people guzzle coffee, tea, cocoa, and those disgusting energy drinks like nothing I've ever seen."

I shrugged. "Guilty as charged. How's Max making a profit again?"

Harry took a handkerchief from his waistcoat pocket and began cleaning his glasses. "To be perfectly honest, I don't think he's planned that far ahead. Creative freedom is more important to him than profit at this juncture. Normally a show like this would be produced by an investment group and the building would be independently owned. Mr. Roman has bought the building outright and bankrolled the production himself. This concentrates the risks but also the rewards, and more importantly, the creative control. He answers to no investors, no patrons, no board of directors. He has complete control. If he fails to make his nut, as the case may be, Mr. Roman is already wealthy enough to pull it off and not affect his lifestyle significantly. And if the show has an impressive run, here or elsewhere, he may well recoup his investment and then some." He held his glasses up to the light, nodding in satisfaction before putting them back on.

I nodded. "Yeah. If. Mutual funds are safer."

Harry shrugged as he neatly folded the handkerchief and put it away. "Mutual funds don't have the prestige of a hit show. He might get a return on his investment, but the real prize is in returning to prominence as a director as much as he has as an actor."

I frowned. "So it's a vanity project?"

Harry waved his hand on the diagonals. "Yes and no. Money and prestige are the coins of the entertainment realm. Money is easy enough to understand, but prestige is far less tangible. More like popularity in high school, only with better drugs and deeper personality disorders. Done right, they feed each other. Being invited to the right parties and featured in the right magazines gets one's next project funded, and may make it a hit all on its own, and the circle goes around again. Mr. Roman is currently cash-rich but prestige-poor, if that makes sense. He has all the money in his pockets he will ever need. But only a success on this scale will put his name in people's minds on the level he desires."

I nodded, remembering Mariah's similar lecture. "Makes sense."

"Does that satisfy your question?"

That cracked a smile. "Actually, yeah it does. Thanks Harry."

He gave me a polite smile in turn. "You're very welcome. Now go away. My spreadsheets await."

*   *   *

It was my turn again to stake out the smoke pit. To my surprise, half the cast arrived with smokes and drinks in hand.

Danny, who I vaguely remembered was playing Mercutio, was the first to light up. He was a slender, handsome black man in a purple track suit. After leaning against a railing, he nodded to me. "Hey, man. Travis, right?"

I nodded. "That's me."

A guy with tousled blond hair nodded at me. A dig in my memory remembered he was Kenny, the guy playing Romeo. "Ghosts been treating you any better today?"

There was snickering all around. I shrugged. "Well, none of them tried to kill me today, I figure that's the best I can ask."

Danny grinned. "An optimist! I like that in an ASM."

Tim, who was playing Tybalt, shook his head. "That's just freaky, man. I'd be nervous as hell." Tim was short and fast, like his world moved a notch quicker than everyone else's.

Ron grimaced. "Shit. I'm already nervous. Never heard of a theater ghost actually killing someone." Ron looked like he was playing hooky from high school. His resume said he was somewhere between legally drinking and good car insurance, but he sure didn't look it. It took me a few seconds to remember he was playing Paris.

Kenny nodded. "Nobody's heard of a theater ghost actually killing someone."

Danny pointed his cigarette like a teacher with a bit of chalk. "You got that right. Even the old-timers are wigged out about it."

I shrugged. "Not the first time I've had people trying to kill me. Just the first ghost."

That got me some surprised looks. Kenny spoke up. "What? You grow up in a bad neighborhood or something?"

I shook my head. "Mostly in the war, man."

That impressed Kenny. "No shit? Thanks for your service, man. What branch?"

I shrugged. "Marines. Assaultman."

Danny looked curious. "What's an assaultman?"

I took a swig of my drink. "A grunt with explosives, mostly."

Ron grimaced. "Better you than me, man. I couldn't do that."

Tim cocked his head. "Afghanistan?"

I took a drag and shook my head. "Iraq."

Tim sighed and grimaced. "Fucked up, that one. Would've been easier if we'd divvied it back up into three countries instead of the one the British mashed together."

I frowned. "I know that. How do you know that?"

Tim shrugged. "I minored in history. Specialized in the Middle East. Thought it was interesting."

I stubbed out my cigarette. "I didn't know actors had degrees."

Ron's face twisted as if he'd smelled something unpleasant. "All of us do. Some of us have Master's."

Tim stubbed out his butt. "Can I ask you something, man?"

I shrugged. "Go for it."

Tim's voice slowed down, almost cautious. "You and the other ASM, the goth chick. You two a thing?"

I snorted before I noticed the interest of everyone but Kenny coming my way. "Connie? Hell no."

Danny frowned. "You just carpool?"

I shrugged. "We're friends. Rocky hired us at the same time, so we figured we'd carpool. Long story, but we're entirely platonic."

Tim grinned. "Good to know. She single?"

I shrugged. "Far as I know."

His smile just got bigger. "Excellent."

I was probably being rude, but was too confused to care. "I'm still wondering how the hell actors get Master's degrees."

That got me a stinkeye from Ron.

Tim shrugged. "Like everyone else, mostly. Add an audition to get into some programs."

I frowned. "How do you pay for it?"

Kenny snickered. "Who says we do?"

Tim nodded. "Yup. I'll still be paying the loans off when I'm dead."

I shook my head. "That just sounds fucked up. No offense."

Kenny and Ron sneered. Tim stubbed out his cigarette. "None taken."

Danny shrugged. "How's it any more fucked up than anything else? You spend your life doing what you love. If you get rich, you pay it off like it's nothing. If you don't, you die owing the government money, so fuck 'em."

Ron nodded. "Definitely not as fucked up as shooting people." He suddenly appeared to care that I was there. "No offense."

I shrugged. "None taken. It's not like I shot them all. Sometimes I used grenades."

Ron flushed bright red as Rocky's voice came in over the intercom. *"Five minutes, everyone."*

Danny thumbed the button as we all said in unison, "Thank you, five."

* * *

The lights of the city marked our drive as we headed back to my place. Connie had a bit of a lead foot, which meant she fit right in with Atlanta's traffic. She passed a minivan on the right, then gunned it. As the minivan receded in the rearview, she shook her head. "I'm starting to like these actors."

I snickered. "They're liking you too."

"Yeah?"

"Tim asked if we were seeing each other. And every male in the cast under thirty was on the edge of their seats listening."

She chuckled. "Tim? Love em and leave 'em himself?"

"I speak the truth."

"My kingdom for better timing. I don't mind the attention. But not while we're busy trying to keep them alive."

I smirked. "And here I thought you were warming up to them."

She shrugged a bit. "Don't get me wrong, they're all flakier than good baklava. But they grow on you. Kinda reminds me of us. Mages, I mean."

I grimaced. "We're like actors?"

She waved a hand in the international sort-of gesture. "Think about it. We get sequestered away from everyone else for a part of school. Really skilled at obscure stuff most people either don't understand or don't believe exists. Spend a ton of time, money, and effort at doing what we do. And it doesn't come close to paying the bills. But they do it anyway. They don't even have the excuse of being magical whether they like it or not. They're just... driven."

I frowned. "I make money with magic."

She snorted. "You make money with magic because a vampire keeps you on retainer. It's not like you advertise in the phone book or anything."

I nodded. "No joke. Only a serious fruitcake would pull a stunt like that."

We drove for a bit in silence before another thought struck me.

"Do they even make phone books anymore?"

"Dunno."

* * *

After dinner, Thumper arranged for us to call an old friend. We all clustered on the couch in the living room. Jazz curled up against my side and Thumper sat on the floor, leaning back against Connie's legs. Thumper opened up a video chat on the TV as Byron started munching popcorn.

Seb's camera showed the inside of his trailer. I could see some of his guitars hanging up on one wall, one of his bows and a quiver full of arrows tucked neatly into a corner. From what I could tell, his webcam was aiming out from the sidewall of his kitchen table. Seb was medium everything in build, with a neatly trimmed goatee, and hair a shade of auburn that some would kill for.

Seb was a classmate of mine and Thumper's, and survived Blue River with us as well. Last year he joined us in taking down Victor Marazzi on top of Stone Mountain. He was a navigator, specialized in magic that dealt with distances. He was also a talented musician, at least third generation, and knew more about bardic magic than anyone else I could impose upon. He had a place in Florida, but for all intents and purposes he lived on the road, performing at Renaissance festivals and such.

Behind Seb, a huge man was sitting delicately on the couch, reading a tablet. He was easily my size or bigger, with a mane of long, dark hair starting to thin on top. A set of hornrimmed glasses too delicate for his face framed his green eyes. A leather pouch the size of a deflated basketball hung from his belt.

Seb waved. "Hey Travis, good to see you. I got all that stuff ya sent me."

"Likewise, Seb. Found something?"

"Long story, man. Short version, there aren't any spells overlaid on what you've shown me. I've watched the video, listened to the rehearsals and read the libretto. There's no secondary effect Jukka or I could find."

The big guy in the back gave a little wave with a huge hand.

I nodded. "Jukka, I presume?"

That got me a thumbs up. A warm baritone rumbled out of him. "That's me. Seb showed me what you got, and he's right. I've seen a lot of music used as trigger effects, and none of that is here."

I raised an eyebrow at that. "Why am I suspecting a big caveat there, gentlemen?"

Seb shrugged. "Just because magic wasn't overlaid in it doesn't mean it's not there."

Jukka nodded. "We're not getting into quantum magic here, but we're getting close. There's a lot of arguments around it, but a lot of old school bards think music is inherent magic similar to the way written language is."

I took a swig of coffee and nodded. "Like the old thaumaturgical theorists? In order to alter reality, you need to tell reality what it is now? That kinda thing?"

Jukka waved one massive hand from side to side. "Sort of. Only we're not sure what music's actually saying. We just have the results. Near as we can tell, music bypasses the language center of the brain entirely and goes straight to the emotional centers. So we more or less know what tunes can stimulate various emotions, even if there's no lyrics."

I frowned. "So music is a natural cognimantic effect?"

Seb and Jukka both shook their heads. Seb took the lead. "That's what most coming into bardic magic from the outside believe at first. The old bards used to catch frauds that way. A cognimancer would play just any old tune and force a cognimancy effect on top of it. But a bard can get the same effect just using the music itself. Focuses more on emotion than conscious thought, but at the same time, it flows better. Like making wire to conduct electricity."

Connie spoke up. "Guys, I'm fascinated. But we got a lot on our plate and normally I can't carry a tune in a bucket. So can you tell me if an evil necromancer is using this rock opera to kill people?"

Jukka shrugged. "Maybe."

I opened my mouth again and Jukka held up a hand to stop me. "Look, we're all mages here. We know anything's possible. So let's talk about likely. And if someone wanted to use this piece for magical effect, they picked a good one. These songs are really well done, and they're hitting the emotional beats they're supposed to. Hard. On top of that, it's R & J. It's a classic for a reason. We've all fallen in love with people that someone didn't approve of. We've all had families that sucked at communicating sometime. The big question you need to ask is, if there's a magical effect here, what's the intended results? Because a story like this? It could have the entire audience calling their loved ones to say what they don't have the courage to say normally."

Seb nodded, then looked me dead in the eye over a shaky internet connection. "Or it could set off a mass murder-suicide. There's just no way of knowing for sure."

Connie grimaced. "Anything you can know for sure?"

Seb and Jukka traded looks, then Seb turned back. "Actually, just one thing. Playing the music to trigger a magical effect is an active act. You can't enchant an instrument or a singer and use them to do it without leaving signs. If this was like the beanstalk giant's harp or the red shoes or something like that, we'd find signatures that we haven't found here. Anyone using this music for magic is gonna be playing it themselves."

I blinked. "So anyone doing that would have to be either one of the musicians..."

Connie finished for me. "... or one of the actors."

Seb nodded. "Yeah, pretty much."

I smiled. "It's more than we had to go on before. Thanks, gents."

"Good luck, folks."

Chapter Thirteen

Guideline Thirty-Four:

Keep it simple.

Especially when it's already gotten complicated.

The next day I spent a break hanging out with the performers who didn't smoke. I was kinda surprised to see it was mostly the older performers, along with half of the musicians. You'd have thought it was the other way around.

"Ah, crap. Damn thing stole my dollar."

Along one wall of the green room was a coffee and tea selection crowding a sink, along with an older refrigerator. A magnet for an HVAC company held up a flyer for the show on the fridge. At the end of the line was a vending machine for bottled sodas. Standing in front of the vending machine was the biggest guy in the cast. My size, more or less. A blue-collar paunch and muscles to go with it. Balding and not bothering to hide it. He looked like the goofy dad on a sitcom, frowning in annoyance at the machine.

I wandered on over, looking the machine up and down. It was one of the older ones that took dollar bills but not cards. I frowned at it in an attempt to be helpful. "This one do that a lot?"

The man shrugged. "Your guess is good as mine, buddy."

I nodded, stroking my goatee out of habit. "Maybe Rocky has a key. Or at least the owner's number."

He shrugged. "Have at, man."

I made a show of frowning at it while touching the buttons. It was a decent cover for what I was really doing, which was using magic to look into the machine and figure out where the stoppages are. Fortunately, it was the same kind of machine I'd learned on in high school. I tapped just under the keyhole with my fingertips a few times, then thumped my fist on a spot just under the keyhole. There was a buzz, a clunking sound, then a bottle of cold soda landed in the out tray.

I stepped back. "There we go."

He chuckled. "Hey, nicely done."

I took a small bow. "ASM's get the job done."

He picked up the soda and shook my hand. 'Thanks.. Travis, right?"

I nodded. "Hey, no problem...Larry?"

"Good call."

Score one for my memory. He was playing Friar Laurence, which jived with his look.

He took a seat on the couch. I pulled up a nearby chair.

"I haven't seen you around, Travis. You new in town?"

I shook my head. "Just to the gig. I used to do some roadie work here and there. Then Rocky called up asking a favor."

"Well, glad to have you with us. Nice guyliner."

"Glad to be here, if the local ghost stops throwing me down the stairs."

I could feel a change in the air, as the various people snacking while checking their phones suddenly all started listening a little harder.

Larry gave a somber nod. "There is that. I knew Grover for fifteen years. Never thought he'd go like this."

"Condolences, man."

"Thank you. The show goes on, as it must."

"How long you been doing this? You a local too?"

"You mean theater? Since high school. Been based in Atlanta my whole life, but you know how it is. A show run here, a season there. I'm just lucky to have a gig this big right here at home."

"That's what everyone keeps telling me."

Larry shrugged. "You get old enough in this business, you try not to look a gift horse in the mouth."

I processed that. "Even with a homicidal ghost?"

He looked uncomfortable but resigned. "Even then."

I nodded. "I never heard of a theater ghost that killed."

Larry took a drink. "Nobody has. I've been an actor since high school, and I've never heard of a theater ghost even hurting someone. Scaring people? All the time. Practical jokes like opening doors and messing with lights, that happens everywhere. This is different. This is new."

Everyone else in the room was nodding somberly. Nobody expected the latest gig to have this kind of twist.

I kept listening, folding my hands. "Anything needs to be done about it?"

He smiled sadly. "Just make sure the show goes on."

I tried to keep the incredulous look off my face. "It's that important?"

Out of the corner of my eye, I saw one or two of the old-timers giving me stinkeye. But they seemed content to let Larry handle it.

He took another drink. "One of the more important things we can do. Ever heard of the phrase, 'making your nut?'"

I frowned. "I think Harry said something about it. Kinda like a break even point? Where it's how much you need to earn before you start making a profit?"

"Very good. It comes from the days of traveling circuses. When the circus came to town, the Sheriff would remove the nut from the axle of the main wagon. Kept the circus from leaving in the middle of the night without paying its bills. The sad thing is that performers who can't perform are usually reduced to prostitution and poverty if they wanted to eat. That's why we were associated with thieves and whores from Ancient Rome to FDR. If we wanted to make it, the show had to make it."

The idea sank into my head. I nodded. "So the show really has to go on. Or nothing else can."

Larry grimaced at the thought. "Exactly. There's so much going against this show. Against any show. Landlords. Sheriffs. Angry Mobs. Poverty. Our own egos. And now angry ghosts. Any of them could stop the show before it happens. Then all of the heart and soul and work that goes into it is all for nothing. Making sure the show happens, as best we can make it happen. That's the goal. That brings us in front of the audience. Where the magic really happens."

That made me look up and meet his gaze. He was smiling with a sadness and fondness all at once. A glance at the room showed the others nodding solemnly. This was a bunch that was in it for the long haul. A ghost may have spooked them, but it wasn't about to stop them.

Then Rocky's voice came over the intercom. *"Five minutes, everyone."*

One of the musicians thumbed the button. "Thank you, five."

* * *

The next week passed without further supernatural murder attempts. I appreciated that. I had my guyliner on every day and some of Connie's salt packets on me at all times, but had no desire to need to use them.

There was, however, plenty of creepy to go around.

With Rocky's blessing, Connie and I explored the upper levels as a team. She was looking for signs of necromancy. I was checking out the building itself. Most of the storage areas were stuffed with old junk. Too dusty to be used for anything else without a decent cleaning, and Roscoe didn't seem to have gotten up to them yet. Theater programs from the various shows past. Lobby cards from movies in the 70's. That kind of thing.

Then one day, there was the mother of all fire hazards.

* * *

We knew the room was going to be problematic. We just didn't know how badly.

One of the first things I learned as an alchemist was how to see through walls. And not just the wall of the girls' locker room, for any curious perverts out there. For what it's worth, the view there isn't nearly as erotic as most teenage boys imagine it is. A lot less pinup poses and a lot more dirty socks.

What I could see, on a second glance at least, was building materials: Insulation. Plumbing. Electrical conduits. Drainage. Gas piping. That kinda stuff. And the room we stood outside was just plain weird.

"I bet it's a disappointment room." said Connie.

I grimaced. "A what?"

She waved a hand at it. "A disappointment room. Where you put the relatives you don't want polite society to know or find out about. You put 'em in a disappointment room."

"You know people who used disappointment rooms?"

"I've met someone who grew up in a disappointment room."

I tilted my head at her. "Seriously? What the hell?"

She shrugged. "It's got a steel door and you said it's got a padded interior."

I rolled my eyes. "This is at heater. Before that, it was a lot of things. Victorian mansion wasn't included in the list."

She smirked. "OK, smartass. What do you think it is?"

I shrugged. "I got no idea. I just don't want to open it without backup."

We were two doors down and across the hallway from the booth. Every other door on this floor was made of wood. This one was solid steel with a deadbolt in addition to the handle lock.

She looked at it critically. "You think Max was really screwed up enough to stick her in a disappointment room?"

I smirked. "If he was, we're about to have company."

I took out the ring of keys we'd gotten from Rocky, then unlocked the deadbolt. It took a little more force than usual, like it hadn't been used in a long time. I could see Connie, all business now, out of the corner of my eye.

I unlocked the handle lock, then slowly let the door open. It looked like it hadn't been touched in years. A thin layer of dust covered everything. Industrial steel shelving that looked straight out of a warehouse covered every wall, all of them loaded floor to ceiling with something.

The light from the hallway illuminated a dusty linoleum floor. I shined a flashlight right into the ceiling. True to my scans, some kind of canvas-looking padding covered the ceiling. Shining the light on the wall by the door showed a light switch. I cautiously flipped it, and a dusty incandescent bulb that had to have been older than I am buzzed slowly to life, illuminating the room.

Connie looked left, then right, then center. "Film canisters?"

I stepped inside, putting my flashlight away. "This must have been storage when it was a movie theater."

Connie started reading the labels on the cans. "*Gator Bait*. This must've been an arthouse place."

I shrugged a little, moving down the row. "This is nicer than a multiplex, I'll give it that."

Connie grinned. "If there's a copy of *Rocky Horror* in here, you think Rocky would let us do a midnight show?"

I snickered. "What do you know about *Rocky Horror*?"

She smirked. "I know you couldn't keep your tongue in your mouth when you and Heather went as Columbia and Eddie for Halloween one year."

I sighed wistfully. "Were we ever so young?"

I took a can near the back corner and tried to open it. It took me a minute to slide the clamshell can apart without spilling film everywhere, but I managed. A scent crossed my nose and I grimaced. "Some of these might be past their sell-by date."

I left the can on the shelf and kept looking. The shelves were just steel frames. The walls behind them were padded the same way as the ceiling. Something was tickling the back of my brain about this. I'd never seen this exact setup before. But something about it was giving me the creeps.

The films seemed to be arranged by date, with the older ones being on the right side where I was. I opened up one of the cans on that side without reading the label. The can opened easily, but it smelled like someone had dribbled acid into an ashtray that hadn't been cleaned out in a year. The smell bypassed my frontal lobes and unlocked something I'd only read about.

I blinked, just to convince myself of what I was looking at.

Then I looked around and did some math in my head to figure out how much there was of what I was looking at. My mouth went dry instantly. My heart sank into my chest, trying not to beat too loud. I slowly licked my lips, trying to will my heart rate to slow down while hoping the room hadn't noticed me holding my breath. All that escaped my mouth was a tiny, "Oh shit."

"Trav?"

I gently laid the can back on the shelf, then took a step back, opening my hands and hoping I wasn't too late. As softly as I could while still being heard, I said, "Ward. The room. Now."

Connie, bless her, didn't stop to ask questions. She turned on her heel, pulled out a sharpie, and started marking the doorframe. I tried to control my breathing until she murmured an incantation and nodded to me. I gripped the shelf, my body shuddering as my heart rate finally started to drop.

She slowly nodded, then murmured. "How bad?"

"All the stuff on the left side and in the back are movies from the fifties through about the seventies. But the ones on this last rack on the right side are all from the thirties and forties. Originals, if they're all like this one."

"And that's bad?"

"If this shit ignites, which it can do spontaneously, the building burns to the ground and can't be stopped without magic."

She nodded. "That would be bad. You sure?"

I pointed to a can I'd opened on the left. "Take a sniff."

She walked over to the can and warily inhaled. Her nose wrinkled. "Vinegar?"

I nodded. "Cellulose acetate. That smell is the chemicals breaking down. It's not dangerous, it just stinks. Now smell the one on the right."

She did. This time I could see her repulsed look before she spoke. "Smells like it already burned."

I couldn't blame her for thinking that. It looked like a huge, rusted to hell cigarette lighter from a car dashboard. "Nitrate. It could catch fire all by itself. And once it did, it'll keep going. It creates it's own oxygen. It'll even burn underwater. Oh, and the smoke itself is toxic as hell. That's why the room has this weird padding. It has to be asbestos."

She nodded. "What doesn't burn us alive gives us cancer, got it. You're the alchemist. What's the plan?"

I waved an arm to indicate the racks. "Keep the Crying Girl from setting off this stuff before we get it all out of the building. I can burn it off safely in place at my house."

"We've got an hour before she can pull anything in here."

I nodded. "Then we better get moving."

We gingerly stepped out of the room, then I keyed my radio. "Rocky, Travis."

"Go Travis."

I gathered my words for a second, then keyed it again. "We have a major hazard on the booth level. I need everyone that can be spared, all of those buckets in the scene shop, and a handful of respirator masks in the hallway behind the booth. ASAP."

* * *

We wound up borrowing Roscoe, all the scenic guys, and about half of the ensemble. Once she knew we had a fire hazard on our hands, Rocky immediately press-ganged everyone who wasn't already occupied. Nobody bitched. Not even Max, Dawn, or Ron. I didn't expect actors to be really big on workplace safety. Apparently, theater fires happened often enough to be a huge thing. Nobody was willing to risk one.

There were a bunch of ten gallon buckets in the scene shop. Our working party hauled them up to the booth level and filled them halfway with water from the bathroom. From there, they came to the storage room, where I carefully submerged the nitrate cans in the buckets. Then down the three flights of stairs the buckets went to be loaded into the back of my Yukon down in the loading dock.

* * *

Rocky tried not to look nervous. "How we doing, folks?"

There were four buckets outside of the room.

I stepped out, a reel in my gloved hands. "Last one."

Connie checked her watch. "Five minutes, maybe less."

I let the reel slip into the bucket, watching the water close over it. "That's cutting it close. Send these last four down the freight elevator with me."

Connie raised an eyebrow and I nodded. We were cutting it close. This time I was deliberately exposing myself to get the last of the hazards out of the building. I picked up two of the buckets, with Rocky and Connie each grabbing one of the others. A quick walk down the hall, and a quicker loading into the elevator.

Rocky stepped out, concern in her voice. "Should one of us come with you?"

I shook my head. "It goes south, I'll need you two to get me out of it."

Connie grabbed Rocky by the shoulder reassuringly on her way out.

I reached for the controls. We had less than a minute left and were on the opposite end of the building.

"See you at the loading dock."

I smiled, pushed the button for the dock level, then looked up.

As the doors closed, I saw the Crying Girl turning the corner in the hallway, a look of fury in her eyes. Her dress spilled out into tendrils of shadow crawling across every surface. She didn't walk so much as floated, her skirt billowing around her feet. She was headed straight for Connie.

The doors closed, leaving me alone with four buckets of nitrate film.

I thumbed my radio. "Connie, Rocky, I saw her just behind you. Watch your steps."

My radio was silent.

My pulse sped up as the motor began to run, cable running and spooling as the old car shuddered its way down the shaft.

I thumbed my radio again. "Any station, any station, this is Travis. Anyone got eyes on Rocky or Connie?"

Not even static answered me.

Two floors down, there was a groaning and grinding of metal before the car shuddered to a stop.

I pushed the button for the loading dock two or three times. Nothing.

Then the temperature began to drop.

I murmured to myself. "Oh, shit."

The bucket by my left foot started to churn and bubble. It had been clear enough to see the film cans through just seconds before. But then it was opaque and brackish and almost looked boiling, even though the room was colder than I'd remembered it.

I spun in a circle. All four buckets were bubbling and frothing and too dark to see.

There was a loud popping, a hideous smell, and then a column of flame burst up from one of the buckets, tongues of flame licking at the ceiling tile. I took a knee and slapped the fire alarm button, which did absolutely nothing. I thumbed my radio while digging in my pocket with my other hand.

"Fire! Fire! Fire! Fire in the freight elevator!"

As I was yelling uselessly into the mic, there was more popping, more stench, and finally more flames. Smoke filled the room just as I found what I was looking for.

I turned and fell on my back, smoke billowing around me. I opened one of Connie's banishment packets and tossed the contents into the air. I have no idea what the combination of grains and powders and dusts actually was, but I heard a faint scream when they flew around the inside of the elevator.

All four of the buckets were still boiling, the columns of flame bright yellow through the black smoke. The chill from moments ago was gone, replaced by a growing heat.

When I hit the deck, I took a breath of the still-fresh air near the floor. Closing my eyes and touching the deck, I started looking throughout the elevator system to find the blockage. I was supposedly only one story up, a fall I could survive if I tried to not be on fire. But the traphouse oven Ginny had kindly set up for me was rapidly turning into a flaming poisonous brick.

Another breath. Tamped down any panic. I'd never looked at an elevator system before and had no idea what I was looking at. So I started with the normal controls. I pushed the loading dock button telekinetically, then flipped the switch behind it to make sure that operated. If that didn't work I was going to follow the control as far as I could, then start breaking things and hoping I lived.

Mercifully, flipping the switch behind the control panel did the trick. The motor rumbled to life and we started heading down. I rolled over, trying to breathe shallow.

The car finally rumbled to a stop, and the doors opened to chaos.

Fire extinguishers roared uselessly as the flames kept going. I heard screaming and swearing from a dozen different throats. Finally someone yelled, "grab his feet!"

Four hands grabbed my boots and yanked. I slid across the concrete floor and out into fresh oxygen. Well, fresh pollen, paint, diesel fumes and old cigarettes accentuating fresh oxygen. Better than the smoke that billowed out. I choked, retched, then finally spit.

The columns of flame were dying down. Roscoe and one of the scene guys were still going at it with extinguishers.

Rocky was at my side. "Travis! Travis, you good?"

I growled. "Knock it off with those extinguishers, godsdamnit!"

Roscoe bellowed. 'They're still on fire!"

I coughed again and got to one knee. "They make their own oxidizer! That's why they're burning underwater! Let 'em burn themselves out! And get some fresh buckets in here so I can transfer the cans still in there!"

The columns dropped, then disappeared, leaving clouds of steam roiling among the smoke and the carbon dioxide. Mercifully, only one can per bucket had caught, and they'd all burned themselves out in less than two minutes.

I staggered to the elevator and locked the open in place button. That was about all the time I wanted to stand up for the moment. As I slid down the wall, I watched the smoke dissipate fast in the open air of the loading dock.

I let out a chuckle that turned into another cough. "At least most of it's in the smoking deck."

* * *

I have no idea how we didn't wind up with the fire department on site. But it turns out the fire alarm hadn't been triggered in the elevator and the smoke vanished from the dock without setting off anything. A couple of big shop fans had been brought out to blow the stink out of the dock. Somehow, the buckets hadn't melted in the elevator, though most of the water had boiled off either during or after the burns. Even more merciful, the three other cans in each of the buckets hadn't ignited in the chaos.

By the time I'd topped off the buckets with fresh water, Max and Harry were going around the crew, asking if they were all right and shaking their hands. The question of the fire department was answered when they got around to me. Max's handshake felt like the kind of genuine gesture that had years of training in it. Harry's handshake, on the other hand, deftly passed along a pair of Benjamin's.

If I hadn't been worried about a homicidal ghost, I'd have just called the fire department to get rid of everything from the beginning. As it was, I systematically violated a whole lot of hazmat laws between loading and transport. I took back roads instead of I-20 or even Memorial Drive to get home, and drove like an old lady besides.

While the buckets were filling a bunker I had out back for sensitive projects, I took a list of names of the films in the cans. About an hour of scouring the internet let me make sure none of them were lost films or anything. After fighting hellhounds, vampires, and werewolves, the last thing I needed to do is get myself killed by an angry film geek because I torched a copy of *London After Midnight* or something.

I did the controlled burn in my backyard forge that weekend. The alchemical challenge was a nice distraction from, well, everything. All I had to do was burn up stuff that could burn and/or explode all by its lonesome, then successfully render all of the lethally toxic gases inert.

It beat the hell out of dealing with an angry ghost.

Or my increasingly convoluted feelings about Jazz, for that matter.

By the time I had cleaned up and showered off, it was still a nice day. So I fired up the grill and cooked for the coven, plus Byron and Jazz. It was cool but not rainy, a nice day before the summer heat would really start rolling in.

Chapter Fourteen

Guideline Thirty-Seven:
Boredom can kill you as easily as anything else.

After the film fire, the rest of the rooms were relatively boring. Although some of the junk throughout the decades would have kept a thrift store happy for months. We mostly rummaged around, then swept for anything magic or related to the Crying Girl. We usually found nothing of note, then locked the door behind us and noted our findings to Rocky.

That said, some of the more interesting pieces even caught my attention. "Is that a cannon?"

I sighed in disappointment at the two feet of tarnished bronze and dusty wood I'd recently unearthed from under a pile of rolled carpets. "Yeah. Just a signaler, though. Ten gauge replica of a naval piece, probably early 1800's style, but made in the 1960's."

Connie shrugged. Artillery didn't get her motor running. "Is it loaded?"

I slid open the breech and peeked inside to find emptiness. "Nope." Since I was there, I poked around with my flashlight, watching it play on the dust and a single lonely cobweb. "It could use a good cleaning." I reached under it until I found what I was looking for, giving it a turn right, then two turns to the left. "But the elevation screw works and the bore looks OK. I wonder if Rocky would let me keep it?"

"For what? Marking time for the neighbors?"

"Don't be ridiculous. I'm about as likely to be an Admiral as you are to be a governess."

She smirked. "Spit spot. Still, it never hurts to ask. Besides, you've already stopped the theater from burning down once."

"I think Harry bribed me into making us square there."

"Point. Still, it's not like production's using it."

* * *

"Wonder what the average rent on a place like this was?"

On the top floor were a handful of actual apartments spaced between the storage rooms. They were single rooms smaller than a roadside motel's, but each one had a bed and a small kitchen with a stove, sink, and fridge. Two closets turned out to be a closet and a tiny toilet and sink combo apiece. Most of them looked cleaned out before they were abandoned, so we were spared any nightmares lurking in any of the fridges.

"Not sure. I'm not even sure who'd live here."

"Janitors, maybe? Someone to be on site in case something happened in the boiler room?"

"Dunno. Probably changed tenants and purposes as often as the rest of the building. Workers that couldn't afford anywhere else when it was a factory, cast and crew when it was a theater. Maybe the projectionist when it was a movie house. Could be almost anything."

"Is Roscoe living in one of them?"

"I haven't asked and he hasn't said, so I'm assuming no for now."

* * *

Another day, I went looking for trapdoors. Three were a part of the stage furniture and were relatively mundane. One I found under a carpet in one of the unused offices. It opened directly into the ceiling above the costume room. I managed to replace it without being seen, and Connie and I agreed that it was probably a remnant from the speakeasy days.

Thumper came on board and turned out to be great with lighting systems. They couldn't reliably respond over a headset, but they could listen easy enough. And they'd be sitting next to Rocky and a sound tech if there were any problems.

They were a bit confused when Connie mentioned that they needed to wear all black on the job. They had their head tilted in the way that said "why?" without going into detail.

Connie shrugged. "Stagehands always wear black."

I nodded. "Yeah. Because of the ninjas."

Connie blinked. "Wait, what?"

"Yeah, you didn't know?"

"I thought it just made sense. You don't stand out with the lights out."

I nodded. "Exactly. Ninjas."

She frowned. "Are you just being stereotypical?"

"No. The stereotype we think about how ninjas look like comes from stagehands."

Thumper watched us going back and forth with interest.

Connie folded her arms. "So which came first, the stagehand or the ninja?"

Reflexively, I said. "Whichever one was the selfish guy."

That got me a gentle smack upside the head. I waved it away.

"No, seriously, Uncle Mac taught me a little ninjitsu back in the day. Real ninjas looked like everybody else, usually servants and that kind of thing. But kuroko, Japanese stagehands, dressed all in black while the actors all wore colorful costumes. So the audience was trained to ignore the kuroko."

Connie smirked. "So what brought them together?"

I grinned. "Showmanship. Ninja are supposed to disappear and reappear out of nowhere. Easiest way to do that on a stage with no lighting control was to make whoever was playing the ninja dress like a kuroko.

Then when they appeared out of nowhere and killed one of the characters, the audience all knew what they were watching was a ninja attack."

She shook her head. "And you thought you knew nothing about theater."

I shrugged. "I just know my ninjas."

Thumper covered their face below the bridge of their nose with one hand, then from the eyebrows up with the other. Their eyes looked out at us in the gap between their hands as they nodded solemnly.

* * *

Most days were filled with the surprisingly mundane details of rehearsal. Even though the story was the simple, annoying one I remembered from High School, presenting it in rock opera style involved a lot of moving parts. Six musicians, sixteen actors, and a half-dozen stagehands (who did look like ninjas, FWIW), plus Rocky, Connie, Thumper, a sound tech, and yours truly. All of whom at least looked highly skilled at their jobs. Most of which were easily distracted as kittens. For all I didn't like Max, he was good at herding cats into a cohesive whole. If he hadn't attracted a necromancer to my city and gotten a ghost pissed off at me, I might actually have liked the guy.

* * *

I did get myself chewed out once. I deserved it, but it was still a pain in the ass.

I was out in the smoke pit on a break, making sure to obviously look at the fake camera and take a glance at the real one. A handful of the cast were outside with me. Mercifully, we'd pressure washed the loading dock and managed to get the stink of burning film out of the area. The smells of bodies and cigarettes were slowly but surely replacing it.

There had been a mass shooting the day before. Some assclown in the Midwest had decided to shoot up a mall. Killed three and injured seven before someone carrying concealed made him the underworld's problem.

Ron would not. Shut. Up. About it.

Of course, all the usual talking points came out. Guns were evil, only the cops should have them, blah blah blah, bullshit bullshit bullshit.

I normally bite my tongue about such things. Especially around people who don't know me. The details of Blue River were still vague to the general public. I couldn't exactly go into too much detail that a big reason I'd survived was by shooting back. A lot. And anyone doing enough mundane digging would find out that a kid who had been one of my best friends was held responsible for most of it.

But Ron was annoying on a good day, and I was tired of his bullshit.

I stubbed out my cigarette and said, "Actually, having one did a lot to keep me alive."

That got heads turning.

Ron, of course, wasn't about to give up what he thought was the moral high ground.

"What?" He said. "In the war?"

I flicked my cigarette into the can and looked him in the eyes. "At Blue River."

That got wide eyes even from him.

I hated myself for bringing it up. But fuck it, it was either that or punch the little shit in the face, so I kept going.

"I'd gone skeet shooting with my friend Bubba earlier that day. Yeah, his name really is Bubba. Gun loving rednecks, right? He's a livestock veterinarian now, so he managed to learn him a book after all that. Anyways, after shooting, we didn't have time to go home and clean up, so we went straight to the party. Fuck it, park wasn't on school property. Had our shotguns in our bags and a pocket each full of slugs. So when the screaming started, that was what we grabbed. I got out with some cuts and a shoulder bruised to hell."

I tapped my head like I was just remembering something. "Oh yeah, and a lot of friends dead." I counted off on my fingers. "Girlfriend? Dead. Best friend? Dead. Other best friend? In a coma. Cheerleader with nice tits? Dead. Football player with oatmeal for brains? Dead. The quiet girl in study hall? Dead. I can keep. on. Going." I dropped my hands and spit on the ground. "And after surviving all that, I got a whole wide world of simpering little maggots like you calling people like me everything but a child of god." I never let my gaze leave his face. "I'm not sure what would have let more of my friends live through that night. But more guns and more ammo would have been near the top of the list."

The speaker crackled with Rocky's voice. *"Five minutes, everyone."*

I let out a disgusted breath in Ron's direction, then walked away.

Danny slowly reached out and thumbed the button. "Thank you, five."

* * *

"What the hell were you thinking?"

We were off in a corner in one of the corridors. I had my arms folded in a cross between glowering bouncer and petulant kid style. "I was thinking you actually had some functional adults in this cast. How was I supposed to know he'd go crying like a little bitch when I poked a hole in his paradigm?"

I'd never seen Rocky this angry. "They're great when you have them doing their actual jobs. You know that! He wasn't at Blue River, Travis. All he knows is the horror stories."

I sneered. "That's his fucking problem."

She pulled out a knifehand worthy of a drill instructor. "No, it's mine. Don't make me make it yours."

I rolled my eyes. "OK, I'll make sure to pat their asses and bring cookies."

"All he wants is an apology."

"Fuck him. I don't apologize when I haven't done anything wrong."

"It would help."

"Rocky, you make me apologize to that little shit and I will feed him to the ghost myself."

Rocky nodded, and the look in her eyes softened. "I know. That's why I told him you saved my life that night. And if that makes him uncomfortable, he can kiss my ass."

That had me. I still wasn't going to apologize. But I wasn't going to feed the little shit to a monster either. I sighed, letting the tension bleed out. "You're a good woman, Rocky."

She cracked a smile. "I do my best. "She patted me on the shoulder. "Try not to scare my cast idiots anymore than necessary."

* * *

In harnesses, with our safety lines triple-checked, Connie and I stood side by side as the ballroom scene played three stories below, I had to admit, it was a gorgeous spectacle. Pounding rock music accompanied the complicated dance number. Brilliantly colored costumes shone under the lights, masks hiding faces.

Then most of the lights dimmed, leaving spotlights on Dawn and Kenny on opposite sides of the proscenium. The two stared in wonder at each other as the music softened and the high energy partying faded into the background. It was a Vegas idea of love at first sight.

Connie leaned against the catwalk with a dreamy look in her eyes. "A part of me always wanted that to happen to me."

I tilted my head like a confused pit bull. "You wanted to kill yourself after a night with a guy you just met and take half a dozen people with you? I know you're a goth, but that's pretty hardcore."

She shrugged. "Can't be a necromancer without a little romance in you."

I snickered. "How long have you been waiting to say that?"

"Oh, I've had that one in my back pocket since freshman year."

"You seriously find this romantic?"

She smiled wistfully. "Yeah. Yeah, I do. Not everything after. Not all the stupid shit. But what they're showing now? Making that million to one connection? Yeah. It's romantic. So quit being a hardass and let a girl dream."

I shook my head and turned back to watch the spectacle. "Dream on. I can't."

There was a silence until she broke it. "You really do have a hair up your ass about this story. Should I know about it?"

I closed my eyes and sighed. "Heather ever tell you about Jordan and Jackie?"

She paused to think. "I think I met their parents once or twice. She was a cheerleader, right?"

I nodded. "She was a cheerleader. He was a varsity running back. And they were the absolutely dumbest mages to ever make it through the epiphany. She was dumber than a bucket of mayonnaise and he somehow managed to be worse. And on top of that, she was a cognimancer! Can you believe that shit? A walking example of the blonde bimbo stereotype, and she's a fucking mind reader. Whoever put mages on the earth had a fucked up sense of humor. Especially when it came to those two morons."

"So you were tight is what you're saying?"

I sighed again, looking at the stage. "I couldn't stand them. Most of us couldn't. They had two saving graces: They were too dumb to really bully anyone. And they were head over heels in love with each other. Then Blue River happened."

She took my hand. I accepted it and went on. "I'm fairly sure I was the first one to find their bodies. When we were cleaning up before the police arrived. Right around when we found out Thumper was still alive. They were holding hands. Jordan and Jackie were." I gripped Connie's hand a touch tighter and remembered to breathe. "They'd both had their guts clawed out. Maybe fifty feet from each other. You could see the drag marks where they crawled. They crawled in their own entrails, making mud with their own blood at every move. They got close enough to hold hands. And then they died."

I shook my head, feeling tears welling up and hating it. "They were idiots. But they died uselessly. They should've gone off and gotten useless degrees and bullshit middle management make-work jobs for conglomerates owned by their parents. They should've bought a McMansion in the suburbs and had stupid kids. He should've gotten bald and she should've gone gray and they both should've gotten fat and lived happy, stupid lives. Instead they're forever 18. Because the responsible adults in their lives dropped the ball so hard it ripped our class in half."

I shoved a tear out of my eye with my thumb before it could fall. "People look at this story and think it's fucking romantic. Such bullshit. You see romance in those of us who lived. Who saw how fleeting life could be and decided to live as full as possible. Lori's got a wife and a husband and I lost track of how many kids between them. Becky Sue's got a daughter she's raising into an awesome diviner. Seb's happily married, sings for his supper every night, and hasn't been kidnapped by mermaids yet."

Connie blinked. "Kidnapped by what again?"

I let go of her hand and managed a chuckle through the tears. "Florida mermaids. They're more like selkies, really. Long story."

"Most stories that start like that are."

I waved towards the stage. "Unlike this. Happily ever after, these two."

She nodded in understanding. "Forever young."

I sighed. "Dying stupid."

* * *

Every now and then, the theater reminded me it was haunted and knew who I was.

There were at least two mystery singers in the building now, a baritone and an alto. It was always the same song, too. "Across a Crowded Room" from the ballroom scene. Connie was hearing them too, now. Usually in one of the stairwells when we were alone. I'd chase each up or down a level, only to find nothing. Nobody else claimed to hear them, and Ginny hadn't ambushed us trying to chase them down, but we kept hearing them.

Connie found what looked like a sigil chalked on one of the set walls. All Thumper and Jazz could tell us was that it was a Conjure sigil. I considered asking Babs, but erred on the side of giving her plausible deniability. We took pictures with our phones but otherwise left it alone. Chances were that Dr. Gull already knew who we were. No need to mess with the Doctor's things until we moved to kill or capture him.

Mabel reported at a staff meeting that a pair of masks had disappeared from her shop. While they weren't expensive or hard to replace, the notion that they were gone was disturbing. A lot of jokes in poor taste were made in that meeting.

Connie and I didn't add that we'd seen people wearing those masks out of the corner of our eyes: on the catwalks, in the balcony, in the house, in all manner of odd corners of the theater. A man and a woman. If we looked at the mask wearers directly or tried to approach them, they vanished. Nothing flashy, they'd just duck into a doorway or in a shadow and never come back out. It didn't feel like either Dr. Gull or the Crying Girl. More was going on here. And since I'd apparently been the designated target since I first came to the theater, I had more to look out for.

*   *   *

After rehearsal one night, I walked past Harry's office and heard him in an absolute row with Max. After pausing, I looked both ways and found myself alone in the hallway, so I stood where I was, listening in.

"What do you want me to do, Max?"

"Make that fucking ghost go away! That's what I want you to do, Harry."

"That's still as tall an order as it was when you made it the first time."

"Well, that lucky charm of Grover's turned out to be pretty damn useless for him, didn't it? The cops backed off for now, but one more ambulance or cop car in here and I could get shut down. All that bullshit with the nitrate film? How in the fuck did we not notice that back when we moved in? As it is, I'm just gonna have to seal that room and deal with the asbestos after we've opened. Shit, ask that little goth girl Rocky hired, maybe she knows a damned exorcist!"

"Look, ghost hunters have a high kook-to-professional ratio in the best of times, Max. That's why I'm taking a different track this time."

I clicked my heels and, moving more silently than I had a moment before, turned and walked away.

When I turned the corner, I felt a cold breeze blowing past. There wasn't an air vent anywhere near me, and nowhere to explain the chill. I stopped and lingered, but felt nothing more. A moment later, I moved on, just a bit more swiftly than before.

Chapter Fifteen

Guideline Forty-One:

Accept the help you can get.

You never know what you'll need.

The next day, there was a priest at rehearsal. Standing next to him was an old friend.

I tipped my water bottle in his direction. "Doctor."

Dr. Cyrus Dowdell, PhD, was another Blue River survivor. We'd had a falling-out for several years, then more or less made up after the Battle of Stone Mountain. We weren't besties, but we could stand to be in the same room as each other. He was a slim black man with hornrimmed glasses, dressed smartly in an academic's tweed and Vietnam-era jungle boots. He shook hands with Thumper and myself and he hugged Connie a second later.

Connie was closer to him than I was, and gave an awkward smile. "What's bringing you here?"

Cyrus pointed to his companion. "Father Wallace here was called in to do some good work. He thought I might have an academic interest in being around, so he was kind enough to bring me along."

Connie nodded to the small, solid-looking priest, offering her hand. "Father."

The priest shook both our hands, a smile creasing his careworn face. "Father Wallace. A pleasure to meet all of you."

Connie gave him one of her shining smiles, which almost hid the ankh hanging from her neck. "Connie Chandler. The big guy's Travis Wayland. The quiet one is Thumper."

Father Wallace smiled gently. "I take it work's been a bit uncomfortable of late?"

I nodded. "You could say that, Padre. Angry ghosts make a bit of a hostile work environment."

He kept the smile coming. "Well, God willing, I might be able to alleviate that a bit."

He said it like he was going to make sure there were enough snacks for everybody. It was kind of comforting. His clothes looked like he'd done some honest work in them over the years. When you live close to a goth as I do, you learn quick what black clothes have seen some wear and tear over the years. Father Wallace looked like a hands-on kind of preacher.

My coven believed in ghosts because we knew damn well they existed. The cast and crew believed in ghosts because they were typical human weirdos who were more comfortable with the idea of ghosts than gas leaks. The padre was more like us than the actors. I made a mental note to ask Cyrus exactly how knowledgeable Father Wallace was.

Connie smiled. "Appreciated, Father."

I nodded. "Yeah, we'll take all the help we can get."

Rocky came in from the back of the house, with most of the cast behind her. I tried not to laugh at the looks on most of their faces. Some were wondering if the ghost had killed anyone else. Others were clearly wondering if their own sins had warranted calling in a preacher.

* * *

I grew up vaguely Methodist and I use a lot of Norse invocations in my magic. So it's no surprise I've only got a pop culture knowledge of

Catholicism. That said, I'm an accomplished mage, and I've been around enough divergent traditions to be comfortable with the "sit down, shut up, pay attention and try not to screw it up" school of ritual witness.

Father Wallace, for his part, knew how to lead a ritual. And the cast and crew knew enough to join in with varying degrees of enthusiasm. Circle up, hold hands, call and response, you get the idea. There wasn't any blame spread around or any actual complaints about the Crying Girl. Just a mention of unrest and upset and wouldn't it be better to sing along with these wholesome artists trying to raise their voices in the service of humanity? It felt almost like the spiritual equivalent of calming down a heckler until the ushers could take over.

I had no idea what anyone's spiritual inclination was, but everyone was spooked by Ginny's presence whether they admitted it or not. Someone authoritative who took them seriously went a long way. Prayers said, holy water sprinkled, actual preaching kept to a minimum. The general vibe was that it couldn't hurt, and if it helped, it would do a lot for the growing unease.

I did take the opportunity to keep my head up and watched when Father Wallace asked everyone to bow their heads. Everyone else closed their eyes. Larry and Ron both stayed silent at the calls and responses. Dawn, Danny, and Tim all crossed themselves at the finish, as did Connie. I filed it all away for later.

When the good Father finished, Rocky called for fifteen and everyone dispersed. Connie, Thumper, and I disappeared along with Cyrus, heading to the roof. We'd found an access door a few days beforehand. Take the backstage right stairwell next to wardrobe and go all the way up. It was mercifully overcast when we stepped outside. Still, the warm, humid air coming at us as we emerged from the air conditioning hit us like the first wave of a sauna.

Connie closed the door behind us, scratched out a few sigils over the door with a sharpie, then spun on her heel. "OK, seriously, Cyrus: what the fuck?"

Cyrus, poker-faced, opened his arms to show them empty. "What do you mean?"

Thumper rolled their eyes. I tried to hide my annoyance and probably failed.

Connie wasn't impressed. "What the fuck are you doing here, Cyrus?"

Cyrus dropped the pretense. "Neary sent me."

Thumper facepalmed.

I almost growled. "What the hell? Vampires got a hit out on you too?"

Cyrus sneered. "What? No! Besides, wouldn't you already know if there was?"

Thumper gave me a look that said Cyrus had me there.

I shrugged. "You'd think so. But we found out about the price on Connie's head from Neary."

Cyrus held his ground. "Neary said nothing to me about vampires. Just ghosts."

Connie frowned. "What?" Then something clicked in her mind and she rolled her eyes. "Oh you fucking sucker! Please tell me you didn't fall for it."

Cyrus frowned, folding his arms. "This place has ghost problems."

I grumbled. "That's why we're here, assclown."

Connie nodded. "Lemme guess: Neary thinks I'm up to some necromantic hijinks and he sent you out to stop me?"

Cyrus grimaced in surprise. "What? No! He's not concerned about you. He's worried about Dr. Gull."

I blinked. "Wait, you know about Dr. Gull?"

Cyrus looked at me like I was an idiot. "He's one of the most powerful Conjurers alive. Of course I know about him."

Connie blinked, then snapped her fingers. "Oh, Cyrus. Don't tell me Neary promised you a line to the Conjurers. It's not gonna work."

Cyrus glared at her, and I knew she'd hit the jackpot. I just had no idea what that jackpot actually was. Thumper and I looked at each other and traded shrugs.

I cocked my head. "Uh, Connie?"

"Yeah?"

"What's going on?"

Cyrus glared. "He does NOT need to know!"

Connie waved a hand. "Put a sock in it, Cyrus. It's not forbidden, just embarrassing."

Cyrus didn't object further, so Connie went on. "Cyrus has been trying to learn Conjure magic for years."

I raised an eyebrow. I was really bad at magical politics. "I can see at least two problems with that. Why does it justify working for Neary and how would it get you a mentor from the Conjurers?"

Cyrus fumed. "A bad misunderstanding that I've put a lot of effort in trying to fix."

Connie rolled her eyes. "We've been in a cold war with the Conjurers since the 70's, Travis. And the Zombie War a hundred years before that."

I blinked. "Wait, Cyrus, you're Nimuen, aren't you? Can't that make you buddy-buddy with the Conjurers?"

Connie sighed, then looked at me. "Who do you think fought hardest against the Conjurers in the Zombie Wars?"

Now I was confused. "The Daedeli?"

The Daedeli and Nimuen were two magical factions. Think conservative and liberal, only not really. I didn't run with either of them, so my knowledge was kind of limited.

Connie shook her head. "The Daedeli were the ones who created the SiS Marshals, who did do some of the fighting. Especially near the end. But the original conflict was more about territory and resources than anything else. Nimuen have always been more rural, which meant the Conjurers were competition for them when the Civil War ended."

I frowned. "Wait. I thought the wizards that fought against the Conjurers hid among the night riders. Joining the mobs that drove freemen away from small towns."

Cyrus groaned in embarrassment. "Here we fucking go."

I did the math and twitched at the answer. "Are you telling me the Nimuen rode with the Klan?"

Connie looked me in the eye. "I told you it was embarrassing."

Cyrus just looked disgusted.

I grimaced. "Yeah, no shit. And here I thought Nimuen were all kumbaya and buddies with the other Councils and suchlike. You're telling me the Nimuen are the ones who drove the Conjurers to the coasts in the first place?"

Thumper was openmouthed in shock.

Connie nodded. "Longer story than that. But basically, yeah."

I turned to Thumper. "I had no idea. What's your excuse? I thought you were Nimuen too?"

Thumper shrugged innocently. Apparently they'd missed the quiz on that one.

I blinked. "So how does that relate to Cyrus? He's too young to have fought in the cold war. All of us are."

Connie sighed. "Cyrus was raised in the study hall system by the Iron Council, just like we were. Then he joined the Nimuen, thinking they were the next best thing. He didn't know about the bad blood between them for years. Like I said, it's embarrassing. You don't tell your newbies about your embarrassments. Far as the Conjurers are concerned, Cyrus is just the latest iteration of the wizards they've been fighting for over a century."

That made more sense now. Magic wasn't the same as ethnicity. Or for that matter, citizenship.

I looked over to Cyrus. "Why bother? You're already a badass cognimancer in your own right. What's so important about learning Conjure magic?"

Cyrus looked really uncomfortable and was trying not to yell. "Because I should've been a Conjurer. At least one of my great-grandmothers was. A hundred years ago, I would have been. And if I can talk to some and gain their trust, maybe I can really do magic that speaks to me."

I nodded. Magic was a part of who we were. Being held back from the kind of magic that worked for you was an itch that was almost impossible to scratch. "So Neary made you an offer you can't refuse."

Cyrus opened his hands again. "I never really learned necromancy in school. The only monitor we really had that was into it was... her. And she only went beyond the basics with-."

"- Ethan and Doug, yeah."

Even this long after Blue River, most of us wouldn't even name our former teacher. Knowing she was rotting in an Iron Council cell somewhere wasn't a comfort.

Cyrus went on. "Then after Blue River and the ban, I got caught the few times I tried."

I nodded. It was starting to clear up. "So Neary's made a bargain with you in case something happens to the three of us. What terms?"

"Stop Dr. Gull from whatever he's up to. Kill him if necessary."

I sneered. "That makes even less sense! Killing Gull won't let you make an inroad with the Conjurers unless..."

Connie smirked. "Unless you're planning to tip the Doctor off. Try to buy your way in by sabotaging Neary's efforts."

I could almost see Cyrus biting his tongue.

Thumper let out a low whistle, cupped their hands under their crotch, then lowered their hands to their knees.

I nodded. "Thumper's right. That is ballsy. Stupid, but ballsy."

Connie shrugged. "It's not as if we'd mind."

Cyrus cocked his head. "What?"

Thumper and I both turned to her. "What?"

Connie shrugged. "Think about it. So far, Dr. Gull hasn't obviously been our problem. The Crying Girl has. For whatever reason, Dr. Gull hasn't made an obvious move to either strengthen her or direct her murderous impulses. Not yet, anyway."

Cyrus frowned. "But why send you all and me?"

We all stopped for a moment. I thought of it first.

"So we'd sabotage each other. Neary doesn't trust us or you. But he's got leverage on Connie, so he went to her first. So if one of us made a deal with Gull, the other would stop it."

Connie frowned. "Doesn't Neary know you and Cyrus are on speaking terms again?"

I shook my head. "That's just it. He doesn't. Cyrus just as easily could've joined in at Stone Mountain for your sake or Thumper's instead of mine. And I'm not a Nimuen, so there's no reason to assume I'd be talking to Cyrus through them either."

Cyrus nodded uncomfortably. We still weren't particularly close.

Connie traded looks with Thumper, then smiled. "Neary bother telling you he gave me a full exemption from the ban?"

Cyrus's eyes got wider. "No. Never."

Connie's smile grew. "That's why we're here. Send a necromancer to fight a necromancer. So I got a permission slip. Complete and total. Covers my coven. As well as any students I take on."

Cyrus bit his tongue for a moment. "Dare I ask?"

Connie nodded. "It's not an introduction to the Conjurers. But walking and talking with the dead? There I can hook you up."

Cyrus smiled in gratitude. "What do I need to do?"

Connie matched his smile. "Be waiting in the wings when we call you. I'll make it worth your while."

The sun emerged from behind the clouds, brightening the day and making the temperature rise by the moment.

In the harsh light of day, they shook on it.

Chapter Sixteen

Guideline Forty-Nine:

Everyone's got a reason that makes sense to them.

The next morning I heard the singers in the hallway again.

Both of them this time. I'd heard one or the other, but this was the first time I'd heard both. I softly headed to the downstage left stairwell and listened. The voices were coming from the top floor.

I keyed my headset and murmured as quietly as possible. "Connie, Travis. Ninja up with Thumper and meet me in the hall above the booth."

A click told me I'd been acknowledged. I looked up and tried to focus on the singing.

On a hunch, I reached into a pocket and sent a surge of power through a talisman. It would mask the sound of my movement for the next several minutes. I crept up the stairwell, going up every flight to the level just below the roof.

When I reached the stairwell door, I found it wedged open a crack with a rubber doorstop. I tiptoed closer as the singers continued. They were down the hall in one of the rooms.

What have we done?
Who have we shattered?

It was only a dance.
A way to be moving.

I took a moment to get a good look at the doorstop, which I hadn't seen before. If it was set by Dr. Gull, there was no way I wanted to set off whatever he'd arranged for it to do. I couldn't see any wires, mechanics, or chemicals in or near it. Looking into the x-ray spectrum showed me nothing unusual. A moment later, I took a vial of powder Connie had given me and sprinkled a little on it. But no, it was just a small lump of rubber, exactly what it looked like.

Safer than sorry, I managed to slip through the stairway door to the upper hallway without being seen or heard. It was warmer up here than anywhere else. None of the spaces on this floor were used, and even with the HVAC system running, warm air rose, and we were just below the roof. The voices were clearer now. An alto and a baritone. They couldn't be heard in the house or the booth, but here in the halls they sounded like a full blown performance.

If I could love you without loving the wartime
I could run the gauntlet of hatred to you
If I could know now what I've hoped for forever
I could step in the light and reveal my face
Across a crowded room.

The singing was coming from one of the old apartments we'd checked earlier. One that still had clothes and furniture and other bits of life's detritus in it. I crept closer as the song ended, the voices trailing off.

Just as they finished, I saw the stairwell door open a little further than it had been, then close softly on the doorstop once more. A glance up and down the hallway told me nobody else was there. I resisted the urge to activate my eyeliner, but I did check to make sure my salt packets were still there.

Then, on my left shoulder, I felt a single tap. A moment went by, and then I felt another tap.

I nodded, then gave a thumbs up to the apparently empty hall before I began to creep forward.

I heard the baritone speak. "What could have been."

The alto followed up. "I thought I'd seen a ghost when I realized it was you."

I frowned. I recognized those voices. Both of them.

The baritone replied softly. "God knows we've seen enough ghosts. She's getting worse. She's tried to kill the big guy twice, and she almost burned the place down doing it. She's just going to keep hurting people. Keep killing people. And who knows how many more until she finally goes after Max? We've got to do something."

"Do what? What can we do to an angry ghost? Max brought a priest in here. If that doesn't work, then what can we manage?"

"I don't know. See it through, at least?"

"We won't have to see any more. Not once the show is up and running. To hell with our show run pay. We can go right after opening night. Far away from here. Then we can make up for lost time. God knows I want to. But we have to see this show open. Just one night. Maybe that's what she truly wants. After all this time. We owe her that much."

"Max is the one who owes her, not us."

I'd heard enough. I stepped forward and looked into the room.

Roscoe and Mabel were wrapped around each other. Clinging to each other, even, like survivors on a life raft. They startled, stepping away from each other. Roscoe let his customary scowl drop over his face. Mabel actually blushed, which I didn't think she was capable of.

I smiled in a way I hoped was reassuring before waving a hand dismissively. "You don't have to get modest on my account."

Mabel cleaned her glasses with her shirttail before smiling up at me. "Travis, was it?"

I nodded. "Yes ma'am."

Roscoe, wringing his hands, finally found his voice. It was weird seeing him contrite instead of sarcastic. "Sorry if we were bothering anyone."

I shook my head. "I'm the only one who got far enough away from the house to notice. No bother, Mr. Burbage."

Roscoe, or rather George, stiffened his jowls.

Mabel, or rather Maria, just nodded, speaking quietly. "So you know."

I nodded. "I know a good bit, Ms. Clive. But there's a lot I don't know yet."

I closed my eyes, and let energy surge into my eyeliner. My face started to tingle. The smell convinced me the eyeliner was working. A whiff of day-old corpse floated past my nose. When I opened my eyes, the world was shades of gray and green. The old furniture looked rotted. Mabel and Roscoe looked ten years older apiece. The creases and lines time had carved into their skins seemed twice as deep in an instant. But what I was worried to find wasn't there.

I touched the doorknob, then raised a finger in a questioning gesture. After a moment, I felt another tap on my shoulder. Satisfied, I closed the door and marked a ward rune above the doorframe in sharpie. It wasn't as well done as one of Connie's, but it would do the trick. When I turned back, Mabel and Roscoe's eyes had grown wider even as they sunk in taught flesh over their skulls.

I licked my lips, pocketing the marker. "There's not much time to explain. Ginny's in the building but she's not in this room, for now."

Mabel's breath caught in her throat. "Your eyes weren't that green a second ago. Who are you?"

I shook my head. "No time. What the hell happened to you? And her?"

Roscoe almost growled. "We got screwed, young man. That's what happened. We'd worked with Max off and on for most of his career. I was Laertes to his Hamlet. I was Banquo to his Scottish Man. And in the end it meant nothing to him. Max screwed us all for the sake of his own career."

I frowned. "How? I know he enlisted, but how did that screw you?"

Mabel clutched Roscoe's hand, her voice more sorrowful than bitter. "If you know who Ginny is, then you know the show that was planned. The contract for the show would've kept all four of us working for five years. You never get that kind of show now. And they were rare as hell back then. That was the kind of show you could put down roots with. Start families..."

She bit her tongue after that. Roscoe held her hand for a sheepish moment, then looked back up at me before he nodded. "But the investors would only go for it if we all went in. All four of us. If any one of us broke contract, it killed the entire deal."

I cocked my head. "So someone made Max break it."

Mabel snorted, laughing with no mirth as she patted Roscoe's hand. "Made him break it, my ass. He did it on his own. The contract was null and void if the show didn't open. He enlisted just before Desert Shield with massive publicity. People were listing him with every star that stepped aside to fight in World War II. His enlistment would be up in four years instead of five for the contract, and a studio waited in the wings, ready to make him ten times the star he was before."

Roscoe spit on the floor. "So he left us all in the lurch. All so he could play at being a war hero and then a movie star. Serves his sorry ass right that he wound up being neither. Sumbitch never set foot outside Saudi Arabia. And when he got back, the studio had gone under in a recession. Nobody else would take his calls. Well and truly a has-been. He's been clawing his way back ever since."

I nodded. "And Ginny?"

Mabel scowled. It was unsettling seeing that much bile in a little old lady. "Ginny got tossed aside like a bag of garbage. She killed herself not long after he'd left. She thought he'd marry her. We thought he'd marry her. We thought he'd take a knee and pull out a ring any day. Hell, they used to live in this very room back then. We all lived in these things."

She waved an arm around the apartment. Roscoe picked up a newspaper, sending a pill bottle rolling across the floor. He waved the paper at me. It was the same headline Thumper and Jazz had found. "Hell, this is still here! Same as the day it was delivered. This is how we found out! In the morning paper! He didn't have the balls to tell us himself!"

I looked around. Still no sign of Ginny, but gods only knew when that would be over.

I frowned. "So the Crying Girl really is Ginny Kemp. I get that. Explains an awful lot, honestly. But what brought the two of you back here? And under assumed names?"

Mabel shrugged. "I was always good at making my own clothes and was about to hit thirty. Costuming paid the bills. Once I decided not to go back, it was easier to live professionally under a different name. This business likes putting you in boxes. Preferably the first box they ever saw you in. If they spent time looking at the kooky little costumer, they don't see the aging ex-ingenue who never made it. As the years went on, all my competition left the business, got married, started teaching. Turnover being what it is, it didn't take long before people started forgetting I ever was competition. Made my own reputation under this name for years. More time than I spent as an actress, now. Then one day, I heard through the grapevine this show was going to happen. Right here, in the same damn theater. Max always did have balls, I'll give him that. I decided I had to be here. Had to see it happen, one way or another. I called in favors with my most likely competitors. Anyone with a better resume suddenly had conflicts. So the job was mine.

And Max has no idea. I didn't expect to see George. And I definitely didn't expect Ginny to..."

She trailed off, tears welling up. I nodded.

Roscoe shrugged. "Burbage was always a stage name. Nobody who wasn't signing checks ever knew what my real name was anyway. I left the business, opened a dry cleaner's. Retired a few years back, doing janitorial to get me out of the house more than anything. Got a gig cleaning properties that were hung up in receivership or probate. Pure luck I was assigned to the building when Max bought it. My contract expired, but I kept the keys and kept working here to... I dunno. I thought about fucking with Max just to show him up. He don't recognize me either. But then I saw Maria was here."

She touched his leg. The look that passed between them was radiant, even looking in the land of the dead. I was watching a love lost across time that had bloomed fresh anew. No wonder they were singing in every spare moment and corner they could find.

Roscoe finally turned away from her and sighed, facing my gaze again. "We never thought Ginny would...but it's the only thing that made sense. We've heard her whisper. We've felt a chill in the room and we knew it was her. I've seen her shadow in the ghost light, late at night when it's just me in the building. I heard her scream when Grover ran. But I've only told Maria about it. Nobody else. Nobody we can tell. And if we did, then what?"

Mabel let tears fall again, shaking her head as they dripped under her glasses. "She would sing to me in the shop when I was alone. The very first day I moved in and started working alone. I was so happy to have a part of her back. I would sing with her. I missed her more than I realized. Knowing someone who's been where you are is enjoying the good parts with you. She was so comforting. The way the best theater ghosts always are. It's special enough knowing the theater's ghost likes you. This one used to be my best friend. And she's been gone so long and now I have her back. Even if it's for just one show run. But Grover, and then Greg, and now you... I don't know what to do."

Roscoe gently brushed a tear away with his scarred hand, then turned to me, embarrassed. "And when people started dying, I figured if I left now I'd be a suspect. Especially if anyone found out who I was. Who we are. I can't defend myself in court by saying the ghost of my friend did it."

I nodded. "No, you can't. Best case scenario you'd trade prison for a psycho ward."

Roscoe wrung his hands, then threw them up in a giveaway gesture. "Anyways, I figured I was here when Max started this crazy show. We deserved to be here when he tried again."

I slowly nodded. "So that's why Ginny's left you two alone. You're Max's victims too."

The looks on their faces told me everything I needed to know.

Mabel held out her hands helplessly. Roscoe took her hand in his, looking resigned. "So that's why Rocky brought you on board. You're no ASM. You're some kind of ghost hunter. That's why Ginny's tried to kill you too. And why you survived."

I nodded. "Something like that. Let me ask you something. Have you seen anyone who shouldn't be here who isn't Ginny?"

Roscoe shook his head. But Mabel nodded slowly. After a moment, she spoke. "One ghost has always been here. Even when Ginny was alive. That one's still here. It's a comfortable one. A proper, good old fashioned theater ghost. One who appreciates the joy and music and energy. But there's another one too, now. A man. At least one. I've seen him wearing the stolen masks. I don't know if he's human or another ghost. But I don't feel right about him."

I nodded. "I know who you're talking about. He's bad news. If you see anything, learn anything else, please, for all of our sakes, tell one of us."

Roscoe frowned. "Us?"

I looked him dead in the eyes, raised both of my hands, and snapped my fingers twice.

Thumper dropped the veil that was hiding them and Connie from sight, though they were both still wearing ninja masks. Thumper waved in a rather goofy way.

Mabel clutched Roscoe's leg as both of their eyes grew wide. Thumper's waving let them both calm down even as what they'd seen sank into them.

After they removed their masks, Roscoe shook his head. "I should've known."

Connie shrugged. "What can I say? I'm gonna be a meddling kid till I'm 40 at this rate."

I breathed, trying to ignore the smell of grave rot that filled the room. "Look, we're all gonna keep our mouths shut about you two. But you're right. We're trying to settle Ginny's hash before she kills someone else. Bad as Max did her, she can't go around killing people with a show going up. We're still figuring out the how, but we're here to stop her."

Connie smiled gently. "If what you told Travis is true, Ginny has no reason to harm you two. Neither does the old timer. But the other one, in the stolen masks? No guarantees there. So look out as best you can. Please."

Mabel looked to Roscoe with so much yearning I almost felt tears welling up in my own eyes. Then she looked down and slowly nodded. Roscoe did the same.

I bit my lip. I could see myself across the years in them. And my eyeliner was showing me vividly how little time they both had left. It broke my heart to see it. I spoke up again. "If you two are smart, you'll disappear together as soon as you can. Right after we take care of Ginny. Or as soon as your contracts will let you. Life's too damn short. Let the show go on without you."

Chapter Seventeen

Guideline Thirty-Six:

Just because it's not your fault doesn't mean it's not your problem.

In the middle of rehearsal the next day, one of the lights started flipping on and off. Then it started moving. We weren't quite into full rehearsal, but it was moving and lighting out of sync with the rest of the plot. I didn't think the cast or Max were noticing it, but it was irritating me. I turned to tell Rocky, only to see that she was watching it too. I put an eye back on the lamp as Rocky keyed her headset. "Connie, does Thumper know what's up with that Fresnel? Middle-left-hand side of the catwalk booms?"

After a moment, she frowned, then turned to me and murmured. "Travis, head to the grid and check on that light, will you? I don't remember the actual number, but it's on our right at the catwalk just behind us."

I was already standing up. "On it."

The trip involved a walk to the back of the house, turning to one of the corner stairwells, up two more flights of stairs, past the booth, halfway down the corridor, and another turn onto the catwalk. I slid a pair of leather gloves on, then buckled into a harness.

It was uncomfortably warm, with the lights burning away and the air conditioning not reaching this far up. More so than the upper hallway where I'd found Roscoe and Mabel. Remembering the story about Greg,

I hooked my harness to the catwalk and made my way across. Beneath me and to my left, the rehearsal went on, starting and stopping as Max gave notes on the fly.

I could hear the malfunctioning light before I could see it. It sounded slightly different than the others like it. Frowning, I stepped up and checked the electrical connection, then the placement. The clamp was tight, the safety cable was connected, and the yoke was secured. The moving head wasn't obstructed. There was nothing electrically or mechanically that looked wrong with it.

I turned towards the booth and made eye contact with Thumper, then made a throat-cutting motion. They nodded. Beside me, the light turned off, the odd sound fading with the light. I counted to ten to myself, then unplugged it. With the rehearsal going on far below me, I quietly counted to 30 by myself, then plugged it back in. Another look back at the booth, this time with a thumbs up. After several seconds, the light turned back on and got back in sync with everything else, sounding normal. From here, I could see clearly down into the booth. Thumper gave me a thumbs up from inside it. Apparently they'd regained control.

I gave the light a minute or so of running normally before getting suspicious. It could've been some ordinary gremlin. But we were in a very haunted theater. If I didn't start looking, I'd get nowhere. I closed my eyes, took a breath, and felt the magic move. It tingled, gathering in the base of my spine before I let a little bit flow up my back, coming around to cover my eyes. My eyeliner went active. The smell of grave rot teased my nose.

I opened my eyes, and the world went gray and green. The catwalk was rusted to hell and covered in cobwebs. Lights were burned out husks. The light I'd just plugged back in was no more or less burned out than the others. It didn't look tampered with at all.

Below me, the rehearsal continued, and drew me like a moth to a bug zapper. The actors below looked more vibrant than I thought possible.

They burned with life and energy and passion. I could see in reds and blues the raw vitality and the temperance of control. And they were all moving in time with each other, telling the competing stories coming to a head. In the center, like the eye of a hurricane, I could see the crowd part as Kenny and Dawn saw each other, raptured at the sight.

The song came to an end, and the lights dimmed. I could finally turn my eyes from the spectacle. When I did, I realized I was leaning over the railing. Almost too far for comfort. I backed away and centered myself before moving on.

I carefully made my way across the catwalk. I had yet to see a ghost today, but I was seeing whatever the local underworld was now. And it didn't look safe. A careful walk got me off the catwalk, into the corridor, and finally into the stairwell. I kept my harness on, tucking my safety line into a pocket. Looking out both ways and seeing nothing, I descended the stairwell to go back to the house.

In the stairwell, I could hear the song starting from below. But it wasn't the full orchestration in rehearsal I heard a minute ago. This was being played out on a single piano farther away. I didn't hear anyone's voices, just the piano. That was new. I took off my gloves and hooked them to my belt. I followed the stairwell down, trying to walk softly while looking at the cracks in the cinderblock walls, the paint rubbed off the railings, and the cracked, peeling and bubbling linoleum on the floor. The sound of the piano grew stronger as I kept going down, into the subbasement. As I stepped into the hallway, a man in a polo shirt and slacks brushed past me, not paying attention. He stormed into the rehearsal hall, where the piano music abruptly stopped. There was a rustle of paper.

"What the hell is this, Max?"

Max's voice came from inside the room. "Looks like a newspaper to me, George."

Max had been onstage just a second ago.

I followed the man and stepped into the rehearsal hall. Instead of a full wall of mirrors, there were two full-length ones in the center of the wall. The rest were covered with old posters from shows back in the day. A small bar, as long as a sofa, occupied the far corner.

Max Roman was a lot younger, and his hair was up in frosted tips. He was sitting at the upright piano and smoking a cigarette. An old speaker, the size of a dinner plate, had been removed from its cabinet long ago and was enjoying a new job as an ashtray atop the piano. I recognized George as the guy in the polo shirt. He was slightly older than Max and a good bit more muscular, but he had a full head of hair. There was no sign of the slumped shoulders that would mark his silhouette a few decades from now. Both of them were slightly translucent, the way Ginny had looked like. George was shaking a newspaper at Max.

"To me it's saying you ship out for the Army in three weeks! When the show is supposed to go into rehearsal!"

Max sighed, as if a puppy had taken a leak where it wasn't supposed to. Then he took another drag. "Dammit."

Beyond George was a big-haired blonde whose eyes grew wide at the news. I recognized Maria from her headshot. And now that I saw her, I could see where she would become Mabel across the years. She touched Max's shoulder delicately. "Max? What's going on? Why didn't you tell us?"

Max pulled away roughly. "I was going to tell you all tonight."

Maria drew her hand back with a hurt look. Before anyone else could react, Ginny stepped into the room. She was already in tears, clutching another newspaper as she strode past me without a look. She somehow managed to look more vibrant, more alive than the others. She held up the newspaper at Max, her voice cracking.

"How could you? How could you, Max? When you knew? You knew how much this meant. To all of us. Especially now. You knew that too!"

The sheer heartache in her voice had me tearing up myself.

Max sighed again, stubbing out his butt in the ashtray. The smoke curled upwards in a single tendril.

George and Maria both looked confused. George's forehead wrinkled. "Knew what?"

Ginny choked back a sob before opening her mouth to respond. Then her eyes shifted from George, looking right at me. The storm in her eyes shifted in moments, from anguish to humiliation before coalescing into wrath. She dropped the newspaper.

Max, George, and Maria all froze in place. The cigarette smoke stopped in mid-curl. The lights in the room began to dim.

Ginny spun on her heel to face me head-on, staring at me like a bird of prey on a mouse, manicured fingernail aimed at me like an inquisitor pointing out a heretic. "You're not supposed to be here."

I backed away, my hands up as I stuttered. "I'm sorry."

The tears on her face melted away, leaving a look of raw rage behind. I could see her fingernails lengthen, thicken, and darken into claws as her lips curled into a rictus. "Get OUT!"

She seemed to vanish even as a storage cabinet creaked away from the wall, tilting my way.

I dove to the side as the heavy metal cabinet came down, smashing into the hardwood floor. I started circling, tucking my hand into my pocket while I looked out, expecting her to come from anywhere. The others had disappeared.

"I ain't leaving, Ginny. And I can't let you hurt anyone else either."

She appeared again, bigger this time. She was a head taller than me now, glowing green around the edges and pointing a twice as long and now-clawed finger at me. Her dress had turned black and flowing, moving around like shadows that were somehow alive. "GET OUT!"

I grabbed one of the salt packets Connie had made for me and smashed it on the floor. Not bothering to wait and see if it took effect, I grabbed the door and stepped out.

I expected to step out into the corridor. Instead I stepped onto the rusty catwalk, across a hallway and several floors above. An eerie screech seemed to fill the building, echoing throughout the house.

There was no way to go back. So I slammed the door, hoping somehow that Ginny would take the long way around after giving me a shortcut here. Not questioning the spatial dissonance, I hooked my harness onto the creaking rail and headed out, the house spread out below me. In the house, rehearsal continued. But the actors seemed small and far away, and the music could barely be heard. Larry, who a corner of my mind took a time-out from sheer terror to remember was playing Friar Laurence, looked up at me funny.

Halfway across the catwalk, I turned back. Ginny, or the thing she was becoming, was there with the green glow of murder in her eyes. She was on all fours but somehow was taller than me, her limbs lengthened as she began to prowl forward. I could see the claws, long as snow crab legs, at the end of her fingers as she stalked along the metal catwalk. I scrabbled for another salt packet as I backed up, knowing I was eventually going to run out of catwalk.

She hissed, sounding somewhere between a giant cat and a snake you'd see in a horror movie.

And then I screwed up. I looked her right in the eyes.

I'd just talked the other day to her loved ones. To a woman who still loved to sing with her years later. I knew what she'd gone through. What she'd been driven to. Or so I thought at the time.

"Ginny?"

I didn't have the chance to look away. I caught sight of the dark voids in her eyes and disappeared into them. I couldn't move. I didn't want to move. I didn't deserve to move. I could feel an icy dread crawling up my spine. My emotions began to spike, coming intense and focused. Like the end was coming for me and I deserved it. I'd done too much wrong to too many people along the way. Hurt too many. Killed too many. I should've died in the war. I should've died at Blue River. I should've died working for Eva. I should've died at Stone Mountain. I should've died on the stairs. I should've died in the elevator.

The musty, humid chill soaked through my harness and clothes, sinking into my very bones. Mist rose as the cold fog hit the burning lamps. I was shivering. All of the fight had gone out of me. The salt packet fell from my hands, tumbling off the catwalk into the audience below.

Before I knew it, Ginny was in making out distance. I thought vampires had cold breath. It was nothing compared to that of a ghost. Screaming dead was even more horrible than hungry undead. She hissed in my face.

"Die unfulfilled."

A force like a truck hit me in the side, knocking me over the booth side of the catwalk. I just managed to grab ahold of the handrail with my left hand. I could barely see out of the corner of my eye the severed safety line falling away.

My shoulder wrenched in pain as my entire two hundred and change-pound body pulled it down all at once. I looked over my shoulder to see Ginny stalking ever closer. I started hearing screams, three stories below me. Out of the corner of my eye I could see the actors far below, looking up and pointing.

Ginny reached down with a single arm, the claws had retracted, leaving her arm looking delicate and feminine. She lay down on the catwalk like it was the edge of a swimming pool, reached out with that arm, and delicately laid her palm on my chest. A chill like nothing I'd ever felt sank into my body, concentrating right where her hand touched me. I could almost see her hand start to sink into the skin of my chest. It was so horribly cold it burned.

So be it. I deserved to burn.

Men like me having hearts was an insult to compassion.

Then I got a stupid idea.

I tucked my legs under me, then slapped my right palm horizontally against the catwalk. Energy coalesced in my chest, defying the unearthly chill, then raced down my arm.

"HAMRAR!"

Just as Ginny lashed out with another claw, I fired a bolt of kinetic energy directly into the catwalk. The wire mesh and steel railing dented as I was launched towards the back of the house. Ginny's claw tagged the cuff of my pant leg as I was thrown into the air. Instead of falling three stories below to my imminent death, I was falling one story to a sharp diagonal into the balcony. Possibly as far as the booth.

I turned just enough upwards to see Ginny perched on the catwalk like a squirming gargoyle, snarling in fury.

Then it was really painful and I lost consciousness.

Chapter Eighteen

Guideline Forty-Three:

If you can't draw a perfect circle, it's OK to just connect the dots.

Rocky is probably the only boss I've ever had who could sound reassuring as she said "Travis, this really needs to stop being a habit."

I could hear Connie's voice punch through my consciousness as the pain started to wake me up. "I didn't find anything broken, amazingly enough."

For some reason, I heard Danny's voice next, saying, "Keep the guy. He's a survivor."

Hannah's voice came up in reply. "Or send him into stunts. Down the stairs, on fire, now off the catwalk."

Kenny joined in. "He any good with a sword?"

I came to in the balcony. I'd smashed a half-dozen seats when I landed. Somehow I'd gone far enough to clear the old segregation barrier. Someone had pulled me into the aisle. I flexed a handful of muscles, making sure I could move all of my extremities. I was battered in a handful of places, the worst being what felt like a cracked rib. Out of old habit, I scratched my balls just to make sure they were still there. Thumper was sitting behind my head, their fingers at my not quite so throbbing temples. Connie was crouched beside me, taking my vitals. I could see Rocky, Max, and several others just beyond.

Connie met my gaze first. "How you doing, Trav?"

I blinked. "I'm auditioning for the role of the chandelier. Do I get a callback?"

Thumper rolled their eyes, then gave a thumbs-up.

Connie took that at face value and turned to the others. "He'll be all right. Just bumps and bruises."

Max butted in. "What happened?"

I opened my mouth before thinking. "Her again."

Rocky frowned. "Her?"

I reached under my butt, wincing as a bruised muscle protested, then held up the perfectly-severed end of my safety line. "Ginny."

Max's face turned pale for an instant before he composed himself. If I hadn't been looking him in the eyes, I might not have noticed. He muttered quietly. "Good to hear you're all right, Travis." Then he clapped once, drawing the attention back to himself. "Everyone else, playtime's over! Places in ten!"

A chorus of, "Thank you, ten!" came from the assembled, who began to trickle out as my chances of grievous bodily harm dwindled. Some were trying to rubberneck and find out more, others looked happy to have an excuse to get back to work. I got a thumbs-up from Danny as he left with most of them. Soon, Connie and I were left alone with Rocky.

Rocky shook her head. "That was less than discrete. But for what it's worth, now the cast thinks you're a lucky charm. The ghost's tried to kill you at least three times and you're still around."

I grimaced. "How does that make me a lucky charm?"

Rocky shrugged. "Ghost's been too busy with you to bother anyone else. That counts as lucky here."

I muttered. "Do I get a cookie?"

What I got was a pat on the the head from Connie.

Rocky got stern for a moment. "All right, guys. I'm glad you're OK. But this ghost needs to go. We got an industry preview opening a week from yesterday and I can't fill this house with a homicidal ghost in it."

Connie nodded. "We still need more info; and I know where to get it. I should've done it the day we knew for sure it was a ghost issue, and I'm kicking myself for not doing it our first night here. I need to stick around tonight after everyone leaves. I'll have Travis and Thumper with me."

Rocky frowned. "Harry wouldn't like it. So I'm not going to tell him. I can get you a spare set of keys and the alarm code. Just remember to leave the ghost light on when you leave and try not to burn the place down."

Connie nodded in all seriousness. "I can't make promises, but I'll try."

Rocky didn't look any happier. "Do I want to know what you're planning to do?"

Connie shrugged. "If it helps any, Travis and Thumper are much bigger pyros than I am."

Thumper grinned like a fool.

Rocky let out a deep breath. "Do I even want to ask?"

Connie shook her head. "It's been staring me in the face the entire time. There's someone I haven't talked to yet. And he knows everything that happens in this building."

Rocky frowned. "Who?"

Connie looked her dead in the eyes. "The Scottish Man."

Rocky bit her lip. Her bosom had stopped heaving enough that I could almost watch as her heart began to sink. "Aw shit. He's real, isn't he?"

Connie nodded. "If I'm right, he's very real. We'll find out tonight."

Rocky licked her lips nervously. "Right. Good. Fight a murdering theater ghost by saying The Scottish Man's name."

Connie shook her head, her jaw set. "Saying his name is for schoolgirls looking for something to be naughty about. I'm one of the best necromancers in the country, and I'm going to summon him."

*　*　*

The coven assembled downstage center.

"So how are we going to play this?"

"Good cop/dumb cop. I do the summoning and welcome. When he arrives, ask whatever comes to mind until I tell you to shut up."

We had waited for the cast and crew to go home. Then I'd found George, who I was remembering to still call Roscoe, and asked him politely to take off. He gave me a raised eyebrow but no argument. We closed the stage door behind Rocky and spent the next twenty minutes doing a quick sweep of the building. As near as we could tell, Connie, Thumper, and myself were the only ones there. The ghost light cast deep shadows across the hall and stage as we stepped up downstage center. Connie set down her bag downstage of the ghost light and sat down, crossing her legs. On her other side, she put down her brazier.

I'd made her brazier for her birthday a couple months before. It was cast in solid brass, with three claw feet. It looked like an incense burner, but was the size of a teakettle. Perfect for small, controlled burnings.

As she carefully opened her pack, she spoke to me over her shoulder. "Draw a chalk circle that gives us all enough room to move. And be ready to turn it into a kinetic shield at an instant's notice. Thump, draw another circle, this one inside Travis'."

I nodded. "Got it. Can I know why?"

Connie looked straight up. Far above our heads, the fly system awaited, festooned with battens, lights, and lines. "Because if I was a ghost who wanted to kill us, I'd start dropping lights from the grid on our heads. Got to be a few thousand pounds' worth of ammo up there."

I gave another nod as my imagination reveled in potential bloodshed. "Noted."

I took four paces downstage from the ghost light and left a chalk mark on the floor, before doing an about-face and taking six paces upstage, nearly reaching the staircase that ran upstage from there before leaving another mark. Repeating the movements stage left and right gave me four equidistant points. I always hated seeing movies where some traumatized teenager suddenly becomes able to make perfect circles with a can of salt from the kitchen. I've yet to meet a magical force or entity that cares about me making my circles via connect-the-dots.

As I was drawing mine, Thumper was drawing a similar circle only a few inches shorter in diameter than my own. We believed in defense in depth. Which is why we also both had fire extinguishers in arm's reach.

By the time Thumper and I had finished, Connie had unpacked her bag for tonight's work. She'd also drawn a smaller circle around herself, between the downstage edge of Thumper's circle and the ghost light.

From her side, she took a small coal, placed it in the center of the brazier's mesh and lit it with a purple cigarette lighter. A thin ribbon of smoke curled upwards from the coal. One by one, she began to pick up and light the objects at her side, letting them burn in the brazier. One by one, she whispered.

"A white rose for opening night."

The smoke took on a sickly-sweet smell.

"A blank cast list for held hopes."

The paper gently crackled as it curled up in flames.

"A shard of mirror for broken dreams."

Don't ask me how she got a piece of a mirror to burn. I didn't ask.

She continued.

"A makeup sponge for the greasepaint."

"A ticket stub for the crowd."

"A grave-stolen red rose for closing night."

"And a page of a playbill, for the memory that remains."

The smoke began to widely circle us instead of dissipating into the house or rising into the flies.

I could feel eyes on us now. Human, ghost, something else, or a combo, I had no idea. But whatever was nearby, we had their attention.

Connie began chanting in a language I didn't recognize and didn't pay attention to. I was busy marking sigils on the backs of my hands with a thick marker. Connie and I had been working together long enough to be complementary, but I didn't quite understand the nuances of how she worked. The feeling was probably mutual. Thumper made their own preparations, involving a specific pattern in their nail polish, then stood on the opposite side from me, ready for whatever was needed.

Connie continued to chant, her energy palpable now.

I was seeing the shadows move, the building itself sensing her actions and taking notice. The big set piece, the second story balconies and staircase looking over the stage groaned, the steel itself shifting. Whatever spirits flowed through this place, they knew we were here, and had a good idea as to what we ever doing.

As Connie's chant heightened, she raised her right hand and called out, her voice projecting to the back of the house. "Macbeth."

Her hand came down, thumping her fist against the deck.

The ghost light brightened for half a second, just fast enough to have maybe been a trick of the light. The building itself seemed to moan, turning inward to see just who had dared to break a rule of the theater so openly. It was like watching a thunderstorm form in the one football field sized space occupied by a particularly belligerent atheist saying what he really thought about Gods.

Thumper and I traded glances, then went back to checking the shadows out of Connie's line of sight.

Again, Connie raised her arm and called out, "Macbeth!"

Again, her fist came down, thumping the deck.

Again, the ghost light flared, brighter this time.

The emergency exit signs flared red again, then began blinking like a car's hazard lights.

The house doors thundered as if they were all kicked open at once, then again as they all slammed shut in near-unison.

Connie's chest heaved as she took another breath, singing rather than screaming, her voice echoing throughout the house, "MACBETH!"

I saw her fist come down.

The moment her fist hit the boards, the ghost light shone bright enough to be painful.

I pulsed energy from my hands into the outer circle.

Thumper's hands were up as well, activating their own shield.

No sooner did the shields come up than the bulb of the ghost light shattered, plunging the house into darkness. The coal in Connie's brazier snuffed itself out. The strip lights in the house marking the passageways were all out. Even the emergency exit signs, that reliably glowed red no matter what the board in the booth dictated, had all gone dark.

The shields glowed just faintly enough for me to see myself, Thumper, and Connie within it.

Long moments of agonizing silence followed.

I started being able to hear my own heartbeat, alongside Connie trying to catch her breath.

Then, from the back of the house, I began to hear a slow, single pair of hands coming together in languid applause.

Chapter Nineteen

Guideline Thirty-Eight:
Remember whose house you're in.

The greenish translucent haze I'd always associated with ghosts in the darkness coalesced into the form of a young man. Younger than me, and prettier, with a medium height and build. He became easier to see as he strode down the aisle like he owned the place. He was dressed in Broadway's idea of Scottish highland dress, with a brightly colored tartan kilt, leather boots to the knees, and the extra length of his kilt thrown over his shoulder. A cross-hilt sword hung at his hip. His poofy-sleeved shirt was open just enough to show off some impressive pecs. He wore a mask similar to the ones the show was using for the masquerade scene. The mask's features were in a half-smile and half-frown, his features unseen behind the eye and mouth holes. After a while, I decided what threw me off was his hair. Everything else about the man belonged on the cover of a romance novel. But his hair looked like an all-American kid from the fifties that hadn't heard about greasers yet.

He kept up his slow applause all the way down the aisle, black leather gauntlets giving each echoing slap a solid weight behind them, until he came to a stop before the orchestra pit. A thick brogue that sounded slightly off emerged from the mask. "Who dar summon The Scottish Man? From his own downstage center, nae less?"

Connie remained sitting in her circle, nodding respectfully in his direction. "Tis I who summon you, Scottish Man. Connie Chandler. Necromancer of some skill and some note."

I shrugged. "Well, he's ~a~ Scottish Man."

The Scottish Man's mask narrowed at the eyes, his hand resting at the hilt of his sword. "Nae a, ye potbellied philistine. But rather The." His brogue marked the capital letter before he spit on the floor. "Tis I. Tis me. Tis m'self. The Scottish Man o' the Pencil Factory Theater."

What at first sounded like thunder rolled. Then I realized it wasn't thunder, but a thunder sheet. An old theater sound effect device. A thunder sheet was a strip of sheet metal kept just offstage. Moving it around makes a noise that passes for thunder for those listening in the house. I was thrown for a moment. There was supposedly nobody else in the building. More than that, we didn't have a thunder sheet in the building.

The Scottish Man turned his leg and gave a courtly bow in Connie's direction. "At yer service, Miss Chandler. Necromancer of skill and note ye are. The dead speak of yer skill, nae tae mention yer courtesy. I know of ye and yer coven, the alchemist an the technomancer. What have lurked in our wings these past few weeks."

Connie gave me a gesture to shut up, then nodded. "You know of our skills. Know of our quest, then. Death stalks this theater, Scottish Man. Tell me of it."

He stepped closer, hand still at his sword. "Death has e'er stalked the Pencil Factory, lass. As it does tae all theaters what have felt their boards treaded by so many throughout the years."

Connie quirked an eyebrow. "Ghosts of the theater are not known to claim the lives of the living. One in your domain has claimed two in as many months. Why?"

The Scottish Man opened his arms. He nearly laughed his answer. "When a' theater ghost kill the living, she asks?" He planted his hands on his hips. "Since when does a murderer use a theater tae do it most foul, then return tae the very scene of the crime? Bold as brass, no less, ye ken?"

Connie blinked, confused. "Do you speak of Max Roman?"

I couldn't see his face, but I could feel him grow tense. The eyebrows of the mask actually curled down to give him a scowl. "Aye. Him." The Scottish Man spit again. "Man o' ye ragged arse bunch. Rude mechanicals n' strolling players, ye are! And him a' the very top. Actor and manager. Head o' the company. With a fresh young ingenue on his arm and coin in his pocket. Aye, murderer, he is!"

Thumper was watching our six. I kept the Scottish Man in the corner of my eye.

Connie looked wary. "Proud, I would call him. And vain as well. Murderer is a title I was not aware of. Since when has he been such?"

Frustrated, the Scottish Man threw up his hands to indicate the entire building, clenching his fists like he was milking a cow worthy of Paul Bunyan. "Since he arranged the terrible deed w'in these very walls, ye ken! Murder most foul, it was! The Crying Lass be his victim true. Cursed tae be held beyond the footlights. Cursed tae remain wi'in the temple of her own broken dreams."

I cocked my head. "The only one connected to Max that died in these walls before recently was..." I stopped myself from using her name. "I thought she committed suicide. You're saying he murdered her?"

The mask gave me a slow nod. "Got it in one, lad. That he did. The Crying Lass were brought low by the man ye name. Pledged her troth tae him, she did. An' saw no less than death than his scorn."

Connie gave me the sign for "drop it" and kept her gaze on the Scottish Man. "The Crying Girl has killed two men. Innocent men. She has threatened my companion time and time again. None of her victims have done her wrong. Yet her murderer lives. Why?"

The mask almost looked pitiful. "Death alone wi' no dry tears o' the Crying Lass, Miss Chandler. She may lash out a' men wi' wandering hands n' eyes. But their deaths bring little respite. As will the death of the alchemist, should he fall by her hand. Death alone left her in torment. Death alone will nae bring her peace. Tis justice must she have. Vengeance. Revenge fulfilled wi' let the Crying Lass rest at last."

I frowned. "Justice and Vengeance aren't the same thing."

The mask turned to face towards me, and the eyeholes seemed to be an infinite void as the Scottish Man regarded me. "Gae long enough wi'out justice, alchemist, and ye learn tae settle for vengeance."

Connie got us back on track. "What will bring justice, if not her killer's death? What stays her hand? What is she waiting for"

The Scottish Man cocked his head, and I thought I could see him mulling something over behind his mask. He turned in a circle, taking in the house and stage before regarding her again. "Nae less than triumph, lass. We thought her tae fade away. So long ha' she shed her tears wi'in these walls. Then all of a sudden, life returned here. Music. Laughter. Art. Magic. All of it. My charges and I rejoiced! The show will gae on once more! But then we learn the horrible truth. The newfound showman is her very own lost love and found murderer. The killer returns tae mount the boards again, ye ken? The Crying Lass aims tae take him ere the curtain falls. Let the show close in one night or gae on for years, it matters not to her. But he seeks the roar of the crowd, and she will nae see him have it. She means tae take the applause from his grasp just afore it finds his ears, ye ken?"

Connie nodded. "She's waiting until opening night."

The Scottish Man snapped his fingers and pointed at her. "That she is, Miss Chandler. Followin the narrative, she is. Await for the scoundrel tae have the desire o' his life in hand, only tae take it 'awa. Just afore the final blackout and the swell o' the ovation. Tis' when she'll strike, ye ken. He will nae leave that curtain call alive."

I filed that away for future information.

Connie asked, "What of the other necromancer? The one who is not I?"

The Scottish Man opened his hands. "Doctor Gull, ye ken? I know nae his work in this. Whether tae help or hinder, he answer tae his own, ye ken?"

I broke in. "I thought you'd know more of what happened in your own theater."

He shrugged. It could have been a trick of the light, but his mask almost looked sheepish. "Had ye asked last season, I would ken every mouse in the walls, alchemist. Every scrap o' wardrobe in the racks, every prop in the closet. Tae my long lament. For years uncounted, we have sat in the dark and silence. And now we come alive! We are a proper theater once more! The glorious chaos of creation make these walls vibrant. Ye can sense better than most what such does tae a theater, alchemist. Ye ha seen the vibrancy coursing through cinderblock and tile. From deck tae rigging! Green room tae lobby! And I are The Scottish Man his own 'sel!"

At that, the ghost gave a bow more suited to a renfaire than a theater. I was getting more confused. "What's a Scottish ghost doing in an American theater?"

The Scottish Man's mask curled into a frown. "Hae ye no sense o' tradition, alchemist? Hae ye nae ken the ways o' the theater? The very stars o' yer age fear the sound o my name proper, and sae The Scottish Man I am."

I stroked my goatee. "But that play was written four centuries ago on another continent. You weren't The Scottish Man when you were alive."

He opened his arms presentationally. "Tis' a role I were honored tae play in life, alchemist. Tis a title I be honored to hold in death."

"So you were an actor." That explained his hair. He wasn't wearing his old clothes from life. He was wearing a costume. And if his hair was from when I think it was... "You died in this theater, didn't you?"

The green glow surrounding his body grew all the more vibrant as he growled. "Hold yer tongue an damn yer eyes! Ye great tub o guts and gaff tape!" His mask curled into an angry rictus. He almost drew his sword, but Connie lifted a hand in what I think was supplication.

"Please, Scottish Man. We have come to you for guidance. Death has come to this place time and again, and now turns towards my companion."

If he'd been alive, I'd think The Scottish Man was coming down from hysterics. "Yer man have grown over personal, he has."

Thumper shook their head in a "can't take you anywhere" look and playfully smacked me upside the head.

Connie kept her voice calm. "He is dense in such matters, and for him I apologize. We seek wisdom, for the very show is threatened."

That seemed to calm him down. "Fer the sake o' the show, I shall guide ye as best I can, ye ken? Provided ye nae speak further of me own past."

Connie's look and tongue would take no argument. "Done."

Mollified, The Scottish Man went into lecture mode.

"Playhouse, theater, they are places o' the dead dreams, ye ken? Fer ev'ry dream come true, a thousand are dashed. For every wish granted, scores lie unfulfilled. Every cast list that bears another's name. Every crowd what sits on their hands. These passions saturate the very walls of the building. The sheer devotion unbound warp nature itself. Every actor whose character dies on the boards may return after their own death to haunt those very boards. There be a reckoning for that sort o power, lass. Especially for an actor who dies and returns with unfinished business. The Crying Lass and her need for justice, I've ne'er seen such power in business unfinished. The Crying Lass, she risks the show itself in her rage. Finish that business. The show must go on, but the curtain must fall if a new cast is tae take their places, ye ken?"

I nodded. "That makes sense."

The mask curled into a neutral look that could almost be a smile. "Bind her fast tae deny her, or pave her road to justice. Either way, I will watch for ye as I may. But The Crying Lass is powerful. And the Doctor all the moreso. Tae defeat them both will take more than the three of ye, I think."

Connie nodded. "We will do as we are able, and bring our allies to bear. Tread your boards in peace, Scottish Man."

"Break legs, Miss Chandler."

He took another flourishing bow, then walked backwards up the aisle towards the lobby. Smoothly, he began to clap his hands. Once, twice.

On the third clap, he vanished, and the house was plunged into darkness once more.

A few moments later, the emergency exit signs began to glow red once more. A second later, the strip lights marking the passageways began to glow anew themselves.

* * *

Headlamps and powerful flashlights cutting through the shadows, we stepped into the hallway for the top floor, then headed straight for the old apartment. We could've just turned on the lights normally, but some unspoken agreement had us feeling better using these. We'd cleaned up the small mess we'd made and replaced the bulb in the ghost light. Even now it burned merrily away, illuminating the house just enough to appease both safety's sake and The Scottish Man's subjects. Connie's eyes glowed green as she checked both ways down the hallway, then nodded. I used Rocky's keys to open the door and let Connie lead the way. She scanned the room, nodded, and headed further inside. Thumper watched our six.

Roscoe had cleaned here and there, probably to make it easier for his private time with Mabel. Old books, papers, clothes, even dishes were still here and there. Most likely they had been all that Ginny owned, and the apartment was never rented again after she died. Roscoe, for some reason, had never seen fit to throw anything out.

We were taking a stab in the dark here. History told us that Ginny had committed suicide. The Scottish Man claimed she'd been murdered by Max. Now we were trying to find out if The Scottish Man was right. If we could confirm it, our need to protect Max dropped far down our priority list.

Unfortunately, we didn't really know what we were looking for. There were no signs of a struggle. No bloodstain residue that I could sense. We were counting on blind luck and Connie's working relationship with death to somehow find a murder weapon.

On the counter I found the old newspaper Roscoe had shown me. The headline of the Arts & Entertainment section detailed Roman's enlistment. It had been folded and refolded, and wrinkled in a few small places. It took me a moment to realize that the wrinkles were from where long-ago tears had fallen, blemishing the paper.

Inside a drawer were a few ancient condiment packets and sets of plastic cutlery filched from takeout places, along with the dead batteries and old pens that usually haunt such drawers. I pushed an old napkin aside, and a pill bottle caught my eye. On a hunch, I took a deeper look at it with magic. As an alchemist, I'm good at seeing what things are made of. I'm also good at noticing things that shouldn't be there.

After a moment, I waved Connie on over and pointed at the pill bottle. She looked it over hesitantly, and I saw her eyes flash a different shade of green. She grimaced, then nodded uncomfortably. I watched her wrap the bottle in a silk handkerchief. Then she passed it to me, dropping the entire thing in a plastic bag.

*　*　*

Thumper and I wordlessly hung our lab coats on the pegs just inside from the garage. We didn't speak until we'd both washed our hands and I'd gotten a soda from the fridge. Connie and Jazz weren't about to ask. I took a breath and let it out before speaking. "It's definitely arsenic."

Connie looked disgusted. "Poisoning her prenatal vitamins? What a sick fuck."

Jazz's look of worry melted into sorrow.

I took a sip and nodded grimly. "Yep. It's a really low dose. Some sort of coating on every one. I'd have to run it by Bubba or Lori to be sure. But if I had to guess, I'd say he was trying to end her pregnancy without her knowing he was doing it. If the memory Ginny showed me is true, then Max knew she was pregnant. If he was living in that apartment, then he had access to her meds. Then when he left, he couldn't control her dosage anymore. But he didn't warn her either."

Connie nodded. "So when she felt worse at him leaving, she kept on poisoning herself."

Thumper gave Connie a finger gun as I nodded. "And when the investigation found it in her system, it was ruled a suicide."

Connie shook her head. "Without even sourcing the arsenic? Fucking lazy-ass cops."

I sighed. "Typical. Easy answer in front of them, nobody left to ask uncomfortable questions, case closed."

Fury overtook Jazz's look of sorrow. She spit on the floor and muttered a complicated curse. My Arabic was lousy, but I'm pretty sure it had something to do with livestock.

Connie almost snarled. "The Sonofabitch. He didn't just love her and leave her. The Scottish Man was right. He straight up murdered her."

I nodded. "So we don't have to worry too hard about Ginny taking him down. But we still have to look out for everyone else in the building, including ourselves. We also still need to catch, kill, or banish Dr. Gull. We don't even know who he is yet."

Connie took a breath and looked more resolved. "No. But we know he's going to be there. Opening night. Ready for Ginny to strike. And help her along if he has to."

Chapter Twenty

Guideline Fifty:

Know when to love, and when to trust.

I opened my eyes and immediately regretted it.

I'd taken as many various healing potions as I dared. While I no longer had a cracked rib that made every breath painful coming and going, I still was a mass of stiffened muscles.

In a sore haze, I took a swallow of water and mentally went through recent events. Yesterday I'd worked a full rehearsal in the theater, been thrown off a catwalk by a homicidal ghost, saved my own life by hitting a theater balcony with my own carcass, finished rehearsal, stayed late, summoned a mercurial theater ghost to pump for intel, searched an apartment that had been vacant for decades, tested prenatal vitamins for poisons, then finally went to bed.

Shrapnel was curled up on the other side of my bed. My groanings made her stir. She opened a single eye and give me a feline look of "so what do you have to complain about?" before deciding to get more comfortable and go back to sleep without waiting for an answer. I scritched her behind the ears, having nothing to say to her anyway. My efforts were rewarded with a subvocal purr and my head throbbing slightly less.

I managed to creak my way into sitting up, only to have Jazz wander into the room with an armload of towels. She'd also apparently discovered yoga pants to go with her crop top collection. A cartoon beaver grinned toothily at me from the top she wore now. The fact that I wasn't more distracted by this should tell you how wiped I really was. She smiled in her usual cheery manner, which felt like the shine of the sun: too bright for my weakened state to handle.

"Afternoon, Master. It's good to see you up and about."

I blinked. "I've only managed the first, Jazz. Don't praise me too early."

That smile just kept coming. "Your next step is the floor anyway, Master. You won't have to manage about for very long."

I tilted my head in confusion as she unrolled a mat on my bedroom floor, putting the towels aside. Another step and she had her hand out, which I took before standing up. "You want me to lay down?"

"Got it in one, Master."

I managed to lay down on the mat, with a pause for Jazz to put a U-shaped pillow under my face. This was new, but I'd learned not to object too hard when Jazz got in a mood to put her master back together. So it was a bit of a surprise when Jazz straddled my waist.

"Um, Jazz?"

Then her hands gripped my shoulders and her thumbs dug in just hard enough for me to completely lose control of my tongue. If I was somehow being assassinated, this was probably the best way to take me out. The morning after getting my ass kicked. A bare midriff and a smile. Easily assembled components to taking down a master alchemist. In his own lair. In his own shorts. It took me a couple of seconds to realize Jazz was being really effective at battering my locked up carcass into freedom of movement.

Convinced I wasn't being murdered, and if I was that I didn't care, I let out a breath and let Jazz work. I wondered how I'd never experienced this before. Then I remembered that I'd never asked. She was incredible. And a lot stronger than I'd given her credit for. Jazz had been trained as a scribe and she'd worked as a librarian for centuries, but she somehow had the grip strength of a blacksmith.

She'd also come prepared. Her hands were covered in some kind of oil. I took a sniff in the air and my brain mentioned something about grapeseed. Then the endorphins made my cortex stop trying to do research and sit back to enjoy the process.

I couldn't say how long she'd worked on me. I do know that by the time I realized she wasn't touching me anymore, I could move again and wasn't nearly as sore. I took my time turning over and sitting up, finding her sitting cross-legged near me with her usual smile, wiping her hands on a towel.

"Thanks, Jazz."

"You're very welcome, Master."

Remembering my conversation with Connie, my face fell a bit. "I don't appreciate you nearly as much as I should."

She shook her head, smiling like I'd made a joke. "Master, you're very appreciative."

I bit my tongue for a moment, then decided to keep going. "No. No, I'm not. I've been hiding my own feelings and trying not to notice your own." I waved my hand dismissively. "I'm probably screwing this up, but I need to say it. I'm not comfortable being your Master, the way that I am. I know you tell me you enjoy serving me, and Gods know I love having you here. But I'm feeling about you in ways I can't let myself act on ethically at all. I don't even know if I'm making any sense here."

Jazz licked her lips gently, then put her hand on mine. "I do understand, Master. You know the ring binds me to the one who wears the ring. I cannot help but serve my Master. I have served many, since I was bound."

Stupidly, I interrupted her with, "I'm not..." Which is about all I got out before she shut me up with a finger at my lips. Those sapphire eyes came closer until I disappeared in them.

"I know, Master. You're not envious of my past Masters, and you're only worried about future ones that would hurt me. But you have no way of knowing for certain how much of my devotion is from my heart towards you as a person, and how much is from the ring. So as long as I am bound, you cannot be certain of my feelings at all. No matter what I say. I understand that, Master. And I understand that, until you manage to set me free in a way that keeps me safe as well, you never will be able to convince yourself that know that for sure."

I closed my eyes and shook my head. "I'm trying not to lead you on. Or myself."

She held my hand a touch tighter. "You're doing neither, Master. What you are doing is beating yourself up over what you cannot control. That doesn't help me. It just hurts you. Besides, I'm only a few centuries old. And serving you gives me plenty to do. I can wait for you to build the miracle you seem determined to make for me. But you have enough beating you up besides adding your own impatience to it."

I slumped, sheepish. "I'm sorry."

She smiled with a bit of frustration. "Master, in my time I have known kind masters and cruel ones. I have had masters who fell in love with me. I have had masters who...used me. But in all my centuries, I have never had a Master so devoted to having me live for myself instead of just living in service to them. For that alone, you stand out beyond them all."

She grabbed my chin and looked me deep in the eyes. "If you devote so much of yourself into ensuring I become my own woman, what will you have left for what lies beyond that?"

I let my eyes close. Then I let my tears fall.

I whispered, "Understood."

* * *

After a shower, getting some odds and sods done, and dinner, Thumper took me aside and into their room. That wasn't a big deal. The more of us living in the house, the easier it was for us to grant each other the privacy that was asked for.

I dropped on the bed at their invitation. Firing up their computer system, they turned in my direction and tapped their temple with a questioning look.

I nodded. "Go for it."

I felt a tingle in the back of my neck, then heard Thumper's accent in my mind. *"Thanks, Trav."*

"What do you got for me?"

"I found out some more about your Scottish Man."

That raised my eyebrow. "Fire away."

Thumper opened several tabs from a website I'd never seen, expanding them to fill multiple screens. *"The Scottish Man is more of a title than a name. It appears to be the identity taken by the most powerful ghost in a given theater."*

I nodded. "That's what I figured. The Scottish Man we met was an actor that died in the theater before. But he seemed real pissed that I figured that out."

"He would. It's related to his weakness. The Scottish Man faces competition from every new ghost a theater gains. When one of them grows powerful enough, they can destroy The Scottish Man and claim his title."

I frowned. "He said that any actor whose character died onstage has the chance to return as a theater ghost. That explains why he wasn't eager to see Ginny. She's been around for a while, she was pissed off when she first got there, and now her killer is directing the first new show in years in her theater. Even if she doesn't know about The Scottish Man, she's a threat to him."

Thumper raised a finger in agreement. *"And taking him down would only make her more powerful."*

I snorted. "Here's hoping she doesn't figure that one out. We've got enough on our hands already."

Thumper turned back to me and nodded. *"Shame he can't help any more on his end."*

"Do I want to know how a ghost destroys another ghost, or is that a Connie question?"

Thumper shrugged. *"Connie, probably. I figure the same way anything destroys each other. Just a lot more vicious about it. After all, they're physically souls. Well, not physically, but entirely. Once they're gone, there's nothing left. Nothing that we know about, anyways."*

"Which means The Scottish Man is running scared, and we have whole new levels of being terrified at what Ginny can do. Peachy."

Thumper shrugged again sheepishly. *"Not sure how we can use that to stop Ginny or take down Dr. Gull, but I figured it was important."*

"It is, Thump. Thanks." I thought of something and my eyes narrowed. "What website is this? I've never seen it before."

Thumper grinned and let their fingers dance across the keyboard, bringing up a home screen. Old leatherbound books chained to shelves filled the background, while one open on a lectern displayed the main menu. *"This is the Conservatory. It's a mage forum for all kinds of magical knowledge. Histories, disciplines, new spell variants, current events, you name it. I found out about The Scottish Man from a bardic mage in London."*

I frowned in confusion. "A website for mages? Who came up with this?"

Thumper shrugged. *"They call themselves the Librarians, but nobody really knows. There's a lot of cross-referencing and corrections going on. I think they're just ordinary mages that have the time and energy."*

I pointed to the keyboard. "May I?"

Thumper backed away. I started navigating. It was structured like a wiki, with no ads. I ducked into the alchemy section and started exploring. After a minute, I could feel my eyes getting wider. This was big. This was years of study hall packed into a few hours worth of articles. More than that, this was post-graduate stuff. The kind of thing you'd normally learn from a mentor. If they thought you were worth teaching. I was seeing spells I'd been trained with listed meticulously, with notes on variants people had tried on them from around the world. I was seeing full copies of books I'd only ever heard about.

I whispered. "Does the Iron Council know about this?"

Thumper grinned. *"Dunno. Fuck 'em either way."*

My blood ran cold. One of the reasons mages haven't taken over the world is that we never really had an industrial or information revolution. For centuries, people who could sense magic learned in apprenticeships or secret societies, things like that. The study hall system in America, which teaches the basics, only really started after WWII. Knowledge really is power, when it comes to magic. It gets hoarded like gold. I have an armored vault for a bookcase in my house for that specific reason.

But this site, this Conservatory? It offered a lot of knowledge, free for the asking. Which means any mage who knew how to find it would get their hands on texts it would've taken them lifetimes to find, let alone study, comprehend, and build on. A lot of people were going to get power without attached restraints or responsibilities really fast. That alone was terrifying. Add in what happened if someone decided to deliberately plant false information? I remembered when certain explosive formulas were put on the early internet. The results weren't what you'd call a comedy.

And my covenmate, roommate, and one of my best friends was using it as a go-to research source.

I sat back and let out a long breath. "This is really gonna piss them off, Thump. I mean, really piss them off. There's got to be a lot of shit in here people consider secret. Duels have been fought over revealing spells like this. Fuck, the Daedeli are going to shit bricks, assuming they haven't already."

Thump shrugged, then their expression grew somber. *"I'm more worried about you."*

I cocked my head like a confused dog as Thumper replaced me in the chair. "Have I been that bad lately?"

They dove down another thread, opening tabs. Thumper eventually found what they were looking for. One page opened up into a high-quality scan of a very old black-and-white photograph. A note at the bottom dated it to the early 1920's. A bearded white guy in a three piece suit and fez was posing for a portrait in a highback leather chair.

Standing at his side, in robes and a headscarf, was Jazz. You could tell even in the black-and-white photo that her skin was notably darker, even if it didn't show the fact that she was really blue. The scarf and her hair were both pulled back, exposing the pointed tips of her ears. Her winning smile and deep eyes shone from across the years in the century-old photograph.

Thumper turned to look me in the eyes. Then they gently reached up and touched my shoulder.

"Trav? How long have you known Jazz?"

* * *

The five of us were back at the dinner table. Everyone had looks of varying concern, from Byron, who knew damn well what was going on, to Connie, who had her own worries. The only one without a care in the world was Shrapnel, who was fastidiously grooming herself from her perch atop the sofa.

I was sitting next to Jazz and took her hand, trying not to get lost in her sapphire eyes. "We probably should have done this earlier." I bit my tongue then shook my head. "No. We definitely should've done this earlier. I should have done this earlier." I turned to everyone else at the table. "And

I'm sorry we haven't been forthcoming before. In the end, I hope you'll understand why."

Everyone waited for me to go on, so I did. "I told you all that I met Jazz in Iraq. Which is true. But it's not the entire truth."

I looked her in the eye and nodded. "Go ahead, hon."

She nodded. "Yes, Master."

She could have changed in the blink of an eye. She chose to change gradually, her skin fading into a royal blue as the tips of her ears pointed and lengthened. She kept her clothes the same, not having planned to make such a revelation in yoga pants and a souvenir crop top from a roadside attraction.

Thumper and Connie blinked, then their eyes both widened in amazement.

I bit my lip. "Jazz isn't a witch. She's a djinn."

I could see Jazz fight the urge to keep her gaze on the ground, looking sheepishly up at the rest of my coven and waving a tentative hand in greeting. Her face and the tips of her ears were slightly flushed in embarrassment.

Thumper's jaw dropped.

Connie gently reached over and closed Thumper's mouth, then whispered. "Oh, shit. We're all gonna die."

I awkwardly tried to pick up the story. "I killed her last master in Iraq during the war, then smuggled her ring out. She's been with me ever since."

Thumper let their jaw shut, then blinked a few times. They looked Jazz over again, then licked their lips. With a whimsical smile, they very deliberately said, "Hubba...Hubba."

Jazz blushed a deeper shade of purple.

Connie shook her head, still amazed. "This makes the most ridiculous kind of sense. I knew something was going on. But I never imagined..."

Byron shrugged. "Neither did anyone else."

Connie's eyes narrowed. "Byron knew?"

I shrugged. "He was there when it happened."

She shook her head. "The Council would have kittens. Not to mention Neary. He'd shit a golden twinkie."

I let out a long breath, then nodded. "You're right. Babs confirmed it. If they found out, SiS would kill me on sight and confiscate her ring. Obviously that's a bad case scenario."

Connie looked over to me, compassion in her eyes and snark in her voice. "So you've been hiding her as a needy submissive? That was your plan?"

Jazz wrinkled her nose. "Needy?"

I held out my arms. "A holding pattern. I'm trying to find a way to set her free that keeps us both alive. I haven't found one yet."

Connie frowned. "You can't wish her free?"

I shook my head. "That would free her from me. But any yahoo who knows Solomanic magic could just bind her into something else."

Connie's eyes narrowed. "You can't take her home and set her free there?"

Jazz frowned. "My home is with my Master."

I shrugged. "She's never been to the City of Brass, and I don't know how to get there. It disappeared from our realm around the time she was born. Which was a couple centuries of sand and warfare ago. Any entrance we could possibly know about is somewhere in the Middle East. Which, depending on what old stories you're relying on, could be anywhere from Morocco to western China. Then it's a Gods know how long trip through some spirit realms I know jack and shit about. The most likely people we could ask for are free Djinn. None of whom I have a phone number for. And by all accounts, any left on this plane are really dickish about mages. Some asshole called Solomon really pissed them off somehow. No idea why. So even if I could get to the City of Brass alive, there's no guarantee I wouldn't be ripped apart by free Djinn before we managed to say hello.

Not to mention the oath I swore to the Wild Hunt, which would probably want to know before I went off on an epic quest without them."

Byron, who was a member of the Wild Hunt, nodded at that. "He's not wrong on that last one."

Connie blinked, impressed. "You have been thinking this through." Her eyes widened in sudden dread. "Oh shit, does Chittenden know?"

I grabbed a drink. "Nope. I was bright enough to cover that. Remember last year when we met again, and my memory was jacked up? Turns out I'd hidden Jazz's ring in a safe box in the Warwell vault and magically blocked my memories of Jazz. Vampires knowing about her wouldn't have been good for anyone. By the time I got my memory back, I figured it wasn't fair to Jazz to keep hiding her from the world. We've been building her new identity ever since."

Connie shook her head. "So that's why you've been keeping her at arm's length."

I blushed harder than Jazz did, then sighed. "Yeah. And it really sucks. I can't let myself act on my feelings for as long as I'm her Master. So I'm obligated to get her ready to be free."

Jazz looked down. "I'm sorry."

Connie snarled, pounding the table with her fist. "No!"

Jazz froze like a trapped rabbit, clutching my hand. Byron and Thumper backed away less than an inch, ready to react. Shrapnel, who had been ignoring us, looked up from grooming herself to see what was going on. Even I raised an eyebrow.

Connie lowered her voice, her eyes locked with Jazz's. "Do not apologize for existing. Our biases, Travis's inability, and the Council's murderous bigotry are not your fault. They never will be. So don't ever apologize for it. You have done nothing but be a good and loyal servant to Travis, and a kind friend to the rest of us." She cracked a small smile. "And I hope you'll keep being one until we figure out how to set you free."

Tears were freely running down Jazz's face when she broke into a smile of relief. I gently let go of her hand as my own vision blurred.

Chapter Twenty-One

Guideline Forty-Six:

If you have the time, review. Make sure you didn't miss anything.

Two days later, Max joined those of us out in the smoke pit. I didn't even know he was a smoker. From the look of things, neither did anyone else. Kenny and Danny exchanged a glance and a shrug as Max lit up like the rest of us.

Hannah took a drag on her own, then tossed me my lighter back. "Ghost try to kill you today, Travis?"

I shrugged. "Not yet, but the day is young."

There were snickers all around. Kenny asked. "You seen her at all lately?"

I made sure not to look in Max's direction. Playing it cool, I shrugged, then thought of something and decided to go with it. "Every now and then." I took another drag, then enjoyed the view of the brick wall beyond the dock. "Just watching. Sometimes I hear her sing. I think she likes this show, oddly enough."

Hannah snorted. "Girl got a weird way of showing it."

I shrugged. "She likes y'all better than she likes me. You been left alone. She's tried to kill me three times so far. No idea what I did to piss her off, but I'd like to apologize."

That got a laugh all around, with the exception of Max. I decided to push it. "Funny thing, though. When I was locking up last night, I heard her screaming."

Danny looked incredulous. "Straight-up screaming?"

I shrugged again. "Yeah. Something about vitamins. It got weird."

Most of the cast looked confused at that one. Max was good. I barely saw him twitch.

Kenny cocked his head. "Vitamins?"

I shrugged. "Maybe it makes more sense to a ghost. I got no idea."

Max stubbed out his smoke and was the first one back through the door when Rocky called five. I hung back and watched the others go before stubbing out my own.

I smiled to myself. "Give o'er the play."

* * *

Connie marked another ward over the door in Rocky's office. It's a good thing George knew what we were really doing or he'd probably have already cussed us out over the "graffiti" we were leaving around the place.

Rocky finished her drink, tossing the can in the trash. "Please tell me you three have some good news."

Thumper and I shrugged. "We're pretty sure we can keep Ginny from killing anyone else. But she won't move on until she's killed Max."

Rocky snorted, smiling humorlessly. "Our meal ticket. Peachy."

Connie nodded. "That's the right attitude to go with. The ghost is Max's old girlfriend. He murdered her, in this theater, and now she's out for revenge."

Rocky blinked as the new information sank in. "What the fuck?" She looked around at all of our deadpan faces, then sighed. "I used to like this job." She took another soda out of the fridge, popping the top before taking a swig.

Connie continued. "We might be able to stop her, but we're gonna be cutting it close."

Rocky flopped into her office chair, putting her booted feet up on her desk. "How close?"

Thumper, in one of the comfier chairs, held up their thumb and forefinger less than an inch apart.

Connie dropped the bomb. "Opening night."

Rocky grinned, nearly giddy from the depths of sarcasm. "Even better."

I felt like contributing. "This show is Max's magnum opus. That's why he's dropping all this money and going with a skeleton crew. It's also why Harry bribed us on the day of the fire. I wouldn't be surprised if some inspectors got paid off too. That's the only reason I can think of for an asbestos-lined room full of nitrate film going unnoticed. Max is obsessed with this show being a hit and making him the kind of star he hasn't been since the 90's."

Connie took the lead from me. "The ghost knows it. She wants him dead just before he makes this show a hit. So she's going to try and take him just before the curtain falls on opening night."

Rocky took another swig. "So can you stop her? Or should I just take out a life insurance policy on Max?"

Connie sighed, then shrugged. "Maybe. Dr. Gull is still running around here. And we still don't even know who he is. He's either a cast member or a musician, but he could be any one of them. I'm sure we can keep Ginny from hurting anyone else. But Max might be toast no matter what we do. Either way, we're going to need more people."

Rocky blew a kiss to the sky. "Well, holy shit. Somewhere I can make a contribution. If you have more people, getting them onboard for opening night is easy. And I won't even have to bullshit anyone about why they're around."

Connie frowned. "What do you mean?"

Rocky grinned. "We just sent out the press release and subscriber emails today. Opening night is going to be an industry masquerade. A lot of local stars and hangers-on in the crowd. Cast, crew, and audience: all in masks."

Connie blinked. From across the room, I could see a plan begin to form in her mind. "That... actually helps a lot. We're just gonna need some comps."

* * *

The coven was assembled around the dinner table. Jazz insisted on serving, since we had a guest. But it was my turn to do the cooking, and I'd made lamb calzones. The remnants on every plate attested to either my skill or everyone's hunger. We had been working a lot lately.

Along with Jazz, Thumper, Connie, and Byron, Cyrus was at the table, putting a toothpick to good use. Glasses had been refilled and digestifs were loaded. Connie looked around the table, nodded to herself, and took the lead. "So opening night's the night. Ginny wants Max dead before the closing applause fills the house. Dr. Gull is somewhere in the building, either helping or hindering her for his own purposes. But by all accounts, he's looking for revenge on Max as well, so I'll take a wild guess and say he's helping."

Byron smirked. "The Phantom of the Opera is here. Naturally, he's from Florida."

I nodded. "Which leaves the million dollar question of exactly who he is."

Connie pointed at me. "Got it in one. We know he's someone in the building. And we know he's not one of us, Max, Rocky, Roscoe, or Mabel."

Cyrus looked quizzical. "No idea what identity he's using?"

Connie shook her head. "Nobody in the cast is visibly a century-old black man from Florida. Which means he's using a Gorlois pendant or something similar."

Gorlois pendants are powerful illusion magic. They can't change you into a specific person, but they can change all of your features. Anything a human looks like can become anything a human can look like.

I tapped the table with my fingertips. "Rocky claims she knows the rest of the crew, so they're vouched for."

Cyrus folded his hands. "So that just leaves what, the cast, the chorus, and the musicians?"

I blinked. "And Harry, the business manager."

Thumper and I traded nods. I went on. "According to Rocky, the band and the chorus have all worked with her before. They're young, but they've all been around the block."

Connie nodded. "How about Larry?"

I answered. "Him too. As well as all the other actors over 40."

Byron stroked his goatee. "That narrows it down. I don't suppose anyone else has conveniently come from Florida?"

Jazz shook her head. "The only member of the company from Florida is Mabel. She's apparently been doing costumes for theme parks and cruise ships for the last fifteen years. But we've already written her off."

Thumper shrugged.

Byron nodded. "Worth the asking."

Connie sipped her drink, then asked. "What about Jerry? The composer? Grover was his partner, and Grover was the first to go."

Thumper frowned, tapped their watch, then shook their head.

I nodded. "Thumper's right. Jerry doesn't have any time to creep around doing Phantom stuff. He's always playing in the pit. Dr. Gull had the time to steal those masks from wardrobe and wear them around. Jerry doesn't have the time to do it."

Connie pondered that. "True. How about Hannah?"

I shrugged. "Girl's definitely got a chip on her shoulder, but it's more about the industry than Max. If anything, she's been grateful for the gig."

Thumper seesawed their hand back and forth.

Jazz smirked. "That's one maybe."

Cyrus, who had been flipping through a stack of headshots, held up Dawn's. "How about your leading lady?"

I tilted my head. "It makes a bit of sense. Dawn's closer to Max than anyone. She gets a lot of stage time, but not so much that she doesn't get breaks here and there."

Byron shrugged. "If I was looking to take down my daughter's murderous old boytoy, arranging to be his new arm candy sounds like a solid method of arranging things."

Thumper grimaced. I nodded in agreement. "I'd be willing to go there myself, but it's had to have been an uncomfortable couple of weeks. Are they really being intimate?"

Connie shrugged. "Max and Dawn? Who knows? Normally I'd say yes. But they're both actors, so hiding their emotions is second nature. Not to mention any actual disorders in the mix. Which, given how often the theater gets used for amateur discount group therapy, I can't really rule out."

Cyrus frowned. "Seriously?"

Connie shuddered. "You have no idea."

Jazz nodded at the picture. "Two for two maybes."

I rolled my neck. "Which just leaves the younger gents." I counted off on my fingers. "Kenny, Danny, Tim, and Ron."

Connie spoke up for everyone else's benefit. "Romeo, Mercutio, Tybalt, and Paris, respectfully."

Cyrus nodded. "Any of them stood out?"

Thumper shrugged.

I smirked. "I got into it with Ron once over some stupid shit. He's annoying, but I never got any malice off of him, y'know? Felt like the kind of guy who's never been punched in his life. Or punched anyone in his life. Not a danger, just a pain in the ass."

Connie waved her hand back and forth "I dunno. He did talk shit about you in the smoke pit once or twice. Maybe it was just a measuring contest, but he might be able to work his way up to something."

Jazz smirked. "Another maybe."

Cyrus shuffled headshots to look at Kenny's. "What about our leading man?"

I nodded. "Definite maybe. He's the most professional of the bunch. Socializes the bare minimum, no stupid shit."

Connie chimed in. "Danny's not quite how Rocky described him. To hear her tell it, Danny would be all up in your personal space."

Byron cocked his head. "He's not?"

Connie shook her head. "No. He's more like you. He'd flirt with a rock if it was shiny enough. But he backs off when a girl's not interested. And he's intuitive enough that I didn't have to spell it out for him."

Byron nodded solemnly.

Jazz smirked. "That does sound like Byron."

I smiled, glad that Jazz felt comfortable enough to throw in a comment that wasn't entirely relevant because it amused her. It was another sign of her growing independence.

Connie gestured with her drink. "Tim, on the other hand, needed a clue-by-four before he'd leave me alone. He did back off once I spelled it out, I'll give him that."

Jazz tilted her head. "Should we eliminate him then? Surely a father on a mission of revenge wouldn't take the time for... intimate liaisons?"

Everyone male at the table suddenly looked uncomfortable. None of us, with the possible exception of Byron, had ever been in that particular scenario. But once we'd had the chance to think about it, none of us quite had the willpower to back Jazz up.

Thumper was snickering.

Connie rolled her eyes. "I think we can safely consider them still in the maybe pile."

I tapped the table. "Then there's Harry. The one headshot we don't have."

Connie nodded. "And Harry's either perfect or a hard no."

Cyrus cocked his head. "Why is that?"

I took a drink. "I wish we'd looked up how long Max and Harry have known each other. They're business partners and it's clear they started this venture together. Harry's willing to do the dirty financial work. He's definitely paid off the crew for looking the other way at workplace hazards. He's bribed building inspectors, and probably cops and first responders too. He knows ghost hunters exist, and he even brought in a priest. That and he's never onstage, so he's got plenty of time to plot when he's supposedly in his office."

Jazz smiled. "One more for the maybes then."

Cyrus had the headshots laid out before him. "Five men, two women. One of them a sickeningly powerful necromancer."

I drained the last of my drink. "Seven potentials, six of us. That's better odds than we had at Stone Mountain."

Cyrus looked over the top of his glasses at me. "At Stone Mountain we weren't in a badly haunted building full of several hundred standers with the Council waiting to come down on us like a load of bricks."

Connie grinned. "We also have more time to plan, and even time to rehearse. Thumper's got ahold of some new toys, and they brought enough for everyone..."

Chapter Twenty-Two

Guideline Fifty-Two:

Move most of your pieces in the opening of the game.

We had a bigger crowd than I expected. Max, the show, and the theater itself had all been attracting buzz for months, and with opening night being an industry masquerade, it was attracting a lot of Atlanta's showbiz names. We hadn't bothered with a red carpet, but you wouldn't know it from the suits and evening gowns filling the lobby. Ushers were scanning barcodes and handing out masks as quickly as they could. We were going to end up filling the house, balcony and all.

It was an hour before places. The cast and musicians had already warmed up, and Rocky supervised the cast as they went over every dance number and every fight scene. They'd done them all dozens of times by now, but apparently it was custom to do them again before every show, just to make sure their bodies have it in them before going onstage to do it all for real.

I snickered to myself. I was starting to think like theater people now. More than one of them had referred to tonight as "the real thing." Given how much time they'd spent in the building, where everything from the air temperature to the ambient light was chosen for aesthetics, it sounded partly delusional and partly arrogant. But here I was, going along with it all.

We weren't supernaturally alone either. Jazz and Byron were already in the crowd, escorting each other. I'd booked them a limo for the evening, just to put them even more in place among the glitterati. Chittenden paid me a nice retainer, I figured I might as well splurge every now and then. Jazz and Byron were decked out as an evening formal take on Aladdin and Scheherazade, and were turning heads easily. Byron was already a social butterfly and played the role perfectly. Jazz, accustomed to being seen more than heard, was charming enough to be eye candy but not so stunning as to distract from Byron's blunt force charm.

From outside the coven, Calista looked lovely in her best Gothic finery. Flense slightly less so, but you could tell he'd at least tried to have what he wore tailored. I noticed Lady Mariah with a local actor whose name I couldn't remember. Henry and Elaine Warwell, of the magically infamous Warwell family, were deep in the crowd, looking every inch the elder upper crust. Lady Sina, a former mentor of mine, was in the mix, on the arm of her majordomo, Glenn.

Over half of the crowd wore the stock white domino masks we were giving out at the box office. The rest had brought their own, with varying degrees of elaboration. I saw everything from sugar skulls to Venetian carnival masks to animal features.

I was hanging out near one of the balcony staircases, wearing a stock mask and one of the comfortable black suits I used to wear to look respectable back in my renfield days. I was killing time drinking a soda in a solo cup as the crowd rolled in. My right earpiece led to a radio linked to Rocky's base station in the booth. My left earpiece was one of Thumper's new toys. It operated a limited telepathic net controlled by a base unit in Thumper's pocket. Thumper was in the booth and Connie was backstage, both of them dressed like I was.

At the back of the crowd, I saw Cyrus step in the door, get his ticket scanned, and don his mask. Satisfied, I let a bit of magic flow into my left earpiece. A gentle pressure against my temple let me know it was activated.

I gently thought. *"The gang's all here."*

Thumper's voice came to my mind. *"All wings report in."*

"Connie, standing by."

I thought again. *"Travis, standing by."*

"Byron, standing by."

"Jasmine, standing by."

"Cyrus, standing by."

"Lock S-foils in attack positions."

"What's an S-foil?"

"Ignore them, Jazz. Thumper's just being a dork."

I dropped my empty cup in a garbage can and headed up the stairs, past a winged fae-looking lady and a red fox in a tuxedo. I thanked whatever Gods were listening that my ex-security self wasn't stuck checking ID's and a guest list.

Then I blinked. Someone I'd never expected had walked in. I'd only ever seen him through a screen, but it was impossible not to recognize Brandon and his mother, who looked bound and determined to make him a proper escort one way or another. From the look of it, Brandon was arguing with her at every step. She looked every inch the grande dame, perfectly at home among the glamorous assembled. His suit looked like he hadn't ironed it since his Senior prom. What conversation his mother was beginning, he either ignored, rolled his eyes, or grumbled. I murmured to myself, "if it isn't fortune's fool," as I watched Brandon pull away and head for the restrooms. I followed as inconspicuously as I could.

Cyrus' thought came over the net. *"Travis, what've you got?"*

I shrugged. *"Just a chance to reinforce some education for America's young people."*

I followed Brandon into the lobby men's room and went to wash my hands, noticing him sit down in a stall not far from the urinals. The only other person in the room finished drying their hands and walked out.

I had seconds at best. If I tuned it right, I'd rattle the walls in here, but not be heard in the lobby. I let a trickle of magic flow into my throat, then spoke in the voice of a demon.

"YOU STILL NEED TO BEHAVE AROUND LADIES, BRANDON."

I turned on my heel and walked out nonchalantly, letting the door close on Brandon's startled cry of, "motherf..."

Within two steps I was back in the crowd. Twenty steps later, I was back at the base of the balcony stairs and could see Brandon out of the corner of my eye, equal parts terrified and enraged, bursting out of the restroom. A few passing guests glanced at him, wondering what all the fuss was about. I kept my poker face on, but thought. *"Education reinforced. We'll see how Brandon does in the future."*

Thumper cut in. *"He's here?"*

I nodded before remembering the gesture was useless. *"Him and his mom."*

Cyrus cut in. *"Who's Brandon?"*

I could see some commotion coming from the stage right-side hallway. *"Long story. We'll tell you later."*

Max appeared from the hallway at the head of an entourage, looking immaculate in a tuxedo of his own, a white carnation in his lapel. He wore one of Romeo's spare masks from the production itself. Dawn was on his arm, dolled up to perfection. Surrounding them were a handful of celebrities I recognized and a double handful of older, very well-dressed people I didn't. I thought, *"Max is in the lobby. Jazz, Byron, you're up."*

"Opening night jitters, Mr. Wayland?"

I turned to see Lady Mariah, in an evening gown that probably cost more than my truck. It somehow flattered her figure and let her fade into the background at will all at once. If she'd arrived with an escort, he'd conveniently disappeared, leaving her looking down her mask at me.

I smiled and shrugged. "Greasepaint's roaring, crowd smells, the usual. The audience being the last part of the show to really make it happen and all that."

She smiled with no mirth. "Found your ghost yet, Mr. Wayland? Or the good Doctor?"

I matched her look. "They're around and about."

She tilted her head mischievously. "My goodness. Are we safe, then?"

I shrugged. "We cut the chandelier scene, if that's what worried you."

Her smile grew. "Ah, so you haven't dealt with them. How exciting."

From across the hall, Jazz opened her arms and let the entire lobby hear her. "Max, darling!"

Max blinked, clearly having no idea who she was. That wasn't a surprise, given that the two of them had never met. But his instinct with a masked face and an expansive bosom approaching him at speed was a warm smile, open arms, and a vague welcome. "Hey! How you doing?"

Her smile dazzled. "Looking forward to your new opus, dear."

She was good. I was watching for it and I barely saw Jazz slip something into Max's tuxedo pocket. As Max was distracted by another well-wisher and Jazz withdrew, I heard her voice in my ear.

"*Package delivered.*"

I turned back to Mariah and kept my tone easygoing. "Been to a lot of nights like this, Lady?"

Her resting bitch face solidified. "More times than you've had hot meals."

"How would you judge the mood tonight?"

She ran her professional eye over the crowd for a moment. "More optimistic than usual for this town. Max is a C-lister, B-lister if he'd had a good year. This show will make him or break him, which is always good for the gossip-mongers."

I nodded, proving I was paying attention. "Think he'll be a star again if this goes off right?"

"Possibly. But I think his current arm candy stands to gain even more."

That was new. "Who, Dawn?"

I swear I saw her fangs flash. "Oh, yes. She's working the crowd like she was born to it. She's just the right... everything. Pretty enough to turn heads, but not so stunning you can't be convinced she's the girl next door. Skilled enough to do much more complex work than she is, but not so heavily trained as to wrap herself around the axle. A success here properly handled and she'll be on the short list to a piece of Oscar bait by Christmas."

A pop came from across the room. The young cast members, in formal wear of their own, were hooting and hollering in Max's wake. I turned to see Kenny holding a frothing bottle of champagne aloft, pouring out for his fellows. Danny headed over with two flutes, passing them over to Max and Dawn. I couldn't hear the toast, but I could see out of the corner of my eye an impending crisis. I didn't know everything about theater etiquette even now, but I was pretty sure celebratory drinks happened after a performance, not before.

Mariah sniffed. "That one's got some solid brass ones on him. Doesn't your stage manager keep a tighter leash on her actors?"

I stepped away from her with a pardoning finger in the air, keyed my radio, and spoke aloud. "Rocky, I'm in the lobby. Are you seeing this?"

"Coming up on your right, behind you."

I turned, seeing Rocky's purple ponytail behind one of our domino masks. I could tell she was pissed, but determined not to let it show. I just nodded. "Orders?"

"Everyone downs their one drink then gets their asses backstage. This kind of shit is for after a successful opening night, not before."

"Copy that." I headed for the crowd and thought into my other ear.

"Travis here. I'm gonna start wrangling actors."

"Byron here, Jazz and I are heading for our seats."

"Cyrus here. I got eyes on Max."

Rocky kept her poker face as she slid through the crowd easily, making it to Max's side. Without hesitation, she whispered in Max's ear. He immediately nodded, pounded down his flute like it was a shot, left the flute on a nearby table and clapped his hands. "All right, folks! Let's get seated! We got a great show for you tonight!"

Dawn kissed him impulsively, then dashed off, passing me as she went. Rocky and myself went to work herding the rest of the cast backstage swiftly. Danny and Kenny giggled like naughty children. Hannah smirked, amused at a joke only she knew. Ron tried to keep from sneering at me. But one by one, they all disappeared into the hallway and to their duties. If fight call hadn't happened an hour before, we might have had a mutiny.

I patrolled like a hall monitor for the next half hour, making sure there were no other opening night shenanigans and trying to burn off some of the nervous energy I'd built up since the audience had started to arrive. You could feel their excitement in the air, like an approaching storm.

By the time I returned to the lobby, the last of the audience were filing into the house and taking their seats. I watched as Jazz, Byron, and Cyrus all took spots where they could keep watch on Max. I watched the last stragglers as they slipped through the closing doors just as Rocky's voice came in on my other earpiece. *"Cross your fingers and hold your hearts. It's places."*

"Thank you, places."

* * *

With the overture beginning to play, I was nearly the only one left in the lobby. A single usher was manning the concession stand, his compatriots all having snuck inside to claim standing room in the far back. George, still in his janitor's jumpsuit, now decorated with a stock mask, was policing up the remains of the toast. We traded nods as I headed down the hallway, past the restrooms and straight to Max's office. After double checking to see nobody else was there, I stuck a tension wrench into the door's lock and shoved it to one side. A few moments with a pick and I let myself in.

I'd never been in Max's office. Unlike Harry's or Rocky's offices, there was a minimum of paperwork and a maximum of luxury. A red velvet couch suitable for either a nap or a quickie, a full bar and fridge, and another one of those boat anchor desks with a laptop and desk phone nearby. Above the desk was a full-length tapestry depicting, of all things, the poster from one of Max's old movies. Opposite the couch was a full-length mirror in an ornate frame. After glancing up to check, I was briefly thankful there wasn't another one on the ceiling.

Beyond the bar was a private bathroom complete with a shower. On the bar was an elaborate bouquet in a vase. A bunch of orange and yellow flowers surrounding a single blossom that was so deeply purple I thought it was black at first. There was no card or anything attached.

I couldn't sense any wards, bugs, or booby traps in the room. But there was more electricity flowing through the room than the décor would normally allow. On a hunch, I gingerly pulled the tapestry aside. Behind it was a bank of screens showing security camera placements. One at the smoke pit, one at the front entrance, one showing the stage, one showing the house, one on the roof, and one in the green room.

That explained the other cameras. Max was in the house directing the show most of the time. So either the feeds from these were recorded and watched elsewhere, or someone else was using Max's office. Before I could look further, I heard a voice in my left earpiece.

"Travis, coming up on you."

I opened the door and Connie slid inside. I closed the door again as she began warding the room. It looked like she was scattering salt and scribbling random graffiti with a sharpie, but I learned long ago not to question the mundanity of someone else's magic. I did, however, warn everyone else through my earpiece about the monitors.

After a moment, she stood and nodded. I drew my wand, indicated the bathroom, and she moved to back me up. I crossed the threshold and cleared the bathroom quickly, satisfied there was nothing unpleasant waiting for us there.

We returned to the office, and then Connie immediately stopped short at the bouquet. Her lips didn't move. I heard her voice in my ear. *"Were those flowers there when you came in?"*

I nodded. She grabbed the vase and handed it over to me. *"Burn them. Quick."*

I headed into the bathroom, pulling a lighter out of my pocket as I thought. *"Dr. Gull's?"*

Connie was scribbling more on the bar. *"Yellow roses for infidelity and greed. Orange lilies for passionate hatred. Sunflowers for delusions of grandeur. And a black dahlia for betrayal."*

"Makes sense." I flicked my lighter, muttered a quick incantation, then blew a thin stream of flame at the bouquet. The fresh flowers dried, then burned up instantly, and with less smoke than an incense stick. I dumped the smoldering stems in the sink and turned on the water, drenching them.

I turned the water off, dumped the wet ashes in the garbage, and stepped back into the office as Connie was finishing up.

She nodded. *"Max's office is warded. No ghost is getting in here."*

I put the tapestry back in place. We both slipped out into the empty hallway as I locked the door behind us, then split up. Connie headed across the lobby to backstage left while I headed to the corner stairs to go down two flights and head backstage right.

When I reached the stairwell, I spoke into my other earpiece. "Rocky, Travis. I'm in place."

"Copy that." I heard in my ear.

* * *

I got backstage right as the applause from the opening number was dying down. The chorus were dropping off their knives from the big opening brawl and getting in place to backup Romeo's "I Want" song. Danny high-fived me as he went past. Hannah gave me a wink before disappearing into Mabel's care to quick-change before her next scene.

The energy in the building was constant now, and becoming addictive. It felt like the emotional equivalent of being near a live electric fence. These performers were at the top of their game. They'd been given the resources to do their very best. Now they were proving how good they could do in front of a crowd of their peers and critics.

And somewhere in the midst of it all was a ghost who wanted their director dead and a necromancer who wanted to help things along. No pressure.

With Rocky's cues in one ear, I kept my other senses out for anything amiss. On a vague hunch I picked up one of the prop knives. It was bigger than I'd expected, being a little over a foot long. It had been machined out of aluminum bar stock. The bevels gave it a fake harmon line, but the point was still rounded and the edge about an eighth of an inch thick. Butter knives in prison cafeterias were more of a cutting hazard. Benny, the fight choreographer, was an old friend of Rocky's who looked like he modeled for romance novel covers. He'd shown me one day how much effort went into making the actors look like they were slaughtering each other without unfortunate accidents happening. Gull or Ginny would have to go to some effort to hurt anyone with Benny's tools. It was still a possibility, which is why I'd checked a knife at random before putting it back.

As Connie and I kept up with our half-dozen suspects, the show kept drawing my attention. I'd seen it in rehearsal countless times. I knew every song and what was going to happen. But watching it happen now still kept clawing back at my attention.

Several scenes later, I didn't even notice Mabel coming up until her hand was already on my shoulder. She murmured in my ear. "Don't mind you getting a good view, honey. But these masks are going to get real popular real quick."

Sheepishly, I stepped out of the way of the mask rack. Moments later, half the cast came in to take and don their own. Familiar faces already painted in the lurid makeup that let them be seen from the seats disappeared beneath carnival visages. Bright colors, glittering sequins and features stretched to cartoon proportions consumed my colleagues, transforming each into true party animals as they broke the legs of the curtain to the ballroom sequence's entrance.

Behind my own mask, my eyes flickered here and there. I still didn't know who Dr. Gull was, or where he'd strike. At least one life still hung in the balance tonight.

And yet, a part of me was content in ways I hadn't been in years. The secret that divided my coven, however uncomfortably, had been shared gratefully. The danger from the Council, the world, that was still there. But my covenmates accepted it, and were as willing to fight as I was. There was an infamous necromancer here tonight, but so what? I had four mages, an elf, and a djinn working in concert to stop him.

Now there was just a murderer to rescue from vengeance beyond the grave and a show to go on. No big deal.

It was taking all of my concentration to keep checking every corner instead of follow the show. I've suspended my disbelief before, but in the middle of all this, I was having to strap it down with duct tape.

The music slowed and shifted, the rowdy choral number becoming what I'd heard in the stairwells so many times before. But this time with the entire band at their prime and with the chorus backing them up. Kenny and Dawn stared at each other amid the swirling dancers, beginning to sing.

What do I see?
What am I feeling?
An angel. A ghost.
A source of this yearning.

Gods, I thought. Was I ever that young? That stupid? A memory floated across my mind. Bloodstained hands reaching out from still bodies. Bodies that an hour before had been young, vibrant, stupid, but most of all hopelessly in love. You could still see echoes of it in their eyes that stared openly at nothing. Approaching them were tracks in the dirt from where, dying slow and ugly, they had crawled to each other. Those same stained hands clutching each other tight in their last grasps, laid on the ground soil of the park turned battlefield of a lifetime ago. The night that so much was taken from us.

Then there was another body. The beautiful eyes I'd been lost in for so long were staring at nothing, the spirit behind them long gone.

Then there was the night before. The planning night. When we knew what we were going to do. When we knew we were probably going to die. How many of us spent that night holding onto each other? Clinging to one of the few who understood and cared when the darkness surrounded us?

The song reminded me of the days before that night. When we were young and in love and fascinated with each other and all of it. When each moment lasted a lifetime, before we learned that lifetimes could only last moments. I could still smell the sandalwood and leather. I could still feel the skin under my hands.

If I could know you without knowing destruction
I could feel like a star from the void out in space
come hurling down uncontrolled trusting
I could slow my approach, and take my own pace.

Kenny and Dawn stepped closer to each other, the dancers around them opening up to let their paths cross without comment. They seemed awestruck, as if each other were the only people in the room. The only people in the world. Their hands met, then their lips.

Over a thousand people in the house fell in love with them on the spot.

I knew in this moment that this was a kind of magic I could barely recognize, and once swept up in it, I'd be rendered helpless. And a part of me wanted it anyway.

Tears welling under my mask, I forced myself to look away, and concentrate on the hunt.

Chapter Twenty-Three

Guideline Fifty-Five:

Plan on the map, but drive on the road.

Knives flashed. Bodies flew. People screamed.

It was easy to see what was going on and who was doing what to who, which is the easiest way to tell it wasn't a real fight. But the play had let everyone care about what happened to these characters, and threatening them was keeping the audience on the edges of their seats.

The duel that closed Act One moved fast and furious. Tim and Kenny danced in vicious crossing spirals, barely missing each other as the chorus called for blood. I knew every step in the dance, every note in the music, and I knew it was all an illusion. I'd also checked every last one of the knives, and I knew damn well they were dull, rounded, inert lumps of aluminum.

But I was swept up again. In the music. In the story. My coworkers had vanished, and in their bodies were two people I'd never met, and they were trying to kill each other. Was this what Seb and Jukka were talking about? It must have been.

In my right earpiece came a steady stream of cues as Rocky called the show. Lights, sound effects, the band, and the set, all changed at her call and command.

The music built to a crescendo as Danny charged the two in an attempt to break it up, and halted just as Tim managed to fake stabbing Danny. Danny's body seized, muscles clenching tight under the lights. I heard a faint whisper of a bassline before Danny's fingers uncurled, his knife landing on the deck. He clutched Kenny, smiling in a way that broke hearts. I heard gasps as Danny broke away from Kenny, staggering. He made it to the central stairs and slowly began to climb. The lights dimmed everywhere else as a shaft of light shone through the stairway. Danny arched his back and let out a scream of anguish, clutching his side.

Everyone's eyes were on Danny. But buried backstage left, I was the only one who saw his face. In the sudden drop in the music, I could hear a guttural murmur I recognized as an incantation. Danny's eyes flashed green for an instant before singing his final notes.

I frantically thought. *"Did anyone else see that?"*

Byron answered. *"The guy playing Mercutio just cast a damn spell up-stage center."*

Connie came in. *"Danny is Dr. Gull. He has to be."*

The band played the last note.

Rocky came in over my headset. *"And blackout."*

The bright stage lights cut out.

The audience roared like a single giant animal with a thousand clapping hands.

Dim blue lights shone over the stage and glow-in-the-dark lines painted on the floor let the cast scurry offstage and away to their dressing rooms. The cast scattered, disappearing into shadows.

Up on the second level of the set, Danny ran off stage left and ran into the wings. As he reached the escape stairs, he saw me offstage right, his eyes meeting mine in an instant. His eyes shone a familiar shade of green and he smiled wickedly before giving me a two-fingered salute, vanishing into the shadows.

* * *

The audience was on their feet and not letting up. I lost sight of Danny, just managing to duck out of the way as the cast fled for their dressing rooms. I resisted the urge to go for either my wand or my gun. This would be an ideal time for Ginny to strike.

I thought. *"I've lost Gull. Someone in the house keep eyes on Max."*

I heard Byron's voice in my head. *"I got Max."*

Connie's voice followed. *"I lost Gull too, but now I know what to look for."*

Rocky's voice came over the headset. *"That's intermission, everyone. Fifteen minutes."*

I clicked my radio and murmured, "Thank you, fifteen."

A moment later, I heard Thumper in my head. *"Trav, Danny's the only cast member who didn't make it to the green room or the dressing rooms. Wherever he is, he's out of my sight."*

I walked into the offstage right corridor and headed for the lobby before thinking. *"Understood. Byron, how's Max?"*

"Just ducked into his office. Looked a little green around the gills."

I nodded, then remembered nobody could see me from where I was. *"Got it. I'm heading down to the scene shop, then up and across the stage right corridors."*

"Connie here. I'm heading to the roof and working my way down the stage left side."

* * *

Thumper would've told me if Danny had shown up at the loading dock, so I didn't bother there. Instead I headed past the stage right dressing rooms, then down the stairs. I saw nobody that wasn't supposed to be there. The cast and rest of the crew were all going about their own business, giddy with the adrenaline rush. None of them were giving me a second glance. The first act had wowed the audience. They were pumped up and now they had to keep their energy up to top it. I forced my urge to join them down somewhere deep in my chest and focused on finding Danny.

As I passed Dawn's dressing room, she opened the door and held out a hand to stop me. Her makeup, which had looked fine under the stage lights, looked garish and uncanny in the harsh fluorescence of the hallway. She'd also apparently caught a crisis in mid-costume change, but at this point I'd gotten used to actors spontaneously running around in their underwear.

"Travis! Please tell me you have some Pepto-bismol or something."

I blinked. "Yeah, it's in my kit. Gimme a sec."

Rocky had actually had time to show Connie and I how ASM's worked, and she believed in being prepared as much as I did. So I was not only prepped for fighting a hostile necromancer, I was ready for a dozen or so minor emergencies. I took a knee and unslung my day pack as Dawn went on.

"Thank God. I dunno what I ate, but it's being brutal."

"Well, you're doing great. The audience is eating it up." I passed over a pink bottle and a green packet. "Here ya go, plus some chewing gum to freshen up once you fix up."

"Thank you! You're a lifesaver."

She grabbed the goods and bolted back into her room. I got up and went back to trying to hunt down Danny. After a second I remembered to radio in. "Rocky, Travis."

"*Go, Travis.*"

"Dawn's got a bellyache of some kind. Doesn't looks serious, but she's been given meds and mints."

"*Copy that.*"

We couldn't discuss Gull or Ginny on Rocky's net, what with various stagehands and a sound tech listening in. But by now, Thumper had passed Rocky a note to keep her in the loop.

The scene shop was empty of people. Tools hung neatly on their racks. The storage bays were nearly empty. With tonight being the first show in decades, there were no old set pieces wedged into wherever they would fit. I could see where fresh coats of paint had been spread before everything had been loaded in. I flashed my light into what dark corners I could find, looking like an ASM trying to find a needed widget in case anyone asked. Nothing caught my senses, so I moved on.

Some of the musicians passed me as I opened up the under stage area. This close to the house, I could hear the murmur of hundreds of people chatting about what they'd just seen. I cleared the room as fast as I dared, noting the undisturbed dust. The remaining musicians looked up as I opened the door and glanced around the pit, but none of them asked what I was up to. An ASM on the hunt can go where they damn well please.

Wardrobe was empty of people, but packed to the gills with clothes. The trapdoor hadn't been used. Mabel was nowhere to be seen. A couple of naked mannequins were lined up, ready to go back into further storage. Two other mannequins near the doors had backup versions of Friar Laurence and the Nurse's ballroom outfits, complete with masks. I touched both to make sure they were still mannequins. In my line of work, you never know.

I turned on the light in the rehearsal hall, but the moment I stepped inside, the temperature dropped several degrees. Danny was nowhere to be seen, but Ginny was here and clearly wasn't happy. I nodded politely and stepped right back out, turning out the light and feeling the temperature return to normal the moment I shut the door. That was new. Either Ginny was distracted by opening night or I'd followed some rules I didn't know for sure. I refused to look the gift horse in the mouth and reported in instead.

"Ginny's in the rehearsal hall. No sign of Gull yet."

Thumper's voice came in my head. *"Still no sign of him on the cameras."*

Jazz's voice followed. *"Max is still in his office."*

Connie chimed in. *"What's Ginny up to?"*

I blinked and thought for a moment. *"Defensive, but not aggressive. It's like she's waiting for her cue."*

Thumper commented. *"No wonder she's occupying the rehearsal hall."*

I went up every level on the right side of the building, checking room by room. No traps, no hidden shadows. No people. Only the gathered murmur of the audience, their tongues loosened by the intermission, following me throughout the halls. My senses were straining, and I was clutching my wand. By the time I went up the last level, I was openly sweating even in the air conditioning.

At the top floor, I could feel the chill begin as I reached for the doorknob of the apartment.

I backed off, turning and heading back down the stairs.

"No sign of Gull, but I've felt Ginny in the apartment too."

Connie's voice came to mind. *"No sign of either of them on the left."*

I nodded to an empty hallway again. *"Heads on swivels. We know Ginny can change where doorways lead, and gods only know what Gull's capable of."*

Byron spoke up. *"Max is out of his office and heading back to his seat. He's looking kind of weird though."*

Connie responded before I could. *"Keep an eye on him, Byron. Cyrus, Jazz, hang back. Hide in the bathrooms if you need to, then join us in the corridors. I have stage left, Travis has right."*

Rocky's voice sounded in my ear. *"Five minutes to places, everyone."*

I took a second to catch my breath. I'd wandered around half the theater ready for a fight in less than fifteen minutes.

My voice had a slight echo as I came down the stairs. "Thank you five."

* * *

As the fire curtain rose and the music reverberated through the building, I stood just offstage right. Kenny high-fived me before picking up his knife off the prop table. I'd double-checked his knife as well as Tim's. I tried to keep my senses up all around. Cyrus and Jazz were both using some sort of illusion magic now. Their masks would only hide the fact that they weren't supposed to be backstage for so long.

The opening to Act Two was intense and fast-paced, showing Romeo's hunting down of Tybalt. I was nervous as a cobra at a mongoose convention, wondering what set piece would collapse or what lamp would fall from the grid. The intense rock music used for the sequence didn't help. Seb hadn't been kidding when he talked about music short-circuiting the brain. I could feel it trying to do that to me, and the story was doing the same thing.

To my amazement, it all went on without a hitch. Tybalt died and Tim, unscathed, was carried offstage, where he instantly got back on his feet and headed back to his dressing room under his own power. Another power ballad covered Romeo's lament and banishment.

As the audience applauded their way into a scene change, I heard Connie's voice in my mind.

"Sound off."

"Thumper. No sign on the screens."

I joined in. *'Travis. Loud and clear, no changes."*

"Byron. Max is right where he's supposed to be. Looks kinda weird though. He's not clapping. Not cheering. Not smiling. Nothing."

"Connie. Thump, Max has access to your camera feeds in his office. Anything in the last few minutes that would've riled him up?"

"Thumper. Nothing that I can tell."

"Jazz here. I'm just past the booth. No sign of our quarry."

Connie replied. *"Copy that. Cyrus?"*

There was no answer. I felt my heart sink.

"Cyrus?"

Chapter Twenty-Four

Guideline Forty-Eight:

Good when you need it is always better than perfect too late.

I've got him! Left hallway, even with the stage!

My feet responded instantly. My tongue fought the urge to be grateful Cyrus was still alive and curse him for scaring me that much. Another burst of willpower and I resisted the urge to cross behind the stage, turning and bolting down the hallway, past the dressing room and around the back. Cast and crew made a hole without being asked. A running stage manager outranks everybody.

With the hall clear before me, I thought. *"I'm on my way!"*

Connie thought a moment after. *"I'll be there in seconds."*

I ran down the hall and curved around, past the loading dock. *"Byron, keep your eyes on Max."*

"Roger that."

I turned the corner and came face to face with Connie coming up the other way.

I blinked, then realized it instantly. Cyrus didn't know the halls connecting to the lobby were a level above the stage. I almost opened my mouth before Connie pointed at the ceiling. I nodded as she ran past, following her up the stairway.

I blew past her at the landing to hug the opposite wall, wand out.

The hall above was as empty as the one below.

Connie and I looked at each other, then thought in stereo. *"STAGE left!"*

We took off in a dead run, curving around the back of the building. We passed the storage rooms without thinking. Connie was normally faster, but I had longer legs. I pulled ahead of her as the corner came up. I drew my sidearm. I could hear the familiar clunking sound of Connie's e-tool unfolding.

As we arrived, we could hear a low, slow whistle. It was a tune I didn't recognize.

We turned the corner, weapons hot. Halfway down the hall, near an open door of one of the storage rooms, we could see the slim form of Dr. Gull. His face was still that of an actor in his late twenties. But his gait was so different. He carried himself like a king now. His eyes, which had been so bright and full of mischief, were as intense as any professional fighter in a life-and-death encounter. He was still in his bloodied costume from Act One. He was also crouched over the still form of Cyrus, who was crumpled in a heap on the floor. Dr. Gull continued to whistle the low and slow tune.

I stopped just outside of knife fighting distance, resisting the urge to breathe deep. I'd been getting a workout in tonight.

Connie beat me there. "Dr. Gull, I presume?"

He stood upright, flashing his bright smile. "Oh, you can still call me Danny, girl."

I lined up my sights on his center of mass. "You're not taking Max. And neither is Ginny."

I saw rage mixed in amusement flash in his eyes. "You're not in a place to say who's taking who, boy." He whistled another verse of the tune I didn't recognize.

"Who's the asshole that's whistling backstage? It's opening night, dammit!"

An irate Ron stepped out of the open storage room door and almost wet his pants. His eyes bulged in my direction. His phone fell from his twitching hands, clattering on the tile floor. Somehow in all of the terror he managed to hiss in a stage whisper. "Travis? What the hell are you doing with a gun in the theater?"

I kept my eyes on Gull but still blinked, not losing my focus. "I'm holding the killer at gunpoint, Ron."

Ignoring my words completely, he nearly shrieked. "But what the hell do you need a gun for?"

I forced my eyes not to roll. "To shoot him if he runs, dumbass. They're really useful that way."

Ron finally noticed, in order, Connie, Gull, and Cyrus, who still wasn't moving. Ron backed into the doorframe, cringing when he realized that brought him closer to me. He was on the verge of panic. "Danny's the killer?"

Connie grimaced. "Well, technically his daughter is. It's kind of a long story."

Ron's jaw dropped. He looked Gull straight in the eyes. "You have kids?"

I gritted my teeth. "Ron, we're kind of in the middle of something. Please go run your lines or whatever."

Ron threw his hands up. "This is crazy! We're in the middle of a show run! Who the hell is on the floor? And what the hell are you doing holding a gun on Danny? I'm calling the cops!"

Ron lunged away from my muzzle straight into Dr. Gull, who grabbed him by the throat with a single hand.

I dropped my muzzle, scooted sideways, and targeted Gull again. "Let him go, Doctor! He's got nothing to do with this."

Ron, eyes bulging, looked frantically at Gull. "You're a Doctor?"

Gull yanked Ron towards him until they were close enough to kiss, his gaze boring into that of the squirming actor. "Take a nap, boy."

I saw Ron's eyes flutter shut and his body slump forward into the Doctor's arms.

I didn't see the packet of gods know what wrapped in gingham that the Doctor tossed onto the floor with his other hand.

Connie did see the packet, and had just enough time to avert her eyes and open her mouth to warn me before the world went white.

* * *

"Travis?"

"Travis!"

I blinked, trying to realize which voice I was hearing and by which method. As my eyes readjusted to the dim light of the hallway, I saw Connie crouched over the bodies of Cyrus and Ron.

Dr. Gull was out of sight.

I was starting to hear Rocky in my ear again. *"What the hell was that?"*

I holstered my pistol and took a knee beside Connie. "Same spell we know?"

She nodded. "It's gonna take me a minute, but I can get Cyrus back up and running."

The spell has had different names at different times and places: Sleeping Beauty, Naptime, Freddy's Hug, Super Siesta, you name it. Essentially drops a human being directly into REM sleep. It's one of the first things you learn in study hall. Makes dealing with single witnesses to magical doings a lot easier. Unfortunately, the side effects can be ugly. Starting with the nightmares. Most mages don't bother with it anymore, as even video evidence isn't something most believe these days. But if you really need it, it comes in handy.

I nodded, then got up. "Got it. I'm gonna go make the show go on."

She rummaged in her bag as she asked. "How?"

I grabbed Ron's feet and dragged him into the storage room. "Marines and actors do it the same scary way. Improvising."

As Connie worked on reviving Cyrus, I thought. *"Cyrus is down. Gull is in the wind. Ginny's waiting to strike when the curtain falls, so we need to prolong that until we catch Gull again."*

Thumper's voice came in my head. *"Standing by."*

I headed to the stairwell and hurried two levels down. *"Connie's reviving Cyrus. Gull hasn't changed out of his costume. Byron, stay on Max. Jazz, you're up. Go to the lowest level and into the wardrobe shop. It's in the back left corner as you're facing the stage. I'll meet you there."*

Thumper's voice came in again as I made it to the costume shop. *"Trav, Rocky said she misses you."*

I grimaced and thought. *"You're right. I'm being rude."*

I flipped on the lights and thanked the Gods that Mabel wasn't there. Then I made sure my radio was on and keyed the mic. "Hey Rocky."

"Hi Travis, I missed you. What the fuck are you doing to my theater?"

I pulled off my mask and shrugged out of my shirt and tie. "Sorry about that. Danny's the necromancer. He's on the loose, but we're working on that. Ron is down. He's OK, but I'm gonna put in his understudy."

Jazz stepped into the room. I pointed to a mannequin, twirled my finger, and nodded. As I unbuckled my belt, she set her own mask aside and undid her top.

"You're gonna what?"

I only took half a breath before grabbing a robe.

* * *

Kenny sang his heart out, breaking audience hearts with every note.

In his lament at the last thing he needed to do, Romeo popped the lock on the gate of the crypt with the crowbar. Chains fell. The iron gate creaked open. Downstage, lit like a classical painting and just high enough to take a knee beside, Juliet lay on a bier. She'd lived fast, died young, and was doing a great impression of a good-looking corpse.

As Kenny knelt by the bier, I stepped into the frame of the gate left behind, and was nearly knocked to the ground by the onslaught of light.

A semicircle of lights I'd spent a week aiming and focusing were all shining on me at once. The vast house was full of gazes. Full of eyes. All intent on what was happening. The lights washed out any individual faces, leaving just a sea of masked silhouettes.

I'd seen the house dozens of times by now. I'd never seen it full of audience and ready to pounce. A terror shot through my body, one that made no sense to me but kept me at the spot anyway. I'd faced more kinds of death than I had fingers. But this was beyond death. This was risking the disapproval of an entire world. A world I was intruding in. A world I had no place in. A world I didn't belong to be in.

It was a place I had to go to keep people alive. So I treated it like a death and charged.

I stepped forward upstage center, dressed in Friar Laurence's ballroom robe and mask. If we all survived, I hoped Larry would forgive me. I did as best an imitation of his voice as I could. It helps that I've got a baritone with an NCO's kick to it.

"You're not going to need that crowbar, son. Paris isn't going to be joining us."

Larry, when he woke up, would forgive me. Rocky, who was swearing loudly in my ear, was another story.

Kenny, in his final set of Romeo finery, stood dumbfounded at the sudden improv. I took that as a cue and kept going. "Nor will you need that poison. She lives."

Kenny valiantly tried rolling with it. "Why come you hither?"

An alto voice called from upstage, right behind me. "Because you two cannot be trusted! You've known each other a few days! Two people have already died for you! And you fools are bound and determined to make it all for nothing!" Jazz, in the Nurse's dress and ballroom mask, strode through the gate like she owned the place. "Perfection or death. That's all you know."

A hush fell over the crowd. Until a few moments ago, everyone knew how the story went, and how it was going to end. They didn't come to find out what was going to happen. They were all interested to see how Max told the story. Now we were in uncharted waters. We'd thrown a wrench into one of the most well-known tragedies of all time. Now, a thousand breaths were being held. A thousand backsides were on the edges of seats. They were all wondering. They knew they were about to see a miracle or a disaster. And all they could do was watch it play out.

Dawn, taking it in stride, rose from the bier. To her credit, she looked around wide-eyed, rolling with the improv that the show had become.

Kenny, staying in character for dear life, gasped. "She lives!"

I slowly nodded. "As I said."

There were chuckles in the audience from that one. They grew into full-throated laughter as Dawn realized Kenny was within arm's reach and nearly tackled him. The couple embraced, breathed, touched, reassuring themselves and each other that what they were experiencing was real. Whatever real meant in the here and now.

My eyes had adjusted to the light. In the orchestra pit, I could see Jerry helplessly shrugging at the musicians, who were all completely lost. A few rows behind them, I saw Max's face. He was giving a warm, gentle smile that was probably supposed to be reassuring, but threw me off.

I thought. *"Something's wrong with Max. He didn't even blink at this."*

Kenny turned back to me. "What becomes of us now?"

I shrugged. "You're the ones who planned to run away together and start a new life. Now you have the chance."

Kenny, playing helpless, took a breath. "You mean?"

He left it hanging. Dawn, swifter on the uptake, grabbed his chin and nodded, a dazzling and above all knowing smile on her face. A few more in the audience laughed.

I nodded. Words finally came to me. "Now you've got the hard way. All of the hard work. All of the struggles. A lifetime together, if you're willing to work for it. Argue about larks and nightingales for the next fifty years, if it works for you."

Kenny beamed. "I had thought our romance to end in tragedy tonight."

I snorted. "Because you're young and stupid and that's the easy way out."

Another round of laughter came from the depths of the house.

Max still hadn't stopped smiling.

Jazz nodded. "Time is strewn with the bodies of star crossed lovers. And their love died with them."

I'm not sure what had taken either of us, but I wasn't about to stop it. I waved a finger in Kenny's face. "But you lost sight of that. Because you tell stories that live and die in a night and are so sure they will rise again tomorrow. Because that's somehow more romantic."

Laughter again rose from the audience.

I took a breath and let my tone soften, but my eyes were locked with his. "Only the dead are forever young. Look her in the eyes the same way in twenty years, son. Then talk to me of romance."

Jazz touched my shoulder gently, looking at Dawn in the eyes. "Your parents don't even know what started the feud. Make sure your children know what ended it."

Dawn joined in, looking to Kenny hopefully. "Our names and places are already gone. Let us make new ones."

I nodded, waving at the upstage stairs. "Go. Live. And for the sake of the Gods, communicate! Tell each other your fears and your dreams. And take their fears and dreams to heart. But more important than that, listen to each other."

Kenny looked every bit as lost and confused as his character. "What shall we live for?"

I looked Jazz in the eyes, and my heart melted. Every frustration, every lie, every denial of how I really felt lined up to point out how I'd screwed up. With my gaze deep in the eyes of the woman I loved, I said. "Start with each other."

Someone stepped into the light above and behind me, and a hush fell over us all.

Then a baritone voice rose from the second level of the set.

What have I done?
What have I ruined?

A rich alto filled it in from the other side.

It was only for fun.
The thing to be doing.

Another Romeo and another Juliet had stepped out onto the balconies. Rocky, still cursing me out through my earpiece, decided to roll with it and had Thumper spotlight them both on the fly. They were dressed in their garments and masks from the ballroom sequence. But even through the finery, all could see that they were older. Grayer. Heavier. Juliet's hair was short and white. Romeo was hunched over and balding. But their voices were rich and intoxicating and so deeply in love with each other that they held the audience in rapture. The story went off into the distance, the tragedy shattering into an epic romance. Their voices entwined and the world ceased to care.

The band, who knew a cue when they heard one, came in to do a reprise bursting with energy.

If I could court you without courting disaster
I could brave the storm, scandals, the rumors, disgrace.
If I could ask now and just hope for what's after
I could step in the light and reveal my face.

The pair of them radiated love. In an instant that's what I'd been feeling within the walls of the building since I first came here. I could feel it on the stage beneath my feet. I could see their younger counterparts feel it in arm's reach. I could feel it spill out into the house and into the fly system. I could feel it envelop everywhere. I could feel it as Jazz stepped closer and curled into me. Tears fell behind my mask as I openly embraced her back. The love of the story was woven into every inch of this building, and it made a magic of its own. I couldn't formulate it. I could manipulate it, but only in the same way that performers had for thousands of years. And now it was sweeping me away, along with everyone and everything else.

In the front row, a part of me that was far away and beyond care could see Max, still staring dumbfounded at the spectacle with his quiet little smile.

The music swelled as the company joined in from the wings, surrounding the couples that were below and the couple that was to be above.

Now I can court you without courting disaster
I can brave the storm, scandals, the rumors, disgrace.
Now I can ask now and still hope for what's after
As I step in the light and reveal my face.
Across a crowded room...

The couples, older and younger, above and below, embraced. The bier below and the walkway above showed in shafts of light the yearning across the ages.

I could hear Connie scream in my mind. *"Heads up! Any moment now!"*

The blackout came, and the house plunged into darkness as the audience roared in approval.

The show had gone on.

* * *

The lights came up for curtain call with everyone still on stage. The spell had been broken.

Not that the audience could tell. The entire house, balcony and all, were on their feet. The clapping of hundreds felt like rolls of thunder.

Thumper's voice called in my mind. *"Gull's onstage!"*

Jazz and I backed up, my hand reaching for my sidearm. From offstage left emerged Dr. Gull, still in his costume. He strutted up close to Dawn and Kenny, then gestured for Max to come onstage. Giving that smile that seemed more mechanical every moment, Max rose and walked along the orchestra pit to ascend the stage stairs.

I thought. *"Something's wrong. Max wasn't phased by the change at all."*

As Max stepped onstage I felt the chill come up my spine, just as it had when I crossed the color line up in the balcony. Downstage center was twenty degrees colder now. I felt Jazz shiver next to me. It wasn't over.

Connie's thought confirmed what I already thought. *"Ginny's here."*

As Max raised his hand to wave I could feel rather than see lamps begin to explode in their sockets overhead. I'd already began to run, heading straight for Max as glass and metal rained down. The crowd shouted into the already momentous applause as I heard the creak of metal overhead. Two different kinds of metal snapped like backfiring car engines as an ellipsoidal gave way.

Dawn screamed as Kenny pulled her away.

I jumped clean over the bier and caught Max in a football tackle, sending us both rolling across the apron of the stage and tumbling into the orchestra pit.

Behind us, the ellipsoidal smashed into the stage, sparks and shards of glass flying everywhere.

I could just barely see Dr. Gull, the ellipsoidal missing him by inches, smiling devilishly as his eyes flashed a familiar shade of green.

The world disappeared.

Chapter Twenty-Five

Guideline Fifty-Three:

Just because they're called strange bedfellows doesn't mean you have to sleep with them.

I rolled, letting go of Max and then getting to my feet in a cold, creepy, familiar world of gray and green. I could feel Max and myself surrounded by life as the applause continued, only to die away in shock and concern. Then a moment passed and the life faded away, taking whatever warmth we still had with it. I tried not to shiver, thankful that I was still wearing the friar's robe. Whatever underworld look at the theater this was, the audience couldn't sense it, or be sensed by the likes of me. I patted myself down, looking for any gaping wounds. I didn't feel pain, but I didn't remember activating my eyeliner or opening any kind of portal, either.

That brought my mind to a screeching halt. I didn't feel any pain. I actually felt kinda numb. I'd been running around for a while, and I still had fading bruises from my last couple of tangles with Ginny. Clearly, I was in some sort of local underworld, and I'd managed to bring Max with me. Did we make it out from under that falling light? Did we land on something relatively soft in the orchestra pit? I couldn't remember.

I heard Dr. Gull whistle his low and slow tune again, but I couldn't see him.

"Don't you know that's bad luck, Doctor?"

I took off my mask and dropped it, then felt a lingering sense of dread creep down my spine. Then my stubborn nature grabbed it and choked it out. Fuck it. If I was already dead, I was going to make sure I got shit done. I drew my wand, then reached over, shaking Max's shoulder. "Max? Hey, Max? You OK?"

Max slowly sat up, and turned to look over at me. I grimaced at the sight, my first clear look at him in this realm. The slack-jawed remnants of his creepy smile was bad enough, but he looked like death warmed over himself. He'd gone from movie star handsome to skeletal in an instant. He hadn't aged. He'd withered. His skin was stretched tight over bones, eyes sunken, flesh shriveled. He twitched, looking an inch from death. Worse than that was the listless, forgotten and faraway look in his eyes. He normally looked so vibrant, so energetic, so full of energy that seeing him like this was shocking. If he'd been sedated for surgery I don't think he'd have been this bad. I think I could've slit his throat right there and he wouldn't have changed his expression.

That said, he didn't look like he was going to attack me or run away, so I clapped him on the shoulder gently and helped him up. He accepted the hand easily enough, then stood, swaying gently. A stiff breeze could've knocked him over.

"Look, Max. Just stick around and don't panic. I'm gonna get us out of here."

I turned around and looked someone new right in the face. Standing a double arm's length away was a slender man in a wine-dark purple suit. He was wearing a ballroom mask that came down over the cheekbones, leaving the mouth free. Mabel's work was easy for me to spot by now. This one looked disturbingly skeletal. As if a skull maybe a tenth over scale for a human had been elaborately carved into a mask. He grinned widely as I looked him up and down.

I licked suddenly dry lips. "Dr. Gull, I presume?"

He removed his mask, showing Danny's face. "Got it in one, boy."

"You know why I'm here?"

His smile didn't falter. "You and your girl, the Iron Council sent. Take me out. Take me down."

I cocked my head for a second, then nodded. "True, but I meant here in specific. I don't remember falling off the stage into some kind of portal or anything."

He snorted. "We all have work to do and too many prying eyes. Easier to do what needs doing here. Far as the standers know, there a trapdoor they don't know about yet."

I nodded. "Good initiative. You know I still can't let you take Max, right?"

He snickered. "You gonna be disappointed, boy."

This was getting weirder by the moment, but I wasn't about to let it show. "Dunno if you've heard of me, Doctor, but I can put up a fight and I have friends."

He burst out laughing, like I'd told a real stinker of a dad joke he hadn't heard yet. I let my eyes twitch behind me to make sure I was between him and Max.

When he'd taken a breath, he winked at me. "You can't put up a fight like this, boy."

I frowned. Something was up. "I know he's a murderer. But he's still human. He needs to face justice, not Ginny's revenge."

It was stupid to say, I know. Max was never going to see the inside of a courtroom for what he'd done. That didn't mean I was going to let another mage with a grudge have a free for all at him.

Dr. Gull just shrugged as he sauntered ever closer to me. "Delay justice long enough, boy, you gonna learn to settle for revenge."

I let out something between a chuckle and a sigh. "Funny. You're the second one to tell me that this month."

I took a swing. It seemed like a good idea at the time.

Dr. Gull ducked it and countered instantly, slamming a punch that felt like a hammer deeply into my gut. When I doubled over, he caught me in some sort of wrestling hold. He was a lot stronger than I expected for someone I outweighed by eighty pounds.

He leaned down to whisper in my ear. "Too late for your justice, boy. I kill Max before the show ever began. Dosed his champagne at opening. Arrogant sumbitch forgot how unlucky it is to celebrate a hit that hasn't happened. He shit himself to death at intermission."

He let go of the hold and shoved me aside.

I turned to look at Max. He was crumbling, like a clay sculpture that dried out and was slowly wearing away. He didn't seem to be in any pain, just that look of dumb confusion. The withering I'd seen earlier turned to desiccation in moments, then flakes of him began to fall away like old bits of paint in a strong breeze. He held up a single hand, watching as nails and finger joints began to fragment and float away on a nonexistent wind. He met my gaze for a single instant before his body crumbled and then blew away like a handful of sand.

As the last grains of dust that used to be a movie star vanished on a breeze I couldn't feel, an unearthly scream came from somewhere. I've never heard a banshee before, but if someone had told me that's what had screamed, I'd have believed them. I turned back to face Dr. Gull, aiming my wand.

"What the fuck is that?"

He snickered. "Unfinished business, boy."

"If he was already dead, what stepped onto the stage then?"

He laughed again, arms open and dancing a step or two. "I'm a necromancer, boy! Has your Council's stupid ban gone on for so long that you don't know a zombie when you see one?"

I almost growled. "Fuck the Council and fuck the ban. But with results like this, I can see why they did it. That was disgusting."

Dr. Gull cursed, spitting on what was supposedly the floor.

I glared at him. "Tell me. Does Danny Larus really exist? Because you look a little young to be Ginny's father."

Another screech came, followed by the sound of clashing steel on steel.

Dr. Gull shrugged. "It was as good a name and face as any."

He reached into his shirt and pulled out a copper medallion hanging from a leather thong around his neck. He rubbed it between his fingers as if wishing for luck. A short murmur later, and I watched him age decades before my eyes. His hair turned white as his skin began to stretch and wrinkle. He laughed again, showing missing teeth. He shook the medallion once before tucking it back into place. "Gorlois pendants are a pain in the ass to make, but they do come in handy."

Again, that eerie screech came, as did the sound of steel.

I opened my mouth but was interrupted by Connie's screaming. "TRAVIS!"

Some fifty yards away, shadows parted to reveal Connie fighting some sort of huge, clawed thing. It was hidden in a roiling mass of shadows, looking like moving thunderstorm clouds. The occasional claw or tentacle emerged from the mass to attack. Connie's e-tool had somehow unfolded into a full-size spade, and the blade was glowing green. Cyrus was at her side with his walking stick and Bowie knife. They were fighting off claws and tendrils that kept on coming.

On the ground behind them was The Scottish Man. He was sprawled facedown, climbing up to one knee. Some sort of ichor stained his sword, and he looked weakened. His mask was twisted into an eerie-looking frown.

Beyond caring how much of a fool I looked like, I bellowed. "What the hell is that thing?"

Dr. Gull put his mask back on, which did nothing to hide his sneer. "Is my daughter, boy."

The Ginny-thing screeched as Connie batted away her claws. Then it vanished into the shadows. Gods only knew how. I couldn't see any equivalent to the theater or any of the backstage spaces. It was just an empty space, with a horizon that only came up a few meters away. There was dust on the ground, but nothing else. After a moment, I realized where I'd last seen something like this. It was when we summoned The Scottish Man. This is what it looked like when the ghost light had shattered.

Ignoring the doctor, I sprinted to Connie's side. "What's the plan?"

Connie kept looking in every corner for the thing, her spade at the ready. "We take her down before she destroys The Scottish Man."

The Scottish Man flicked the ichor off his blade with a flourish, his mask looking grim. "Glad I am tae see ye, alchemist."

"He's doomed if you go that route." said the Doctor as he strolled up to us.

I drew my holdout pistol and aimed right at his center of mass.

Dr. Gull laughed, holding up his hands. "You that determined to take me, boy?"

I blinked. "Hey Connie?"

She didn't take her eyes off the shadows. "What?"

"Do bullets work here?"

Gull laughed all the louder. "You don't want to find out, boy!"

Connie faced him. "Don't be impatient, Doctor. You're on my to-do list."

Gull snickered. "Ah, yes. Your Council sends someone half competent to kill me. I was worried the boy was the best they'd sent."

She shrugged. "Kill, capture, banish. I got options."

He grinned and clapped his hands. "Ah! Now we get to it."

Her lip curled in a smile. "You looking to bargain?"

Dr. Gull's eyes glowed a familiar shade of green. "Choose banishment, and I'll take my daughter with me."

I recoiled. "What?"

Cyrus didn't look surprised. Connie explained for my benefit. "She got this powerful on the prospect of taking Max down, body and soul. But that didn't happen. His show is a hit and he's dead and escaped her. Now she's chasing power out of sheer spite. Left to her own devices, she'll destroy The Scottish Man and take his title for her own. Then this theater will be stuck with a murderous ghost for god knows how long."

I could feel a tingle of dread up my spine. "So that's what we're fighting now."

Connie shrugged. "Better than fighting for that murdering asshole."

The Scottish Man, his mask a rictus of despair, nodded. "She speaks the truth, laddie. The Crying Lass comes fer me now."

Cyrus and Gull sized each other up, then mutually nodded.

"Doctor."

"Doctor."

I made the obvious known to all. "Connie, I don't even know what our options are. This is your call. However it goes, I'm backing you."

She shrugged a little. "Going solo, even with you and Cyrus helping, all I can do is banish her. But in a day, a month, sooner or later, she'll come for The Scottish Man. And she'll destroy him. I don't know how to capture her soul or put her to rest for good."

I nodded. "Still your call."

Connie nodded. "Doctor?"

Cyrus halfway opened his mouth before Gull spoke up. "Yes, girl?"

She spun on her heel, then planted the butt of her spade on the ground, looking Dr. Gull in the eyes. "We'll back you up. Nobody else dies tonight. Do what you must to collect Ginny. Then leave town. Tonight. Don't let the sun rise on you until you're back in Conjure territory."

He grinned wider than his mask could contain. "Done."

He spat in his hand. Connie spat in her own and they shook on it.

Business settled, I holstered my pistol. "So, how do we stop her?"

Connie spoke up. "Just keep The Scottish Man alive as long as possible." She grimaced as she realized what she'd said. "I mean dead as long as possible. I mean, you know what I mean."

Dr. Gull shrugged. "Intact?"

Connie nodded. "Yes, thank you. What the Doctor said."

Dr. Gull didn't hesitate. "Miss Chandler backs me up. The rest of you keep The Scottish Man intact."

Connie offered me her spade with a questioning look. I shook my head, then pulled the friar's robe off and kicked it aside. After rolling my shoulders once, I murmured at my wand. It glowed for a moment, then slowly morphed into a rigger's axe. With my free hand I activated a kinetic shield ring. In the underworld, it glowed slightly, the same as my wand. The glow showed the outline, the rim bigger than a garbage can lid.

Connie watched me take her place at the Scottish Man's side, then nodded to her new coworker. "Your patient, Doctor."

Chapter Twenty-Six

Guideline Fifty-One:
Some days you save,
other days are saved for you.

It didn't take long for Ginny to attack again. The ambient light hadn't gotten good enough for any kind of landscape to be seen, but she was somehow more defined in form than she had been before. For some reason, she was formed into some kind of damned shadow dragon, all teeth and claws and tendrils. Her torso alone was the size of a school bus.

I quickly lost sight of Connie and Dr. Gull, praying that they were doing whatever they needed to do fast. It was easier to do that than hope three on one against the Ginny-thing was going to be enough. Cyrus and I formed a wedge with The Scottish Man between and behind us.

Mercifully, our weapons seemed to work on her. Axe, knife, and sword bit into claws and limbs and tendrils, sending them back to the mass of shadow that kept coming. Claws skittered off of my shield, giving me a second here and there. I suddenly had a horrible thought.

"Cyrus?"

He was twisting his cane in a fencing move. "I'm a little busy, Travis!"

I hacked a tip off another tentacle with my axe. "How exactly can she harm us here? I mean, claws, tentacles, I get it. But what do they actually do here?"

A clawed arm bolted out of a shadow. I turned to avoid it, then slammed the edge of my shield on it, grinding the arm against the ground. Another shriek and the arm vanished.

"To be completely honest," Cyrus slashed open a tendril with his Bowie knife, "I'm not entirely sure."

A claw got past me and was lopped off by the sword of The Scottish Man, his mask locked in a war cry. He shook his head, fear and exhaustion in his voice as he joined in. "Is this truly wa' occupies yer thought of tae moment, alchemist?"

I shrugged, knocking away another tendril with my shield. "I mean, it matters to us at least. No offense."

His sword swung, and another set of claws flew away into mist. "None taken."

With my axe, I cut off another claw, which dissolved into black mist. "So what gives, Cyrus? She's still a ghost, right? What's with this shadow dragon thing?"

"Well," another tendril was smacked with his walking stick, sounding like a baseball bat hitting a mattress, "we're physically in the underworld right now."

Claws raked off my shield. "And that's a bad thing?"

Another claw went flying under the knife edge. "Generally not recommended. Going at all ain't exactly a good idea. But if you do feel the need, what you want to do is go astral."

I tried to remember a lecture from high school on that very subject. Unfortunately, I'd probably been drawing pictures of race cars instead of paying attention. After a moment, I gave up and chopped two more clawed shadows away. "You mean leave your body? Silver cord, all of that shit?"

Another claw went for The Scottish Man. Cyrus used his cane to curve it out of line with one of those twisty French fencing moves, then cut it off with the knife. "Yeah. Normally, you get fucked up enough here, the cord yanks you back to your body. You wake up sweaty with a splitting headache, but that's about it."

In the distance, I could just barely hear Dr. Gull chanting a spell that I'd never heard of. After a few moments, I could hear Connie joining him. I could smell burning tobacco and dark rum.

The Scottish Man cut down another claw with his sword. I saw another one coming from the side, caught it on my shield, and cut it off. "But unless I missed something, we're here in our bodies. No silver cords or nothing."

"Right." Another shadow beaten, another claw counter-slashed.

"Lemme guess. We die here in the Underworld, in our bodies, it's gonna be worse than a headache."

"Pretty much. No bodies left to go back to. We're here body and soul. Nowhere to go except whatever's beyond the Underworld. It'll definitely screw with your plans for next week."

"So don't get killed by the ghost dragon-actress. Got it. Thank you."

"Glad to help."

A tendril of shadow came in under my axe and tagged me right behind the knees, knocking me ass over teakettle. I landed on my back just in time to see another one knock down Cyrus coming the other way.

I scrabbled to one knee just in time to see Ginny's claws come around for another pass.

We were back in a grinder. A stalemate grinder.

"Cyrus?"

"What now?"

"Does cover exist here? Bunkers, caves, that kind of thing?"

"This is the underworld, dumbass! You see any cover down here?"

I saw nothing but the ground, the shadows, us, and the grinder.

"Fuck you! I've never been here before. Blame a man for exploring options!"

"There's a time and there's a place!"

My response was interrupted by a tentacle, thick as a telephone pole, slamming into me like a defensive line. I went down again, my shield barely keeping a swipe of claws away from me. I saw Cyrus' stick go flying as he swore.

The Scottish Man stood alone, the lips of his mask narrowed into a thin, grim line. He raised his sword in a challenge and beckoned Ginny to him.

Claw after claw fell under his blade. Though he carried a sword that must have been made to clang loud for an audience, it cut through every attack Ginny brought at him. No wasted motion, no fancy swinging. Just an efficiency of combat that drew a monster into a stalemate.

It wasn't enough.

Cyrus and I were both back on our feet, but couldn't hack our way through Ginny's attacks to reach The Scottish Man. It was all we could do to keep ourselves away from the sharp, glittering claws.

The Scottish Man lopped off three of Ginny's claws, sending them dissolving into the mist. Two more came screaming out of the roiling cloud of shadow from different directions. They both slammed through his chest with no resistance, pinning him to the ground.

I threw my rigger's axe at the claws only to see it bounce harmlessly off a third.

The claws impaling the screaming Scottish Man curved past his back, holding him like a hooked fish. I saw Cyrus' Bowie knife fly, only to bounce off a tendril. The hooked claws lifted up The Scottish Man, taking the struggling ghost off his feet. I hacked and slammed away at the mass of shadows, unable to do so much as take a step forward.

The long, curved claws, buried in the chest of The Scottish Man, slowly rotated, the ends of the claws facing out instead of down. The Scottish

Man writhed in agony as the claws twisted inside his torso, preventing his escape. The long shadow arms holding up the claws flexed once, then slowly began pulling him apart. He began to fade, the shadows growing around the claws in his chest. Instead of bones cracking and flesh rending, I heard a low keening, like the banshee screech Ginny had made, but this was coming from the mask of The Scottish Man. The Scottish Man faded further still, tendrils of his essence hurling away under the force of Ginny's rage.

Finally, the Scottish Man was pulled in half, like cotton candy in the rain, each side of his body dissolving into the winds like incense smoke. In seconds, The Scottish Man was gone.

His mask, frozen in a rictus of pain, fell to the ground alongside his sword.

The claws and tendrils roiled back into the mass of the Ginny-thing, which rumbled and roiled. Then it seemed to grow bigger, green highlights around the edges of the mass growing brighter.

I've never seen Cyrus' eyes so wide. As his hand closed around his Bowie knife, he murmured, "Oh, fuck."

I took up my axe, heading for Cyrus. "Fall back to Connie and the Doctor! We gotta get them more time!"

He made it to his feet. "Easier said than done!"

I barely made it to him before bringing up my shield just in time for a claw to bounce off of it.

I could see the Ginny-thing clearer now. It began to swell like some kind of necrotic pustule, absorbing whatever was left of The Scottish Man as it grew bigger.

I drew my sidearm and fired twice, the rounds disappearing into the roiling mass of shadow, to no other effect. Cursing, I holstered, ready to go again with axe and shield.

In the distance, Dr. Gull and Connie were still chanting.

One tendril slammed into my shield like a runaway box truck. I barely managed not to fall on my own axe. I dug my heels into whatever passed for the ground in the underworld, ready to push.

Three tendrils at once caught Cyrus, two planting his feet to the spot, the third clenching the wrist of his cane hand, yanking him forward onto his knees. With his Bowie knife, he hacked away at increasingly intangible shadows, obscuring him more and more by the instant.

My axe managed to slice away a claw trying to carve its way around my shield. Another tendril wrapped around my knees and lifted me like a wrestler, sending me tumbling onto my back. I kept a hold onto my axe, but another tendril caught my wrist, pinning it to the ground.

Cold was too mundane a word to describe the touch of that shadowy soul stuff on my bare skin. I've felt the chill of a vampire's breath against my neck, and this was so much worse. Mundane cold eventually numbs. This chill burned as it went through skin and flesh into bones, then began to curve inward from the bone marrow up my arm. Beyond my axe, I couldn't see Cyrus anymore. He was buried in a mass of writhing, eerie shadows.

For the moment, my shield arm was free. I swung my shield around, smashing tendril and claw against the ground, but my legs had been pinned down as well. I could feel myself tiring.

On the same hand as my shield ring, which was beginning to weaken and fade, Jazz's ring also gleamed. A rush of paradoxical joy rejuvenated me. If the Ginny-thing truly was capable of destroying me in this place, body and soul, then the ring that kept Jazz in servitude to me would be destroyed as well. I smashed another tendril with a hearty laugh. No matter what the crazy bitch did now, the woman I loved was going to be free. That was a pretty awesome thought to die on. More tendrils came, more than I could block. More than I could attack. More than I could avoid.

I drew my sidearm again and dumped the rest of the magazine into the Ginny-thing. Hot lead and muzzle flashes did nothing to stop her onslaught. At best they were a tiny bit of comfort. A candle in one's hands as a blizzard raged outside.

Then the slide locked back.

No way to reload.

Nowhere to run.

No way to fight.

A tendril wrapped around my gun hand like a singletail whip, then yanked, pinning my gun hand to the ground. Out of the writhing shadows came the dragon head, green glows shining from the eye sockets and the depth of the throat. I'd never been close to something that looked like a dragon before, let alone one with an inhuman smile that absolutely dripped sadism.

The Ginny-thing hissed triumphantly, then screeched in pain. The dragon head reared back, bellowing in agony.

From the edge of my vision, a rapier flashed, sending a black and green tendril off into the distance.

Three more slashes and my arms and legs were free. The Ginny-thing screeched in pain and rage, the tendrils backing off. I reloaded, then holstered, taking up axe and shield once more. Out of the corner of my eye, I could see Cyrus again, whole and getting to his feet.

Standing between Cyrus and I was a swordsman with long, dark hair falling beyond his shoulders. He was dressed in a black-and-gold ensemble that looked like what you think Hamlet should look like in high school: tights, a poet's shirt, and doublet. His hands were filled with a rapier and dagger. His face was hidden behind one of the domino masks we'd passed out by the dozens to the audience tonight.

The Ginny-thing howled louder and deeper than before. Her clawed tendrils coiled in tight before attacking the newcomer.

I thought I was decent in a fight. I was nothing on this guy. Every attack that came at him either found him no longer there or countering with one of his blades. He moved like a dancer, turning to his own tune as claws and tendrils spun off into the darkness as his blades cleaved them away.

After some moments I began to realize the attacks were coming slower and less frequent. Against all odds, the swordsman was winning.

Cyrus called out. "Travis?"

"Yeah?"

"Who the hell is this guy?"

"The one who's saving our asses! I'm kinda satisfied with that!"

Cyrus and I stood back with our weapons at the ready, but unwilling to join in lest we throw our newfound ally off his groove.

The swordsman retreated a single step, paused for a single moment that seemed to last forever, then sheathed his blades.

We could hear Connie and Dr. Gull still chanting in the distance.

Reaching into his doublet, the swordsman drew forth a small bouquet of dead, drying roses. Even in the gloom of the underworld, I could see how red and vibrant they had been. In death they had dried to gray-brown stems and dull burgundy blossoms. Cradling the bouquet in one arm, he stepped past us. With his free hand he doffed his mask, leaving it on the ground behind him.

His rich baritone voice called out. "Ginny. Enough. It's over."

The tendrils coiled in on themselves, shrinking ever further as the howling died down. The dragon head disappeared into the shadows. The swordsman continued to advance with the bouquet in hand as the tendrils recoiled from him. The mass of writhing shadow shrank and dissipated, revealing the kneeling, sobbing form of a young woman.

The swordsman took a single knee, a gesture as sincere as a proposal. Holding out the bouquet, he spoke almost too gently for me to hear. "He's gone, Ginny. He's finally gone. You've gone without rest for so long. Too long."

Ginny reached out with a trembling hand, grasping the swordsman by the arm. I could barely hear her speak. "The show must go on."

He murmured. "And so it will."

Ginny reached out her hands and gently accepted the bouquet. As she brought it close to smell the blossoms, she began to dissolve. Not like Max had crumbled to dust, but fading away until she seemed to be a sculpture made of smoke. Breezes we couldn't feel took wisp after wisp of her away, until she and the bouquet disappeared into the light before the shadows.

I could no longer hear the chants.

The swordsman rose, his face still in shadow as he stepped away. A few steps away, he knelt again, picking up the fallen mask of the Scottish Man. With all of the solemnity of a priest, the swordsman donned the mask, securing the strings tight behind his head.

Still on one knee, he drew from inside his doublet a length of tartan cloth in a familiar pattern. Draping it over one shoulder as a sash, he tied the ends in a simple knot at the hip opposite his sword before rising to his feet.

The new Scottish Man of the Pencil Factory turned to face us. Compelled by some instinctual protocol, Cyrus and I raised our respective knife and axe in salute. The Scottish Man gave a courtly bow in response.

"Travis?"

We turned. Connie stood alone, dripping with sweat and leaning on her spade. Dr. Gull was nowhere to be seen.

She caught my gaze and continued. "Time to go. It's probably chaos out there now."

I nodded. "Good to go." I pointed a thumb at our new companion. "The new Scottish Man saved our..." I trailed off as I turned around. The Scottish Man had vanished. Only the domino mask, one of hundreds in the theater that night, was left behind.

Connie shook her head, then folded her spade back up into the e-tool that slid into her purse. "Holster your weapons and tell me later. The Doctor's gone."

I slid my wand into a pocket and deactivated my shield ring. "What now?"

The smile of a job well done shone in her eyes. "We get out of here. Hold hands."

Cyrus and I obeyed as we held hands in a circle.

"Close your eyes. This might get uncomfortable."

I closed my eyes.

It was uncomfortable.

* * *

"Travis? Connie?"

I came to with a serious pain in my side. Connie had been right. This was uncomfortable. I was going to have to start working with a net or something. I opened my eyes and light stabbed into them. I winced, swore, then winced again as I tried to move muscles that insisted they had better things to do, like recover for a week. At least that creepifying chill was gone.

I slowly opened my eyes to realize the lights were from the grid high above. I was on my back in the orchestra pit, my head facing stage left. Rocky was crouched over me, looking worried. I stretched and winced, looking around at the mass of cast, crew, musicians, and audience hanging around.

"What did I miss?"

Rocky stood up, then pointed at the smashed remains of the ellipsoidal. "That. By inches, if I was looking right." Her face curled into a worried frown. "Unfortunately, you didn't save Max."

I got to my feet in time to see paramedics wheeling away a covered body on a gurney. I pointed my thumb. "Max?"

Rocky shrank a little and shook her head. Beyond Rocky, curled up onstage, I could see Mabel on her knees. Her eyes were twisted shut, ugly sobs wracking her chest. A pair of abandoned masks were lying on the deck in front of her. Hannah was on one knee beside her, looking protective.

Rocky found the words. "That's Roscoe. He and Mabel were the old Romeo and Juliet. He collapsed right after the ellipsoidal fell. I thought he'd been hit by something at first, but EMS told me it looks like a heart attack. They couldn't revive him."

I blinked, thinking of a mask fallen and retrieved. "Roscoe? Just now?"

She nodded. "But Mabel keeps calling him George."

Chapter Twenty-Seven

Guideline Fifty-Six:

Surviving is easy enough.

Carrying on after doing what needs doing can be a lot harder.

Amazingly enough, I didn't spend the night in jail.

Not that Ron didn't go to a lot of effort to try and make it happen. He would not shut up about the fact that I was armed in the theater, and couldn't seem to wrap his head around the fact that that wasn't a crime. In the midst of his babbling, he did confirm that Dr. Gull had attacked Cyrus and was held at gunpoint by me. Rocky backed us up, and in the end all Connie and I got was a lecture about investigating without licenses and an advisement not to leave town.

I'm sure the fact that Marshal Sims was smoking cigarettes outside with some of the cops had nothing to do with it.

Connie sent off her report to Neary declaring Dr. Gull banished from Iron Council territory with a minimum loss of life. She also named Thumper, myself, and Cyrus as "allies and apprentices" sharing her exemption from the ban on necromancy. Chucky had been happy to make the trip down to Atlanta to act as courier for both report and response.

The opening and closing night of "Romeo & Juliet: The Rock Opera!" made a minor buzz in Atlanta's arts scene. There were all sorts of arguments about the hubris of meddling with a classic versus championing hopeful romance in a dark world, that kind of thing. But with Max dead, Danny missing, and the show closed permanently, it quickly became one of those "you had to be there" events.

*　*　*

Byron had helped Jazz sneak backstage and change back into her own costume. They escaped into the crowd with nobody noticing. Hannah insisted I had an accomplice, since she had been waiting in the wings for curtain call. But in the excitement, who the new nurse had been was one more mystery in a dozen, and one that hadn't resulted in death, destruction, or a fugitive. Cyrus had also faded away into the crowd once they'd returned with Connie. One more audience member in a mask among hundreds.

Thumper, Connie, and I closed up with Rocky when the last of the cops and looky-loos left, then offered her a late dinner at Wa'cross. There, we filled her in on what really happened and what we'd told the cops. We also told her what we'd seen of Roscoe's ultimate fate.

Rocky put down a forkful of Loretta's blueberry waffles and took a breath. "I'm never gonna be able to talk about this, aren't I?"

I shrugged. "Tell who? And to what end?"

Connie nodded. "The fact that there's more than one Scottish Man is already at least rumored. Now when you're in the old stage manager's home you can say you used to work with one. That's gotta be worth a drink at bingo night."

I raised a glass of Dr. Pepper. "Nights close, curtains fall, shows go on."

Rocky finally cracked a smile. "We'll make a romantic out of you yet, Travis Wayland."

We all drank to that.

*　*　*

A month later, Babs filled us in on what the cops decided. Apparently, Danny Larus (who, to nobody's surprise, turned out to be a false identity) believed a conspiracy theory that Max Roman had murdered Ginny Kemp back in the day. He got himself cast in the show to terrorize and eventually murder Max, using rumors of Ginny's ghost as a cover.

An autopsy found poisons in Max's body. Max's office still had evidence of how Dr. Gull hadn't exaggerated about how Max met his end. The cops figured that "Danny" poisoned Max's opening night champagne. Dawn had caught a bit of it by kissing Max, which is why she was feeling ill at intermission. And when that didn't work as planned, Danny sabotaged the light rig.

The fact that Max had been dead for the entire second act somehow wasn't apparent on the autopsy table. The deaths of Grover and Greg and the attacks on me could've been accidents or Danny covering his tracks. Rendering Ron and Larry unconscious during the show was chalked up to the same thing. In the end, Danny was wanted for Max's murder. George Burbage, on the other hand, was just an old actor who died on the night of a glorious comeback. Not a bad way to go for a career actor.

* * *

We got home past the witching hour. Byron and Cyrus had gone to their own homes long ago, but Jazz waited up for us. Connie drove off after a quick goodbye and Thumper discreetly went to bed soon after we arrived. I took a quick shower, then stumbled out in a clean pair of shorts to find Jazz waiting for me in the doorway to my bedroom.

"Jazz?"

She was in pajamas that looked like a bedlah at first glance. "Yes, Master?"

I hugged her tight. "Thank you."

I could feel her surprised thrill at the affection, which she quickly reciprocated. "You're very welcome, Master!"

I lingered for a moment before making myself pull back. I met her gaze, trying not to get lost in sapphire eyes. "I mean it. I'm not sure how we could've pulled that off without you."

She smiled bashfully. "I did my best, Master."

I nodded. "But I haven't been doing mine."

I sat back on my bed at her puzzled look. I took a breath before continuing. "I almost died tonight. And I did it without telling you what you deserve to know." I waved a hand uselessly. "I mean, you probably know. But you deserve to hear it from me."

Jazz wordlessly knelt on the floor beside me, keeping her gaze to mine.

I breathed. "I've been terrified of telling you this." The words finally fell from me. "I love you, Jasmine. I can't.. I won't act on it. You know why. But I've been fond of you since the day we met. I've loved you since you began to serve me. And now I'm falling in love with you."

She slid her hand into mine. I held on, holding back for fear of hurting her as I continued. "I won't be your Solomonic Master and your lover at the same time. It goes against everything I am. I'm going to find a way to set you free or die trying. But if I fail, you deserve to know. More than know. You deserve to hear it from me. And I'm tired of hiding from that."

I took both her hands in mine, and somehow looked even deeper into her eyes.

"Jasmine Al-Bakr, I love you."

How she responded is none of your business.

Chapter Twenty-Eight

Guideline Sixty:

Accept pleasant surprises gracefully.

Two days later we were back in the theater. The cops had gotten every-thing from the building they wanted to, and Rocky had called us back in. We'd expected a workday, even though our covers were more or less blown. But Rocky had a surprise for us.

"A bonus?"

Connie frowned at her check like it had just started hitting on her. Thumper shrugged and tucked theirs into a pocket. I just gave Rocky a confused look.

"More like severance, really." She shrugged. "It was in all of our con-tracts. Max was so dead set on making sure the show happened at all that he loaded the contracts with perks. One of them was a severance package of three month's performance wages if the show shut down unexpectedly after at least one performance."

Thumper gave a low whistle.

I pocketed my own check. "That had to have wreaked havoc on Harry."

Rocky shrugged. "He seemed pretty on the ball about it. I guess if you handle finance for a celebrity, you wind up being ready for all manner of wacky shit."

I nodded. "So what needs doing?"

Rocky shook her head. "Nothing really. Just say your goodbyes. Do a sweep if you want. Just to make sure, you know?"

We all nodded. Connie spoke up. "Give me an hour with some paint and I can get rid of the wards. Make it easier for The Scottish Man to move around in his own home, y'know?"

Rocky's smile grew softly. "Thank you. All of you. More people would've gotten hurt if you hadn't been here."

Connie let herself crack a smile. "Glad we could help."

We hugged it out and left Rocky to her paperwork while we headed for the roof.

* * *

We did a full sweep. As full as we could, anyways. We worked our way down from the roof, backing up Connie as she took down her wards, my wards, and Gull's wards one by one. I resisted the urge to ask Rocky if I could keep the cannon in the attic. Trying to cleanse artillery of questionable spiritual residue just isn't a backyard project. Not one that I personally have the time for, anyway.

Connie did take the newspaper from the old apartment. She paused before taking it. I never asked if she had been asking George for permission.

Ron passed us by on his way out of the dressing room. He started looking daggers at me the second he noticed us, but didn't say a word. Thumper gave him the finger as he walked away.

Hannah found us on her own way out. She didn't glare at me. Just gave me a wee-need-to-talk look. I let the others go on and hung back with Hannah.

"So, you gonna tell me who that was?"

I shook my head. "If it helps at all, it's nobody you know."

She visibly tried not to roll her eyes. "I knew there was something up with you."

I smirked. "Good eye." I walked past her. "Take care of yourself, Hannah. You're good people."

"Why do I believe you when you say that?"

"I'm not an actor."

*   *   *

We found Mabel packing her personal gear in the wardrobe room.

"I'm sorry about George, Maria."

She waved me off with a silk hanky before tucking it into an enormous sewing bag. "Just stick with Mabel, dear. It's what my living friends all call me now."

Connie smiled in sympathy. "I never did get to tell you how lovely a singer you are. Both of you, really."

Mabel's grin cracked at that one. "Thank you, dear. You'd think we made careers of it or something."

Thumper gave her two thumbs up.

I leaned against the doorway. "You have another gig lined up, Mabel?"

She shook her head. "I was thinking of retiring anyway. And I'm never gonna top this show, on or offstage. I got a place in Florida and some ins with the parks and the cruise lines. I figure I can be a wine auntie to some of these bright young people trying to make a name for themselves in this crazy business. Maybe be a good example." She shrugged. "And a bad one. Whatever's needed, really."

Connie kept her smile going. "Sounds like a nice ride into the sunset."

Mabel's own grin got misty. "I think so. I cursed George for a bastard, going out like that so soon after we'd finally reconnected after so long. But I think the romantic old fart couldn't have arranged a better exit. We got one more song together. The last thing he saw was the footlights. And the last thing he heard was the crowd."

I saw a tear run down Thumper's cheek.

Connie nodded slightly. "I'm sure he'd agree with you."

Mabel shouldered her bag, tears welling up behind her glasses. "Just in case he listens to you instead of me, do be sure he knows I said so, dear."

With a wink to the three of us, Mabel strode out of the wardrobe room without another word.

*   *   *

Connie stood downstage center, the ghost light at her back. Thumper and I flanked her, looking out into the house. The faint passageway strip lights and the dim emergency exit lights were all we could see in the distance, the ghost light only marking the edges of the shadows everywhere. The set had already been struck, and the lights taken down and stored for load-out at the docks below us.

For the first time, I had the sense of how many people had been watching when I stepped out in a stolen mask a few nights and lifetimes ago. How many people had been caught up in story and song. It felt like being in a church the night before services. Had actors come out here to commune with this space like we were now? Like squires standing vigil the night before being knighted? We'd come here to hunt a murderous ghost, and we had. But along the way, we'd become a part of magic I'd never experienced before. Something only bards like my friend Seb even had a chance of articulating, let alone analyzing.

It was a magic beyond me. I knew chemistry and physics. I knew metal and wood and stone. I knew fire and electricity and magnetism and hydraulics. I even knew the rudiments of the human mind, the rapidly evolving connections and distances of technology. I'd begun to see beyond the vale of tears, to experience passion beyond death. I'd thought I understood death after Blue River, experiencing the butchery of loved ones and sworn enemies alike. I thought I'd understood death after Iraq, after the chaos of firefights and the constant threat of explosives from any innocuous corner. But here, in this shrine of storytelling, I'd seen deeper aspects of death, of life, of romance, and of passion.

In the growing awkward of the silence, I shook my head. "Y'know, I'd never been on stage before."

Connie nodded. "A couple of haflas. A solo in one of them. But never a place this big."

We looked to Thumper, who shook their head gratefully.

I looked out across the line of the balcony. "Y'know, I don't think I'm seeing the underworld any better than I used to. But I'm seeing this theater better than I did. It's like seeing a car that someone loves. I can pick those out of a car lot, y'know? It's not the newest ones or the most expensive. It's the ones with the care mixed in with the wear. That's what this place feels like. The casts, the crews... they loved this place. Even with all the heartache and the bullshit. They loved it."

Connie nodded. "Max treated people like things. That's what ended him, in the long run. Maybe all these people treating this place like a person made a difference?"

I shrugged. "Maybe. They loved it and it still almost killed them. That's definitely people for you."

Connie smirked. "You know, it kinda makes sense, us coming in on the crew making the difference. Especially you."

I snorted. "Yeah?"

She nodded. "Thumper was telling me about the old theaters back in Ancient Greece. When they wanted Gods to show up from heaven or hell they'd rig up a crane or a trapdoor to make sure they came up or down to where the mortals were. Called it deus ex machina."

I frowned. "I thought that's when something stupidly powerful shows up out of nowhere and wraps up the story."

Thumper rolled their eyes at me.

Connie smirked. "Yeah, but they did it with the cranes and the trapdoors. That's what deus ex machina means. God from the machine. These days, they'd probably call it technomancy."

I managed a smile. 'I can live with that."

A single piano note rang out, followed by another. Our eyes all turned to the corner of the orchestra pit, where a single upright piano from the rehearsal hall had been left. In the shadows left by the ghost light, we all saw the piano keys fall and lift with no human player sitting at the bench. Within sixteen bars I recognized the tune of "Across a Crowded Room."

Something made me look up, above the balcony and into the catwalk so recently stripped bare of lights. In a small patch between the shadows, the ghost light illuminated a man in Elizabethan garb of black and gold, his face hidden behind an ancient mask both laughing and crying at once.

As the piano played on, I could see Connie raise her arm to The Scottish Man in the curtain call gesture of acknowledgment, bowing her head. Thumper and I did likewise.

The Scottish Man gave a flourishing bow, then stepped back into the shadows and vanished.

The piano stopped, the last note lingering in the still air.

Connie silently led us down the offstage stairs, into the house, up the aisle, and through the double doors into the lobby. I was the last one out, giving a single lookback to the empty theater, lit in the dim comfort of the ghost light.

THE END

Epilogue

The gaggle of excited young women departed in a pack, phones clutched in hand, sunglasses shielding their eyes, beach bags slung under their arms. They were all young and pretty and dressed for the comfortable warmth of the Florida coast. Although heads didn't turn in their wake, more than one set of eyes behind their own sunglasses took an extra moment from the day to watch them leave. It was early May, in that dull roar between the riots of spring break and the months-long marathon of summer vacationers.

Mabel was left behind, her white hair with its fading blue streak bound up under a sun hat big enough to be used as a signal flag. Her fruit juice alone adorned the table. The girls had been conscientious enough to take their empties with them. They were good girls, Mabel thought. Smarter than she had been at that age. Every last one of them bouncing with excitement about the adventures of cruise ship entertainment life. All of them far too savvy to fall head over heels for the first straight and pretty boy to catch their eyes. At least, she told herself, that's what it looks like so far. Best of luck to them.

Not for the first time, she contemplated snowbirding. In about a month, the tourists would be here nonstop and the hurricanes coming in when least expected. Mabel had some old friends that were still wandering around in the Catskills. If nothing else, summering there for the first year might make it a nice change of pace.

A nondescript and middle-aged black man sat down a chair away from her. He looked the picture of a bachelor uncle in board shorts, a bright aloha shirt, and off-white panama hat. On the table, he put down something blended with a pineapple wedge on the rim. He politely nodded to Mabel before going about the business of cutting and lighting a cigar.

Mabel sipped at her juice before commenting. "I forgot you smoked those on the regular."

He shrugged. "I can quit any time I like. You saw me switch to cigarettes for two months of rehearsals, no less."

"I can't argue with that, I suppose. Does it go well with whatever it is you're drinking?"

He took a sip, deftly avoiding the pineapple wedge. After a moment's thought, he nodded. "It does at least for my palate."

"To each their own, then."

He took another puff, then grew somber. "Thank you. For letting me know."

She sighed. "Did all of that really have to happen?"

He blew a smoke ring towards the sea and sighed. "Roman would not have survived no matter what happened. The others... I underestimated my daughter's passion. Not for the first time."

Mabel shook her head. "I can only imagine what raising Ginny must have been like."

At that, he smiled. "Rewarding. It was rewarding as it was difficult."

Mabel downed the last of her juice. "So what happens now?"

Dr. Gull blew another smoke ring. "Hope the next storm that comes is a hurricane. Those, I know how to deal with."

* * *

The Iron Council considered itself the first and last word when it came to the human practice of magic in North America. Despite the fact that there were numerous disputed and even more uninhabited territory on the continent proper did not change that. From a massive cavern system under the Cahokia mounds, near St. Louis, The Iron Council did what they could to establish control, community, and justice while still fulfilling Solomon's command to guide and guard humanity whenever possible.

Despite the imposing name, the Council was not a large organization. With perhaps ten thousand living mages within its territory, the Council held only thirteen members. Twenty-four Monitors around the continental United States were on duty at any given time, as were about fifty Marshals.

Small and magical though it was, the Iron Council was a governing body still. As such, it created paperwork. Chucky Brubaker counted herself lucky that the technomancers managed to keep the old and temperamental printer up and running. The beige casing was covered in various technomantic sigils laid down in a dozen different manners over the last few decades.

Satisfied, Chucky arranged the three copies of her report in different folders: one to go to the Council archives, one to be kept in the knowledge office for short-term retrieval, and one to Councilor Neary, as the point of contact on the project.

The cave had been worked on considerably since the Council had first discovered it in the early 1800's. While relatively new by magical standards, the décor was more along the lines of "castle" than "cave." Even that was helped with some fine-tuned track lighting. Old school wizards were used to gloomy. But the young and upcoming mages that made the maintenance and support staff were slowly bringing the cave around to something more charming than a typical office but not as depressing as an oubliette.

Councilor Neary's secretary wasn't in the anteroom of his office. Every now and then, some young mage suggested renaming the title to something like 'executive assistant' only to be quietly shot down. Occasionally, the young mage in question believed their elders were believers in the days when a secretary was a combination of social roadblock and office décor. Other young mages, who realized that some traditions were older than others, realized that the Council dated rather farther back than that. Rather, to the days when a secretary was a position of some importance. It also amused the older mages to let their younger colleagues believe them to be stuffy, sexist old traditionalists. Really suspicious mages, like the Marshals, noted that it wouldn't be all that difficult to fill both positions simultaneously, and were accordingly courteous. Given the hour, the secretary had likely gone home. Chucky, no stranger to the office protocol, knocked directly on Neary's oak office door.

"Enter."

Neary's office looked like a school headmaster's from a century ago. Dark wood paneling, bookshelves filled with leatherbound tomes and the occasional knicknack that could be a trophy, artifact, or project. Sofa and easy chair for the occasional leisure time. Door to a private bathroom beyond. A steel filing cabinet for such paperwork that, despite the Councilor's effort, managed to remain in his office, instead of going off on whatever adventures they choose to pursue.

He was dressed for leisure, which is to say his jacket was off and sleeves rolled up. His tie, a burgundy shade that managed to invoke old furniture instead of dried blood, was still firmly in place under his waistcoat. He was in the midst of writing, fountain pen ready at hand. His inbox was empty and outbox was full. Without small talk, Chucky dropped off Neary's copy of her report and slid the accumulated paper from the outbox onto her other copies held in her other arm.

"That the Atlanta report, Miss Brubaker?"

Chucky pushed her glasses back into place. "Yes, sir."

"Excellent." Neary set down the pen and folded his hands. "If it's at the level of your fieldwork so far on this case, I must say I'm impressed." He went on without waiting for a reaction to the unexpected praise. "I was about to ask how you were getting on in the archives? Sister Narges has nothing but praise for you."

Chucky blushed. "I like working the archives, sir. I don't think I'll ever be bored there."

Neary nodded solemnly. "The reason I asked is that Logan will be moving on. He's going to be the Monitor Secundus for the SouthWest this coming fall semester. Which will leave me in need of a secretary. You've proven you can manage a desk, the field, and autonomy. With your leave, I will ask Sister Narges if she can spare you."

Chucky could barely be heard. "Oh."

Neary waved a hand magnanimously. "You are of course free to refuse if you wish."

She licked her lips nervously, then pushed her glasses back into place. "Can I think about it, sir?"

Neary nodded. "Just let me know either way by the end of the month."

Chucky cracked a smile. "Thank you, sir."

"Goodnight, Miss Brubaker."

* * *

Two hours later, Chucky had gone home to her threadbare apartment. Nobody visited her. If they had, they would have noticed a complete lack of individual touches in the rooms. No art. No family pictures. No evidence of hobbies. No pets. Minimal furniture. This was an apartment for sleeping in, not for living in. If Chucky had been an ordinary office drone, then it might have been unnoticed. But Chucky's personal look screamed that a nonconformist existed somewhere in the pantsuit, even if it wasn't getting out anywhere on duty.

Next to the remains of a simple supper, Chucky typed away at her laptop.

A browser opened, showing the homepage of The Conservatory.

She had a new message waiting. She clicked it.

Hey, thanks for all that info on theater ghosts.

Really came in handy.

Lemme know if you're ever stumped searching for something and I'll see if I can find it for you.

~ Thumper.

Chucky gave a smile none of her coworkers had ever seen, and probably never would.

About the author

Jay Peterson has a resume that would let him take over the world, but he's seen the paperwork and wants none of it.

When not writing, Jay is a film and TV actor with a streak of supernatural creatures under his belt. Most recently he's been a computer troll in *Red One*, the ghost of a plantation owner in *The Piano Lesson*, and a demon-possessed corpse in *The Conjuring: The Devil Made Me Do It*.

He lives with his family outside of Atlanta, GA.

You can follow his exploits at Jaythebarbarian.com.

www.ingramcontent.com/pod-product-compliance
Lightning Source LLC
Chambersburg PA
CBHW071409300726
48976CB00006B/2041